The Tobias Ad Agency is in the running for the coveted Golden Storyboard, and Tobi couldn't be more thrilled—until she discovers it's literally an award to die for.

It's an honor just to be nominated. But, let's get real, Tobi wants to win. The St. Louis Advertising Awards are like the Oscars for her field, and Tobi is up for its most prestigious prize, Best Overall Ad Campaign. The competition is always fierce, but this year it's killer . . .

Despite her high hopes, Tobi isn't exactly shocked when she doesn't win. But she is shocked when the winner, Deidre Ryan, takes the stage only to plummet to her death as a platform suddenly gives way. After the police discover foul play, Tobi's Grandpa Stu wastes no time in nominating suspects. But was Deidre the intended victim—or was someone else meant to take the fatal fall? Now it's a race to catch a killer in the spotlight, before another nominee gets the booby prize and Tobi gets trapped in a no-win situation.

Books by Laura Bradford

And DEATH Goes To...
30 Second Death
Death in Advertising

Published by Kensington Publishing Corporation

And DEATH Goes To...

A Tobi Tobias Mystery

Laura Bradford

LYRICAL PRESS
Kensington Publishing Corp.
www.kensingtonbooks.com

First Electronic Edition:
eISBN-13: 978-1-5161-0210-5
eISBN-10: 1-5161-0210-X

First Print Edition:
ISBN-13: 978-1-5161-0211-2
ISBN-10: 1-5161-0211-8

Printed in the United States of America

For Joe…

Thank you for helping me see the shoreline at a time it seemed so very far away.

~Chapter One~

You know the kid who lurks at the top of the stairs, listening to adult conversations they're not supposed to hear? Or the one who rummages through the closets in the weeks leading up to Christmas because they have to know what Santa is bringing?

Yup, that was me.

And while I no longer qualify as a kid (freckles be damned) and now live alone in my own one bedroom apartment, I still lurk (only now it's from behind curtained windows) and I still peek (or try to) every chance I get.

Unless, of course, my best friend, Carter McDade, is running the show.

You see, Carter is the epitome of the surprise-loving, rule-following, anti-peeker my mother always wished I was. And if you try to go behind his back and peek—as I was at that moment—he was known to get a little testy (not a good thing when he had both a hot curling iron and a bottle of glue within arm's reach).

"Oh, Sunshine, you are sooo going to be the belle of the ball tonight." Carter took a half step back only to hone in on the side of my head like a vulture spying residual roadkill on the side of the road. "Waaaiitt! Don't move."

In a flash of movement even a fighter pilot would find impressive, Carter commandeered the still warm curling iron from the folding table he'd erected in front of me and brandished it above my right ear. In went the strand…tug went my head…spin went his hand…and, after a Mississippi-count to ten beneath his breath, out came the now-curled strand I could just barely see in my peripheral vision.

He set down the curling iron and applauded his own efforts. "Oh. My. Gosh. I. Am. A. Genius. Andy is going to bust a serious move when he sees yooouuu!"

"A *serious* move, huh?" I started to turn toward the mirror I knew was just over my shoulder, but before my chin had even made it a centimeter past the position I'd been ordered to hold for coming up on thirty minutes now, he leaned forward, his breath warm on my ear.

"Don't. Even. Think. About. It. Sunshine."

I groaned, loudly. "Has anyone ever told you how infuriating you can be?"

"Yes. You. About"—Carter checked his royal blue Swatch—"five minutes ago."

I crossed my arms in front of my minuscule (no, really...trust me) chest and let loose a dramatic sigh. "Good."

Carter stuck his tongue out at me and then grabbed my makeup bag off the table.

"Wait. You already did my makeup," I protested.

"Your *foundation*, yes. But that's simply the canvas. Now it's time for the artwork." He grabbed a second bag, unzipped it, and pulled out a plastic container with two sets of false eyelashes.

"Hey... You've always said you like my lashes!"

"I do. But tonight calls for long and lush." He ordered me to shut my eyes and, when I did, stuck the lashes into place with the aforementioned glue. When I blinked, he barked. When I protested, he barked. And when all was as he wanted, he moved on to my eyelids. "The teal of your dress, combined with *this* shadow palette, will really play up the green hue of your eyes—rowwww."

"Since I'm afraid to open my eyes lest I get beaten, I guess I'll have to trust you on that."

"As you should." He stepped back, contemplated his efforts thus far, and then took in the part of my dress he could see peeking out from under my smock. "That dress really is spectacular on you, Sunshine."

"I know. You told me that when you helped me pick it out, remember?" I held my chin and my gaze steady as he moved on to the mascara, my thoughts moving beyond my friend's apartment to the reason for my makeover. "I still can't believe I'm going tonight."

"You've gone to this shindig before, haven't you?"

"Yes, but this is different, Carter. I'm a nominee now. An actual, honest-to-goodness nominee."

"You act like that's such a shocker, Sunshine. But it's not. You're really good at"—Carter's fingers guided my head to the left—"all that slogan stuff."

"But we're talking about the St. Louis Advertising Awards here. They're like the Oscars for people who do what I do." I stopped myself mid-fidget and looked up at Carter. "You have no idea how many times I've pinched myself today alone, just to see if all of this is real."

He stepped back, surveyed the canvas that was my eyes, and capped up the mascara. "Oh, *it's real*, Sunshine. You're in that dress, aren't you?"

I looked down at the part of my dress I could see and felt the same thrill I felt when I'd put it on in Carter's bathroom less than thirty minutes earlier. The sparkly silver stilettos he'd gone nearly postal over in the store were simply the icing on the cake that was the princess (read: not normal) version of myself.

Since the moment the letter announcing my nomination for Best Overall Ad Campaign had arrived via certified mail, my feet had barely touched the ground. Thanks to Andy Zander (my super cute boyfriend), the milestone of being nominated had been celebrated via a candlelight dinner and a horse and carriage ride along the grounds of the St. Louis Arch. Mary Fran (my next door neighbor and best bud along with Carter) had thrown an impromptu dance party on the front lawn when she found out, and even Ms. Rapple, the old biddy who lives in the apartment below Mary Fran's, had been surprisingly pleasant, though that probably had more to do with her deepening relationship—shudder—withGrandpa Stu. And Grandpa Stu had been so proud of my accomplishment he'd subjected himself to the nearly four hour bus ride between his independent senior living complex in Kansas City and my Central West End digs just so he could be here for my big day.

"You should see your face right now."

I shook myself back to the present and stared at Carter. "You're kidding, right?"

"What?"

"*I should see my face right now*? Seriously? What do you think I've been waiting to do this whole time?"

"I'm not talking about the makeup and the hair, Sunshine." Carter pulled out a big wide brush, stuck it into a canister, and brushed the contents across my cheeks. "I'm talking about the part that's all you. You're absolutely glowing."

I felt my cheeks warm at the praise, but before I could respond, Carter capped up the canister and traded it for our agreed upon lipstick shade. "Validation of your talent obviously agrees with you. You should bottle that; you'd make a fortune."

I didn't need a mirror (although I desperately wanted one at that moment) to know he was right. I was literally living my dream. How could I *not* be glowing?

Still, I felt the need to explain said glow. "At the risk of further beating a dead horse, you need to understand these awards are huge. *Huge.*"

"You might've mentioned that a time or two"—Carter looked up, bouncing his eyes from left to right as he counted silently—"or...*ten.*"

"Well, that's because they are. Shamus Callahan of the Shamus Callahan Foundation was a veritable legend in the St. Louis advertising community and beyond. Remember that commercial when we were kids—the one for that wind-up cat that was all the rage?"

Carter's eyes widened. "*Ms. Pretty Kitty?*"

I nodded.

Clutching the lipstick tube to his chest, he slumped back against the wall, a dreamy expression playing across his face. "I loved her."

"Yeah, me, too. But do you remember the jingle they played in the background of those commercials? The one that invariably made you beg for a Ms. Pretty Kitty of your own?"

He lifted his gaze to the ceiling, closed his eyes (no, not long enough for me to sneak a peek at myself), and began to hum a few bars of the ad campaign responsible for making the mechanical cat the top selling toy across the country for its inaugural holiday season. "Ms...Ms. Pre-ty Kitty...love her...pet her...she's the one..."

I joined in for the final few lines and then followed them up with a laugh. "Yes! Nice!"

Carter slowly pulled the lipstick tube away from his body and smiled down at it as if it was something entirely different. "I took her *everywhere* that year."

"And you—or, rather, *your parents* have Shamus Callahan to thank for that. He made *all* kids want that toy."

Carter walked around to the front of my chair and studied me closely. "So this guy was the real deal?"

"That's putting it mildly. And that wasn't his only national campaign. He had lots. But he never forgot his roots."

"His roots being St. Louis, I take it?" Swapping the still unused lipstick tube for the big brush, he added another swipe of blush to my cheeks.

"That's right. He was the driving force—and money—behind this award show. And he kept it going for thirty years. And when he died, the foundation created in his honor took it over."

"Who runs the foundation?"

"His wife, Mavis, and his son, Kevin. Kevin is now president of Callahan Advertising."

"Is Kevin's mom in advertising, as well?"

"Kevin's *step*mom. Kevin was the byproduct of an affair Shamus apparently had forty some odd years ago. And no, Mavis was simply the supportive and dutiful wife from what I've been told.

"Anyway, that first award show was small. Maybe ten categories. But the crowning jewel was the same Best Overall Campaign category I'm up for with my New Town campaign." I stopped, made myself take a much needed breath, and then dove back in again. "And while the award show has grown and more categories have been added over the years, that category—*my* category—has remained the most prestigious of them all."

He stopping fussing with my cheeks and moved on to my lipstick. "So what does it look like?"

"What?"

"The award. Is it a naked bald guy like old Oscar?"

"I'm not so sure Oscar is naked."

"Google an image one day, Sunshine. No man looks like that in clothes—trust me."

I must have licked my lips when I laughed, because I got a hand smack and a quick lipstick touch up. "Can I answer the original question, please?"

"If you can refrain from licking, yes."

"All but the big award is a golden briefcase."

"And the big one?" Carter asked as he nodded at my face.

"A Golden Storyboard." I held my sigh back as I rushed to share the rest of the picture that had been playing itself out in my head for weeks. "It's the last award of the evening. The nominees are read, just like in all the categories, but as the winner walks on to the stage, a red velvet curtain opens up to reveal a spiral staircase. After the winner is handed the award, he or she gets to walk up the spiral stairs to a special platform. When they reach the top, another velvet curtain opens to reveal a screen. And as the winner and the audience watch, his or her winning campaign is played for all to see."

Carter's answering laugh snapped me back into the moment.

"What?" I asked.

"You're glowing again."

I plucked the lipstick from Carter's hand and set it on the table. "If I am, it's because I can't believe I'm nominated for that award. Last year, when Cassie Turner won for the Ross Jackson Agency, I literally had tears running down my face I was so happy for her—and I really only know her by name. And the year before that, when another one of the Ross Jackson crew won, I was so taken by all the pageantry of the award as the newbie that I was, my boss actually threw an elbow when it was time to clap."

"I take it this Ross Jackson agency is a powerhouse with two wins in two years?"

"Make it five wins in the past five years, and yeah, they're a powerhouse—a powerhouse who was nominated in just about every other category this year *except* Best Overall. And that's despite the work Cassie Turner did again this year—for Remy Electronics."

Carter looked past me for a moment in thought. "Wait. I remember that ad. I'm not an electronics guy and I was intrigued."

"I know. Crazy, right?" I let loose an honest to goodness squeal that made Carter jump just a little. "I'm living my dream. I have my own agency, I have real paying clients, I'm a car owner for the first time in almost thirty years, and I'm nominated for the biggest award in the industry! I-I can't even begin to tell you what an honor it is to have my name alongside the likes of Ben Gibbens, Lexa Smyth, and Deidre Ryan!"

"And I'd be willing to bet they consider it a dream-come-true to have their name alongside *yours*, Sunshine."

I didn't mean to laugh, I really didn't. But I couldn't help it. "I doubt that. I've only been in this business—in this town, in fact—for a few years. Ben and Deidre both interned here during their college days and grew their careers here."

"You're growing your career here, too," Carter argued like the true and loyal friend he is.

"*Growing*, yes. But they've *grown* it."

"And the other one? With the trendy name?"

"Lexa?" At his nod, I picked up the brush that had finally been retired from my face and twirled it between my fingers. "I'm not really sure how she got a nomination other than the fact that she's now working for the Callahan Agency, but there are probably some who are wondering how *I* got nominated, too, so..."

He shook his finger at me. "Stop that. Stop that right now."

"Sorry." I tossed the brush back onto the table and met Carter's disapproving eyes. "Momentary self-esteem setback. I'm over it. I promise."

"Good." Carter puckered his own lips in demonstration and then, when I mimicked to his satisfaction, he moved in for what I hoped was one final swipe. "If all goes well, we'll have *two* winners to celebrate before the night is over."

It was hard not to smile as his words redirected my thoughts to Mary Fran Wazoli's sixteen-year-old son, Sam. Like me with advertising, Sam's passion for photography had been born before he was ten years old. And while many might have considered me crazy for employing a teenager to shoot my agency's stills, I never had any doubt. The fact that his work was good enough to earn him a nomination alongside professionals two and three times his age just backed up what I'd known all along.

My squeal was back. Only this time, it came complete with an echo—Carter's.

"Oh, Sunshine..." He capped the lipstick, tossed it into his bag of tricks, and clapped his hands once. "You could be on a runway right now."

I parted my freshly colored lips in anticipation of the self-deprecating remarks that were poised to announce themselves like the trusty soldiers they were, but, in the end, I swallowed them back. After all, a promise was a promise, wasn't it?

Instead, I took a deep breath, hooked my thumb over my smock-clad shoulder, and smiled up at my best friend. "May I?"

He started to turn me, but stopped before I'd made it more than an inch or two.

"Now what?" I asked.

Reaching behind my neck, he unsnapped the smock and folded it against his chest. "There. *Now* you can look."

I completed my turn until I was face to face with the floor length mirror propped against the back wall of Carter's living room. My first glimpse sucked the breath from my lungs.

Whoa!

"That's...*me?*"

"It sure is."

"But—"

"The makeup may be me, but the gorgeous is *all* you. Always has been, Sunshine. Now go break a leg."

~Chapter Two~

On some level, I suppose I was aware of my colleagues milling about the Regency Hotel's grand ballroom, shaking hands, patting backs, and trying not to talk shop while waiting for the award show to begin. But really, at that moment, all I could truly see were the people seated around me at my table—loved ones who were there to support me in what might very well be the biggest night of my life, career wise.

Seated to my immediate left was JoAnna Kincaid, my secretary (aka lifesaver) at Tobias Ad Agency. Without her doing what she did on a daily basis, Carter wouldn't have had any reason to transform me into the princess Andy hadn't been able to keep his eyes off since he picked me up at my apartment thirty minutes earlier. To Andy's right was my Grandpa Stu, beaming back at me like the proud grandfather he was. I returned his smile while trying not to shudder at the woman seated next to him.

Truth be told, Ms. Rapple wasn't my first (or even my bazillionth) choice for a spot at my table (or anywhere in the ballroom, for that matter), but inviting her had made my grandfather happy. And since Mary Fran's new boyfriend, Drew, was away on business and couldn't attend, my grandfather was quick to suggest Rapple for that seat....

Mary Fran, in turn, was so beside herself with pride for Sam and his nomination, she wouldn't have noticed Ms. Rapple if the ornery little shrew was bedded down on her lap.

"Have I told you how beautiful you look tonight?"

I redirected my focus to the handsome man beside me and answered his smile with one I was pretty sure dominated my entire face. "You have, but it's okay to repeat yourself on occasion."

"You're beautiful." He captured my hand off its resting spot on the edge of the table and brought it to his lips. "And I'm so very proud to be here—to be *anywhere*, *anytime*—with you."

"Wow. I should have Carter do *this*"—I gestured to myself with my free hand—"to me more often."

"You're beautiful in sweats and a ponytail, Tobi."

I felt the familiar pang that was my good fortune at having Andy in my life and quickly blinked away the tears Carter had forbidden me from shedding lest I ruin the masterpiece (his word) that was me. "Thank you, Andy. For being here, for being in my life, for being...you."

He opened his mouth to answer, but closed it as Carl Brinkman, local network news anchor and the M.C. for the evening, stepped on stage to a ballroom-wide round of applause.

Over the next ten minutes, Carl entertained the crowd with advertising-related jokes and puns before moving on to the first award category of the night—Best Fifteen Second Spot. The previous year's winner came out to the podium, gave a fun description of the category, and then announced each nominee, leaving time between names for the swell of answering applause from both the represented agency and the crowd overall. When the moment of truth came, the presenter ripped open the sparkly gold-edged envelope and read the winner's name aloud—a name I knew, but a person I didn't.

Cheers from a table on the right side of the ballroom led my attention toward the forty-something winner who stood, kissed the woman beside him, and jogged toward the stage with an excitement I felt clear down to my toes. The woman tasked with handing out the evening's awards gave him his and then gestured him over to the podium for his allotted two minute acceptance speech.

I tried to listen, I really did, but honestly, I found myself thinking what I might say if the unthinkable happened. Grandpa Stu had encouraged me to write out a speech, but I'd resisted for fear of jinxing myself. Yet now that I was there, listening to the eloquent words of the man holding the first award of the night, I couldn't help but question my decision just a little.

Before the mental browbeating could reach a crescendo though, the wait staff came out with salad plates while Carl Brinkman reappeared with a fresh round of jokes—some invoking laughter, others inciting muted groans and more than a few traded eye rolls. Eventually, he announced the next category—Best Photograph in a Print Ad.

Everyone at my table stopped eating and turned their collective attention on Sam as last year's winner came out to the podium with a gold-edged envelope in one hand and the list of all four nominees in the other.

"As everyone here tonight knows, the right combination of words really does make a difference. It can mean the difference between success and failure for a new company, it can mean the difference between sought-after and ho-hum for a new-to-market product, and it can mean the difference between customers and no customers for a brand new restaurant or coffee house. But sometimes, depending on the method of delivery, the right words are only *part* of the equation. This is never truer than in a print ad. Because, let's face it, pictures make people stop and look… And unless they stop and look, that really great combination of words you're hoping will suck a prospective customer in, won't matter a hill of beans. To that end, I present to you the nominees for this year's Best Photograph in a Print Ad. Please stand when I call your name.

"Mark Walton, with the Ross Jackson Agency, for his contribution to St. Charles Brewery's Autumn Days/Autumn Nights campaign."

A swell of applause from a table directly in front of the stage intensified as the nominee stood and waved politely at the crowd.

"Jess Summer, also with the Ross Jackson Agency, for her work on Dr. Wyatt Morgan's Perfect Smiles campaign."

A second, louder swell of applause rose up behind me and I turned to smile at the petite brunette who rose up on shaky legs.

"Tim Dalton, with the Beckler and Stanley Agency, for his work on the Davidson Clinic's Healthy Lives campaign."

I traded glances with Carter as my former boss slapped his nominated photographer on the back so hard the man literally winced.

"And Sam Wazoli, with Tobias Advertising Agency, for his work on the Pizza Adventure campaign."

In the interest of professionalism, I tried my best to curb my desire to hoot and holler, but even if I'd failed, I'm pretty sure it hadn't been noticed anyway. Because really, anyone looking at our nominee at that moment was likely wiping their eyes over the way he pulled Mary Fran in for a hug. After a few seconds, he stepped back and nodded appreciatively at the crowd before taking his seat once again.

For a moment, I just watched him, marveling as I always did, at the maturity and class the teenager exuded twenty-four/seven.

"He's really loving every minute of this," Andy whispered in my ear.

"As he should," I whispered back. "I'd be willing to bet he's the youngest person to ever be nominated for one of these awards."

"And that's because of you."

I pulled my attention off Sam and fixed it, instead, on Andy. "Sam is here for one reason and one reason only—*his* ability, *his* talent."

"Oh, I'm not minimizing that in any way, shape, or form. I know Sam is good. He's proven that again and again for Zander, as you well know. I'm just saying you gave him an opportunity to showcase that talent."

"It's been a win-win for me, as—"

"And this year's winner for Best Photograph in a Print Ad is..." The woman stopped, slit the envelope's seal with her index finger, and then cleared her throat as she pulled out the slip of paper. "Sam Wazoli!"

This time, I didn't care about professionalism or volume or anything like that. I simply pushed back my chair and ran around the table for the hug I'd imagined more than a few times since word came of Sam's nomination. He returned the hug, added a kiss on my cheek, and then trotted up the center aisle and onto the stage to receive his golden briefcase. When he took his spot behind the podium and the applause finally stopped, he looked down at the award and then back up at the audience.

"Some of you are probably wondering why I'm up here. And honestly, there's really only one reason. Your colleague and my friend, Tobi Tobias, believed in me. She saw something in my work that wasn't negated by my age and she gave me a chance to show that to all of you. Thank you, Tobes. For giving me a shot...for believing in me...for trusting in me."

I sank down onto Sam's chair and stared at my friend's son—a young man who was wise beyond his years in so many ways. He looked so poised and so mature, and I couldn't have been prouder if I'd given birth to him myself.

"I'd also like to thank Andy Zander of Zander Closet Company for not balking when Tobi brought me on as a photographer for their campaign... and Mr. and Mrs. Poletti for doing the same with the Pizza Adventure campaign that earned me"—he lifted his Golden Briefcase in the air and then grinned as he brought it back down to the podium—"this unbelievable accomplishment and honor. And, last but definitely not least, I'd like to thank my mom. Your love taught me to have faith in myself. I love you, Mom!"

I'm pretty sure there wasn't a dry eye in the house by the time Sam headed backstage with his award. Somehow though, Mary Fran managed to get herself together enough to locate her phone, text the good news to Drew, and then hightail it toward the lobby to congratulate her son and snap a few photos of her own.

I, in turn, made my way back to my own seat and Andy, the smile on his face mirroring my own. "Wow. Just wow."

"I couldn't sum it up better myself." Andy gestured toward the stage, his voice hushed as the award show continued. "The other night, when you were telling me about past award shows and your category in particular, you mentioned a spiral staircase. Is that what's behind that red curtain on the right side of the stage?"

Following the path forged by his finger, I felt my stomach churn with excitement. "Yes. And at the very top, behind the platform where the winner stands, is the screen where they will play his or her award-winning campaign."

"I prefer *your*."

"Your?"

He tapped the tip of my nose lightly and followed it up with a soft kiss. "As in the screen where they will play *your* award-winning campaign."

I didn't mean to laugh. And I definitely didn't mean to snort with that same laugh. But, well, preposterous ideas tended to elicit stuff like that from me. Still, I was glad my fellow nominees and advertising colleagues were either focused on applauding at the appropriate spots or working on their own meals. The last thing I needed was for my propensity for odd noises to become public knowledge.

Andy drew back. "C'mon, don't tell me you haven't thought about it— about walking up those stairs with your award…about standing in front of the screen while you smile out at everyone…about mentally reviewing the speech you're about to give in which you break the hearts of every single guy in here by expressing your undying affection for yours truly…"

This time, when I laughed, I managed to refrain from snorting. Instead, I leaned forward, buried my head in his chest for one brief, wonderful moment, and then pulled back to address the obvious. "Yes, I've thought about it. Many, many times. But the reality is I'm still a newbie in this field. And honestly, when I say I'm just honored to be *nominated*, I mean it. As for the part about the broken hearts? That, too, goes without saying."

The dimples I adored appeared beside his mouth before he swept my attention back to the red curtain. "It's quite an elaborate set-up for an award, don't you think?"

"I guess. But there's not an industry person in this room who hasn't dreamed of walking up the spiral staircase with their award."

"I don't doubt that. In fact, between you and me?" He leaned away from the table to allow the wait staff to replace his salad bowl with his dinner plate, and then continued. "When you first described the whole thing to me on the phone the other day, I actually pictured *myself* going up the stairs."

I grinned and then directed Andy's attention to the table in the front center of the ballroom. "See that table there? That's the Callahan table. Shamus Callahan passed away years ago, but his wife, Mavis—she's the woman with the graying hair—and his son, Kevin, have kept the Callahan Foundation going ever since."

"Why?"

"Well, for starters, Kevin is in the business. In fact, when Shamus passed, Kevin stepped in as president of Callahan Advertising Agency. And, in case you're wondering, he's the one seated to Mavis's right."

"He's the president? He can't be more than forty years old. Tops."

When I saw that everyone at our table had their dinner, I sliced a piece off my flank steak and took a small bite, the rubbery consistency in keeping with the venue if not the price of the ticket. "Said the thirty-four-year-old pot to the kettle."

It was Andy's turn to laugh, and laugh he did. "Okay, okay, point taken. But let's be honest here. Callahan Advertising Agency is a helluva lot bigger than Zander Closet Company."

"For now." I plucked the ornamental green leaf off my potatoes, leaned in front of JoAnna, and handed it to an eye rolling Carter. "Anyway, Shamus and Mavis never had a child of their own so the running of the company was left to Kevin. I've only met him very briefly once or twice, but I didn't really get the appeal."

"He's not good at what he does?"

"No, I just mean his not so subtle flirting didn't really do anything for me."

"Why would it? You have me," Andy teased.

"Exactly." I dipped my butter knife into the pat of butter atop my bread plate and slathered it across the bottom of my dinner roll. "Besides, he doesn't have dimples like you do *and* he has a wife and a baby who, based on the empty chair and highchair I can see from here, are around here somewhere."

"Oh."

"Uh huh. And the little blonde with the curlicues on Mavis's other side? That's one of theirs, too."

"Why does that little girl look familiar?"

"She's been in a few of the ads Callahan has done. Most notably the one for last fall's Boo at the Zoo commercial."

"That's it! I knew I'd seen her before. She's a real cutie." He took a bite of his salmon and then looked again at the head table. "Mavis looks positively enamored with that little girl."

I smiled over the top of my dinner roll. "She does, doesn't she?"

"That's the same way Stu looks at you, you know."

I let my gaze travel around Andy to the bald man on his opposite side, my heart swelling at the sight of a man I'd loved my entire life—a man who was so enthralled with the housecoat-wearing woman on his far side I couldn't help but cringe. Like it or not, Grandpa Stu saw something in my next door neighbor I would never understand.

My grandfather...

And Ms. Rapple...

I must have shuddered for real because Andy set down his fork and patted my hand in a show of understanding. But even with that, I had to look away from the pair before my rubberized flank steak found its way back up my throat.

Category by category the show advanced—Best Humorous Slogan, Best Emotional Slogan, Best Jingle, Best 30-Second Spot, and, finally, just as dessert (chocolate cake!) was finishing up, the lights dimmed, Kevin Callahan's wife and baby reappeared at the head table to Mavis's obvious delight, and Carl Brinkman returned to the stage, this time in a top hat and tails and brandishing a cane he spun in the air like a baton.

"Well, folks, we've come to the pinnacle of the evening—the very award the late great Shamus Callahan built this entire award show around *forty*"—the anchorman–turned–master of ceremonies stole a peek at the head table for confirmation—"*one* years ago."

Applause broke out around the room only to subside as Carl held his hands up in a silencing gesture. "In fact, the coveted Golden Storyboard statue specific to the night's top award was designed by Shamus's wife, Mavis."

Clearly uncomfortable by the renewed applause now aimed at her, Mavis smiled quickly and then busied herself with her granddaughter and the just-returned grandbaby now seated atop her lap.

"And the humiliation just goes on and on, doesn't it?" JoAnna whispered in my ear.

"Humiliation? What—"

JoAnna swept the air between us. "Forget that. This is your night. Are you ready?"

"I'm scared to death, quite frankly," I whispered back.

"Enjoy the moment no matter what it brings."

And that is why I loved my secretary. She had a way of cutting through the background noise to get to the part that matters—at work, in life, in love.

I felt Andy's hand encase mine a split second before Grandpa Stu winked at me and Sam and Mary Fran flashed a dual thumbs-up. Swinging my gaze to the left, I met Carter's proud glance with what I hoped was a thankful one on my part. I was blessed and I knew that. No matter what happened in the next ten minutes, I had what mattered more than any award could ever mean.

"To present the Golden Storyboard, for this year's Best Overall Ad Campaign, is last year's winner, Cassie Turner, from the Ross Jackson Agency. Cassie?"

The model-thin advertising executive strolled onto the stage in a gold floor length dress that hugged her curves like a second skin. Her trademark blond locks hung down her back and across her shoulders in such glorious ringlets that even Carter had to sigh. But I didn't care about any of that. My focus, my heart-pounding attention was fixed on the plain white envelope in Cassie's bejeweled hand as she fairly glided into place behind the podium.

"Well, well, well, we meet again," Cassie said around a dazzling smile of bleached teeth. "Only *this* time, and rather surprisingly I might add, I will remain at the bottom of the staircase"—as if on cue, the red velvet curtain beside the podium parted to reveal the famed spiral staircase, as well as the platform and screen it led to at the top—"while this year's winner carries his or her Golden Storyboard to the top."

I looked down at the napkin in my lap and then back up at the stage, my face warm from my tablemates' renewed and not so subtle attention.

"So, without further ado, I present to you the nominees for this year's Best Overall Ad Campaign.

"Ben Gibbens of The Beckler and Stanley Agency for the creativity that was this year's *St. Louis and You* campaign for the St. Louis Tourism Commission.

"Deidre Ryan, of The Whitestone Agency for the creativity that was this year's *Books Can Take You Places* campaign for the St. Louis Public Library System.

"Lexa Smyth of The Callahan Agency for the creativity that was this year's *Get Moving with MetroLink* Campaign."

Andy brought his lips within a few centimeters of my ear. "I didn't know you were up against someone from the founder's agency."

"I am. But it's okay. Really. It's an honor to be nominated—"

"Get Moving with MetroLink? I remember that one," Ms. Rapple whisper-gushed from the other side of my grandfather. "Best commercial I've seen in years."

I started to look at Carter for the commiserating eye roll I knew I'd find, but then Cassie moved on to the fourth and final nominee—*me*.

"And Tobi Tobias of The Tobias Agency for the creativity that was New Town's *Where Vacation and Life Become One* campaign."

Like a robot, I started to applaud just like I had for the first three names, but stopped when JoAnna's hand reached out and stilled mine. "This is *your* moment, Tobi. Savor it."

And savor it I did. I savored the applause from the tables around me, the smiles from my loved ones, and the sweet kiss on my temple from Andy.

Yes, it was official. I would never, ever forget this moment for as long as I lived.

"And now, I present to you, the winner of this year's Golden Storyboard for Best Overall Ad Campaign—Deidre Ryan!"

A gasp from the front center of the room was followed, a half second later, by a squeal from the vicinity of Deidre's table, and, finally, the thunderous applause of the crowd that drowned out all but the sound of my own heart beating inside my chest. I felt Andy's squeeze on my hand, and JoAnna's breath on my ear as she said something I assume was sweet and supportive, but all I could do at that moment was stare with utter fascination as Deidre ran onto the stage, accepted her award from Cassie, and made her way up the spiral staircase to the platform at the top, her face a mixture of stunned surprise and little-girl joy.

I knew, on some level, I was supposed to feel bad—disappointed that it wasn't me standing on that platform, staring down at the Golden Storyboard like it was the Holy Grail. But I didn't. I was actually happy for the diminutive brunette I'd met a half dozen times over the past few years—a quiet, unassuming woman who'd likely dreamed of this moment as often as I had.

The applause continued as a smaller red curtain, positioned behind the platform, opened to reveal the screen tasked with sharing Deidre's campaign with the audience. But just as the shot of the man and his little boy—decked out in Cardinals gear—appeared on the screen, I darted my attention back to Deidre, my confusion mingling with hers a split second before the platform she was standing on gave way, and she, and the stage lights above her, fell to the ground with a deafening thud.

~Chapter Three~

I tried to focus on the Yay-Us party JoAnna had graciously orchestrated for Sam and me at the agency immediately following the awards show, but it was hard. I understood her rationale in going ahead with the soirée despite the horror we'd all witnessed, but still, every time I tried to lose myself in conversation with one of my friends, I heard the sound of Deidre's body hitting the stage and the delayed, yet no less bloodcurdling screams that had followed.

I knew I wasn't the only one who kept traveling back to that horrific moment, but I also knew everyone—myself, included—was trying really hard to keep things light for Sam. After all, winning an industry award at any age was exciting, but to win one as a newly turned sixteen-year-old was something else entirely. Yet the fact that Grandpa Stu had disengaged himself from Ms. Rapple's flappy (*ewww*) arms and was heading in my direction with worried eyes, was a pretty good indication my efforts at being upbeat and cheerful were falling short.

"Have I told you how much you look like your grandmother this evening?" Grandpa Stu pulled me in for a sidearm hug and a kiss on my temple. "With your hair all curled and framing your face the way it is, it's like I'm thirty all over again, too."

I captured his hand in mine and held it close to my cheek, the rasp in his voice a tribute to the love he'd shared with my grandmother—a love that had spawned my mom and, eventually, my brother, my sister, and me. "I miss her, too, Grandpa Stu."

"I know you do." He gestured toward the table of treats JoAnna had erected against the back wall in the conference room and, at my nod, tugged me over to the plate of Napoleons I was sure he'd already sampled a few times over the past hour or so. "So you doing okay, Sugar Lump?"

I took the dessert plate he held out to me and tried to focus on the plethora of options JoAnna had obviously been slaving over in the hours leading up to the award show—cookies, brownies, individual tarts, cupcakes, and the aforementioned Napoleons. My eyes knew everything looked amazing. Heck, even my hands were itching to start piling one of everything onto my plate. But my stomach was a different story. Instead of the feed-me rumbles that usually accompanied any and all sugar-related visuals, there were warning gurgles. And considering the fact my agency's bathroom was a one-staller, I didn't want to chance a line should I ignore the warning and end up paying the price.

"Actually, as good as everything looks, I'm not terribly hungry. I-I guess I'm still full from dinner."

"*Full?*" Grandpa Stu eyed me closely. "I saw your plate when that fella from the hotel took it away. You ate no more than half your steak and no more than a quarter of your potatoes."

"I ate my chocolate cake!"

"You ate *some* of your chocolate cake—not all of it."

"I was excited for Sam." I looked from my grandfather, to my empty plate, and back again before returning it to the pile. "And... I was busy talking to Andy."

"He ate *his* food," Grandpa Stu pointed out.

"I don't know, Grandpa, I can't explain it." I fussed with the container of plastic forks and when they were neat and orderly, I dropped my hand to my side. "It was a big night, you know? I guess I was just busy soaking everything up."

He polished off his umpteenth Napoleon of the night, tossed the plate into the trash can in the far corner, and then motioned for me to follow him down the hallway and into my office. Once inside, he flipped on the overhead light and pushed the door closed enough to give us privacy but not enough to be rude to my guests. "Talk to me, Sugar Lump."

"Grandpa, I can't be in here. JoAnna went to a lot of trouble to put this shindig together for me and Sam. In fact, that's the only reason we're even still doing this—because of Sam."

"And Sam is loving every minute of it." Grandpa Stu made his way around my desk and dropped into my chair with an audible *oomph.* "I'm mighty proud of that young man, Sugar Lump."

It felt good to smile if even for just a few moments, so I gave into it as I wandered over to my draft table, my eyes barely registering the pitch it housed for yet another client I was trying to woo over to Tobias Advertising Agency. "I have no doubt it will be the first in a long line of awards for our Sam. He's incredibly talented. Tonight just proved I'm not the only one who sees it."

I turned at the sound of my desk drawer opening and then closing. "Do you need something, Grandpa?"

"Nope. Just fiddling with things the way you've been fiddling with things all night."

I made my way back to my desk and sat down on the chair normally reserved for clients. "I haven't been fiddling with things."

My grandfather's left eyebrow rose halfway up his forehead. "Oh? You tellin' me JoAnna didn't have to shoo you away from the candy jar on her desk within just a few minutes of you getting here?"

"She's always shooing me from that jar."

"Because you're getting into it, not playing with it."

I started to deny the accusation but when I realized I was obsessively running my finger across a faint scratch on the top of my desk, I pulled my hand back, shoved it under my thigh, and said nothing.

"And when Carter was using his finger to re-curl that one strand of hair next to your ear"—he pointed to the left side of my face—"you kept messing with that folding chair out in the reception area so much Sam actually wedged a coaster under it so you'd quit making that sound."

"The legs were uneven."

"It's a folding chair, Sugar Lump. No one expects it to be premium seating."

To argue would be futile. My grandfather was right. I'd been fidgeting pretty much non-stop since I got in the car with Andy for the ten-plus mile drive from the award show venue. "I still can't believe what happened to Deidre."

"I know. I've thought about it a time or two myself since we've been here. And I've said a few prayers for that young woman and her family. But playing with jars and chairs isn't going to change anything. And this was a very big night for Sam and for you. Don't let things that are out of your control taint that. Although, truth be told, I think it's your name that shoulda been called for that fancy gold storyboard thingy."

"Thank God it wasn't." Andy peeked around my office door. "Mind if I crash?"

My chair (or what was normally my chair) squeaked under the decreasing weight of my grandfather's body as he pushed back from the desk and stood, the smile I'd loved my whole life on full display. "Not at all, young man. Especially since the sight of you in that doorway managed to get this one"—he pointed at me—"to smile for the first time since this party started."

"I've smiled!"

"Not like that, you haven't." Grandpa Stu came out from behind my desk, stopped beside my chair just long enough to kiss the top of my head, and then smacked Andy on the back as they passed one another in the doorway. "If you can get her to keep that smile longer than a minute or two, I'll buy you a beer before I head back to Kansas City."

"I'll do my best, Stu." Andy waited until my grandfather closed the door completely, and then made his way over to me. "I meant what I said, you know. I'm glad you didn't win that award tonight."

When he perched on the edge of the desk and reached for my hand, I gave it willingly. "I'm sorry I was such lousy company on the way here. I guess I was still in shock."

He squeezed my hand ever so gently until I really looked at him. "If you remember, I didn't say anything during the drive, either."

I thought back, and he was right. "I keep hearing that sound, and seeing her face just before it all happened. And when I'm not seeing *her*, I'm seeing the faces of her husband and parents as—" I tugged my hand free of Andy's grasp and used it to try and push away the image in my head. But all it did was advance forward to the moment Deidre's husband backed away from the huddle of people around his wife to let loose the kind of tortured scream I wasn't sure I'd ever be able to forget.

Andy raked his hand through his hair. "And I'm hearing and seeing all that same stuff and thanking God you didn't win that damn award. Because if you *had*, that would have been..."

His words disappeared behind his fist as he turned and looked out my office window to the small side alley that separated my building from the drycleaner next door. But it didn't matter. His anguish and the reason behind it were crystal clear.

But before I could gather my own emotions enough to string together a coherent response, his focus and his hands were back on me. "That woman is dead because of a wrong place/wrong time moment. And it could have been you, Tobi."

I looked down at his hands on mine and worked to steady my breath. "So you saw it, too?"

He drew back but his gaze never left mine. "Her fall? Yeah. Her family's anguish? Yeah. That look on her face as I imagine she felt the platform starting to give way? Yeah. I saw it all just like you did—like everyone in that entire ballroom did."

"I'm talking about the look just before the platform gave way," I whispered, though why I felt the need to whisper in a closed office was beyond me.

"I think she felt something we couldn't see."

Again, I took my hand back, and this time I used it to push off the chair. "I don't think that's what it was at all."

"I'm not following, Tobi."

I wandered over to the window and gazed out over the moonlit alley. "It's like you said before...about the wrong time/wrong place...only it was more than that. Her *being there* was wrong and I think she knew that."

Andy's footsteps drew near until he was standing right behind me. "Meaning?"

I took a deep breath, let it out through my lips, and then turned so I was looking at Andy rather than a dumpster. "I think Cassie said the wrong name."

"The wrong—"

A quick knock thwarted the rest of his sentence and sent our focus toward the door and JoAnna. "I'm sorry to interrupt, but Carter is all geared up to give a toast and he's insisting that you come out and stand beside Sam. And Tobi? This toast fills up both sides of a standard piece of paper."

Despite the seriousness of the conversation she'd interrupted, I still managed a smile. Carter was aces. Always. And the fact that he had a two-sided toast meant he'd spent a good deal of time preparing for this moment. To decline it would be cruel.

"Okay, I'll be out in one minute."

"We'll give you three." JoAnna studied me for a few seconds and then hooked her thumb over her shoulder. "I'm sorry if I shouldn't have pushed to still have this. But I just felt so bad seeing Sam's night end like that and—"

"It's okay, JoAnna, really. Sam earned this. And I'll be out in three, I promise."

"I'll let Carter know." JoAnna gave me an encouraging smile and then quietly closed the door in her wake.

Hooking his finger beneath my chin, Andy guided my attention back to him. "You were saying?"

I took another, deeper breath. "I don't think that award was meant for Deidre. I think it was Lexa's."

"Why do you say that?"

"Because in the split second before Deidre fell...when she looked over her shoulder at the screen...she realized it wasn't her ad they were showing."

Andy stared at me, his confusion palpable.

"Deidre's ad…the one she was nominated for…was the *Books Can Take You Places* campaign. You saw it, right? The one where people open a book inside the library and, suddenly, you see them reading that same book in a completely different place—like inside a castle or on a ship or deep in the woods…"

"Yeah, I saw it. It was clever, for sure. But not as good as your New Town ad, in my opinion."

I waved off his sweet bias and reclaimed the conversation. "Okay, but you know the ad I'm talking about, yes?"

"Yes."

"Well, that's not the ad that was starting to run on the screen just as everything came crashing down on top of Deidre. It was actually Lexa's ad for the *Get Moving with MetroLink* campaign."

"Are you sure?"

"It was really fast, and I'm guessing everyone else was still looking at *her* more than the screen, but yeah… I saw the father and son in their Cardinals gear and that's how Lexa's ad starts…with the pair parking their car in a lot alongside a congested I-70 and then stepping onto the MetroLink for a stress-free and traffic-free ride downtown. Only it was literally the first two seconds of the ad—where you see the father's ball cap and the little boy's glove and then—wham!—the platform gave way, pulling the screen and the spotlight down, too."

Andy's eyes closed briefly at the memory just as mine had done many times since it happened. But this time, I kept mine open, so I could see his reaction when he fully grasped what I was saying.

It didn't take long.

"And you think she knew it?" he asked.

"She was looking at the same screen I was. And I saw it register for her, but then she went down and all hell broke loose."

He raked a hand through his hair, his accompanying exhalation moving a few of my curls away from my face. "Wow. I don't even know what to say. I mean, maybe the tech guys just played the wrong video. But if they didn't, and she wasn't even the one who was supposed to be on that platform, can you imagine how much harder this is all going to be for her family?"

It was the same question that had gone through my head a time or two since it happened. Although, in the grand scheme of things, it was probably silly. Because really, in the end, it didn't matter who was standing on the platform when it malfunctioned. The end result would have been the same. And no matter how much any of us might have wanted that golden storyboard, no award was worth losing one's life in such a horrific way.

I shivered against the chill that skittered down my spine and willed Andy's answering embrace to make it all go away. But I knew it would take time. I hadn't known Deidre all that well, but I'd always found her to be quiet and unassuming—rarities in a business that had a reputation (well earned, I might add) for being extremely cutthroat.

He held me for what was surely three minutes all on its own before he finally stepped back. "I'm pretty sure we've used our allotted time and then some. What's say we rejoin the party and celebrate the good things that came from tonight?"

"Sam really knocked it out of the ballpark, didn't he?" I asked as I fell into step beside Andy on the way to the door.

"He did, indeed."

"And Carter managed to make me look like an actual princess with his box of magic."

At the door, Andy stopped and looked down at me. "Trust me, Tobi, you made his job easy in that regard."

I raised up on my tiptoes, cupping his face between my hands. "Awww, that's an awfully sweet thing to say."

"It's the truth."

I kissed him hard on the mouth. "Thanks for being there for me tonight, Andy. Having you there meant the world to me, even if I didn't win."

"And you *not* winning means the world to *me*. Seriously."

~Chapter Four~

I tossed my sparkly little handbag onto the catch-all table just inside my front door and tried my best to block out the image of my grandfather accompanying Ms. Rapple onto her front porch and possibly leaning in for a goodnight—

"Martha is inside, safe and sound."

I turned and took in my lifelong mentor as he came through my open doorway with an impressive spryness considering his advancing age and the late night (or should I say, early morning) hour. "That was a quick good-bye," I said, my tone rather euphoric.

Grandpa Stu closed and locked my door and then kicked off his freshly polished "party shoes" (his term, not mine) en route to the couch where I, myself, had just landed. "I was afraid if I lingered over Martha's lips, you'd be asleep by the time I got back."

I tried to rein in my answering shudder, but I'm pretty sure I was unsuccessful. Especially since said shudder resulted in a throw pillow (or two) slipping off the couch and onto the floor. If my grandfather noticed, he didn't let on, his focus now trained on and around the sofa cushion to my left.

"Did you lose something, Grandpa?"

He slipped his hand into the gap between the two cushions, felt around, and pulled out the remote control with a triumphant *ah-ha*!

"You do realize it's nearly two o'clock in the morning, right?" I pulled my feet off the coffee table and dropped them to the ground with the intention of standing if my eyes could stay open long enough to do so. "In fact, I probably shouldn't be sitting here, since this is your bed for however long you're staying with me."

"Sit. Sit." Heeding his own advice, my grandfather dropped onto the cushion next to me and pointed the newly recovered remote at my TV. "They repeat the eleven o'clock news at two."

I watched the screen come to life and then eyed the wiry bald man I called Grandpa. "I don't understand when you sleep. You're up when I leave for work, you're up when I go to bed, and other than an occasional powernap while I'm pulling together dinner, you're awake. That can't be good for you."

"I'm still here, ain't I?"

He had a point.

Before I could mount a counterattack, he started pressing the channel changing button at such a dizzying speed I had to look away. "Still, I can't remember the last time I was this exhausted and yet here you are, still revved and ready to go. Maybe you should've laid off the Napoleons a little, you know? Sugar before bed really isn't a good idea."

My grandfather laughed and I knew why.

I, Tobi Tobias, was a sugarholic—morning, noon, and, yes, night. So my lecturing anyone about the dangers of ingesting sugar under any circumstance was, indeed, laughable.

Rather than cop to my hypocrisy, I changed the topic. "JoAnna really did a nice job with that party tonight, didn't she?"

"You scored big with that one, Sugar Lump."

And I had. JoAnna Kincaid was truly the best business decision I'd made thus far. In fact, I'd be kidding myself if I didn't attribute a big chunk of my agency's success over the past few months to my secretary. Because truly, if not for her, I might have caved under the weight (and unpaid bills!) of small business ownership long before Andy and his brother, Gary, had strode through my front door with my first big break.

This time when I shuddered, it had nothing whatsoever to do with Ms. Rapple and everything to do with the *what ifs* that could have been if I had given up.

No Zander Closet Company ad...

No shiny new car parked alongside the curb with my name on the title...

No Andy...

No St. Louis Advertising Award nom—

The jingle of Channel Four's eleven o'clock news yanked me off memory lane in time to see my grandfather point at the TV. "It's starting!"

Sure enough, Bryce Waters, the eleven o'clock news anchor, appeared in the center of my fifteen inch screen with a dour expression. "Good evening, everyone, I'm Bryce Waters and this is the eleven o'clock news."

"At two a.m.," I muttered.

"Shhh!"

"The St. Louis advertising community is reeling tonight in the aftermath of what can only be described as a horrific tragedy—one that played out in a very heartbreakingly public way. Let's go to Matt McKeon who is live outside the Regency Hotel, the scene of what is now being described as an apparent murder."

I felt the intake of air through my lungs, but the true source of the gasp was anyone's guess as my grandfather and I stared at each other, wide-eyed.

"Did you hear that, Sugar Lump? He said murder!"

I think I nodded, I'm not really sure. But it didn't matter as we both turned back to the TV and the forty-something reporter standing outside the same ballroom where we'd been less than four hours earlier.

"It was supposed to be a night of fun and food, a chance to celebrate the best of the best at the annual St. Louis advertising community's award show. And it was exactly that until the final category of the night—a category tasked with honoring the truly creative elite."

I allowed myself a split second of preening at the creative elite tag but it was short-lived thanks to the full screen photograph of Deidre Ryan now gracing my television set.

"Deidre Ryan was a real up and comer in the local advertising community. Just thirty-seven years old, the mother of two was the brains behind the *Books Can Take You Places* campaign for the St. Louis Public Library System. The TV and print ads transported us to some of our favorite and most memorable fictional locales in a way that made you want to drop everything you were doing and go racing to the library. That ad earned Ryan a nomination—and subsequent win—for Best Overall Ad Campaign at this year's St. Louis Advertising Awards Show. But it was while accepting that award this evening that Ryan's life was cut short in what some are calling an intentional act."

The onsite reporter returned to the screen, only this time he was standing beside an older man in jeans and a flannel shirt. "This is Doug Winton, a member of the crew brought in to set up the stage for tonight's award show, including the elevated platform that gave way beneath the victim. Doug, what can you tell us about what happened tonight?"

The man, identified as a stagehand supervisor beneath his name, cleared his throat. "My crew has been assembling this exact set year after year for decades now. The same spiral staircase, the same suspended platform, the same video screen, the same red curtains."

"Any chance the equipment used to elevate the platform was faulty?" the reporter asked.

"No. It was checked multiple times, as it always is. And the picture I was shown by one of my guys on the scene in the immediate aftermath of the accident proves that."

The reporter leaned closer. "Why do you say that, Doug?"

"Because the suspension cables were loosened between when I did my final sign-off on the platform's safety at five o'clock and the accident at ten o'clock."

"Sources are telling us an unfamiliar screwdriver was found backstage—a screwdriver that appears to have been wiped clean of any fingerprints."

I'm pretty sure the stagehand kept speaking, but I couldn't be sure thanks to the not-so-dull roar in my head. Before I could process the horror show unfolding, Matt McKeon handed the story back to Bryce Waters who gave a little background on the award show and its founding father, Shamus Callahan, before breaking back to the scene and a segment obviously taped in the immediate aftermath of the accident. One by one, Matt McKeon asked onlookers about the moments leading up to and following Deidre's fatal fall, and one by one they gave the only answers they really could....

"It was awful."

"One minute she was so happy, and the next she was dead!"

"I-I just can't believe it."

"I'm so thankful her children weren't present."

And on and on it went.

When the reporter tried to get a statement from the late Shamus Callahan's widow, Mavis, the seventy-year-old woman simply burst into tears before being escorted to a waiting car by her daughter-in-law.

I tried to swallow over the lump I felt forming midway down my throat, but it took more effort than I could give at that moment. Instead, I glanced at my grandfather and noted the same general shock on his face that I felt on my own.

"Wow." I know it was a lame thing to say under the circumstances, but in addition to giving me more time to process everything we'd heard thus far, my one word summation fit.

Grandpa Stu cupped his hands together, brought them to his lips, and exhaled. "I can't imagine someone wanting to kill anyone, let alone someone with such a genuine smile."

And it was true. Deidre may have been quiet by nature, but when she smiled, her face, her eyes, her entire being lit up like a Christmas tree—or a *bazillion* Christmas trees as was the case when she'd stepped onto the stage to receive the coveted Golden Storyboard from Cassie Turner just a little over four hours ago.

My grandfather was right. If what had just been reported on the television was true, why would someone have done that to Deidre Ryan of all people? And, even more importantly than why, *who*?

"What do you know about them other folks you were up against tonight?"

"For the award? It was Deidre, Ben Gibbens, Lexa Smyth, and me. Why?"

"It's one of the biggest motives."

This time, there was no pause followed by understanding. Instead, I started clueless and remained clueless. "You lost me, Grandpa."

My grandfather closed the fingers of his left hand around his chin and rubbed it slowly, pensively. "Sure, there are the usual suspects in a situation like this—revenge, greed, money, hatred, et cetera. But jealousy is on that list, too."

"List? List of what?" I asked.

"Motives for murder." Grandpa Stu let his hand fall back to his lap as he scooted forward and off the couch. "Every episode of *Detective Time* comes down to one of them on that list, and last week's murder was on account of jealousy. Like this one."

"You mean Deidre's?"

"Of course."

"But that's assuming what they just said on the news is even true."

"Someone killed her," my grandfather said as he moved around my living room in a sort of aimless fashion. When he reached my drafting table, he stopped and made his way back in my general direction. "And seeing as how she was receiving her award when she was killed, jealousy makes the most sense, don't you think?"

His words hit their mark. "Wait. You think someone killed her because they were angry she won?"

"People have killed for far less than that."

On its own, it was a point I couldn't argue, but in terms of what happened to Deidre, I could. "First of all, I know Ben and Lexa. I know Ben probably a little better, since my time at Beckler and Stanley overlapped with his, but I've seen Lexa at plenty of industry workshops and events. Granted, I'm far from a fan, but branding her a killer is a bit much. Especially when none of us—myself, included—knew who the winner was until the moment Cassie opened the envelope and announced Deidre's name."

"So maybe the motive wasn't jealousy at all. Maybe it was something else," my grandfather huffed, clearly not happy with the possible error in his initial theory. "Either way, someone had to know this young woman was going to win, right? A committee? A group of judges? Family members of the winner tasked with making sure their loved one attended? The M.C. or the one who handed the award to that woman in the first place?"

I pondered my grandfather's list, moving through it point by point. "I imagine the foundation committee knew, sure. The judges—usually retired ad execs and other notables in and around St. Louis—go without saying. But I've never known a nominee *not* to come to the award show."

"And the M.C.?"

"Carl Brinkman. He's one of the local news anchors. Channel Five, I think. I'm not sure what motive he'd have to tamper with an award show platform."

My grandfather stared at me as if I'd grown a second head (which I checked via my hand, just in case). "Maybe his job at the station is in jeopardy—I mean, I found him kind of stiff at times this evening."

"So you think he killed someone because he's stiff?" I asked.

"No, to save his job by being on scene when a major story broke." My grandfather tapped his chin and then made a beeline back to my drafting table where he secured a piece of paper and a pen and began to write with gusto.

"What are you doing, Grandpa?"

"Writing down theories the way they do on *Detective Time*."

"You can't seriously think Brinkman did it? I mean, first of all, it's a stretch. Second of all, you have no reason to think his job was in jeopardy. He's had the anchor chair the entire time I've been here and I'm pretty sure they tout his longevity with the station in their promos."

He silenced me with a wave of his hand, jotted down a few more things, and then pointed the pen at me. "Tell me about the other one—the one who handed our victim her award."

Our victim?

Uh oh...

"Cassie Turner. And Grandpa, the cops will figure this out. It's their job."

"A job we just happened to do better than they did when that body dropped onto your feet in that house last fall, *and* when that woman died on the set of that commercial back in January."

I wanted to argue, but I couldn't. Still, the meaning behind his words landed like a grenade at my feet.

"No, no, no." I held up my hands, surrender like. "We are not getting involved in this, Grandpa."

"You're already involved, Sugar Lump."

It was my turn to stare at him as if *he'd* grown two heads. "How on earth do you figure that?"

"Maybe this young woman was the target. Maybe she wasn't."

"Meaning?"

"Maybe the *category* was targeted rather than a specific winner."

"The category?" I echoed as I sat up tall. "You think someone targeted the category?"

My grandfather's seemingly nonchalant shrug was busted by the smile creeping across his face. "It's the most coveted award of the night, isn't it?"

The most coveted award...

This time, when I looked at my grandfather, I didn't really see him. Instead, I saw the wisdom in what he was saying. Yes, there was a chance Deidre was targeted, but the notion that it was the *category* that was targeted, rather than a specific person, made a whole boatload of sense, too. Maybe even more so.

"Now tell me about this Cassie Turner person. Besides, of course, the fact that she's quite a looker and that she won this same award last year."

Part of me wanted to tease him about his description of a woman nearly half his age, but a bigger part couldn't ignore his line of thinking. What if he was right? What if the winner—no matter who it was—had been the target?

"Sugar Lump?"

I snapped my thoughts in line with my field of vision and gave my grandfather what he wanted. "Cassie Turner is one of the darlings of the St. Louis Advertising Community. At least she has been the entire time I've been part of it. She's quite good at what she does and, as you already pointed out, she's attractive in an almost model-esque way."

"Think she could have been irked her reign as winner was over?"

"Well, there was that snide little remark she made before she announced our names, remember? But if she was irked, as you say, she didn't appear outwardly so."

"*Should* she have been nominated?"

"I think she should have. Her St. Louis Coffee Shop ads carried through on the emotional aspect in a way Lexa's Metro Link ad didn't, in my opinion. But I'm one person. The judges apparently felt differently."

"Think maybe she could've tampered with that platform because she was angry she wasn't nominated? Because that'd give her motive *and* means considering she was backstage and all."

I wanted my grandfather to be wrong, but there was no denying the unease working its way up my spine. Yet just as I was entertaining the possibility he could be right about Cassie and the category as a whole, I found myself back in the Regency ballroom, watching as Deidre's smile slipped from her face a half second before the platform gave way.

Deidre's ad hadn't been the one playing on the screen as she reached the top of the spiral staircase. Maybe no one else noticed, but I had. And from what I could tell just before she fell, so, too, had Deidre.

~Chapter Five~

Now that Tobias Advertising Agency was finally standing on its own two feet, one might think my occasional pang of longing for my former weekends-only gig at To Know Them Is To Love Them pet shop was a bit odd, and, on the surface, they would be right. Working there, part-time, had been a nuisance nine times out of ten—especially when I wanted to: one, sleep in; two, do something fun with my weekend; and three, keep my hands and arms scratch-free. But there had been good things about it, too.

Like alone time with Mary Fran.

Granted, that alone time had included bathing and grooming dogs who weren't necessarily eager for such services (see above mentioned scratches), but now that I no longer needed to be there to pay my rent, I couldn't help but notice the hint of emptiness I felt on the occasional Saturday and/or Sunday. Sometimes, when the emptiness was impossible to ignore, I even had to admit I kind of missed Rudder Malone.

Rudder Malone was an African Gray Parrot who resided at the pet shop. Mary Fran liked to pretend no one had ever expressed an interest in purchasing the bird, but I knew better. In fact, I'd heard no less than six offers for Rudder during my time at the shop, but Mary Fran always had a reason he couldn't be sold that particular day. When I'd questioned her, she'd pointed to some inexplicable "vibe" she got about the person— something that "worried" her, or "didn't sit right." But Sam and I knew the truth. Rudder had successfully wrapped the pet shop owner around his little beak.

How, exactly, the winged irritant had accomplished that, I'm not sure. Especially when you took into account Rudder's personality which, on the best of days, was downright cantankerous. He was bossy, impatient, sarcastic, relentless, and a troublemaker of epic proportions. And he loved to yank my chain, reminding me every time he saw me of a certain little habit I was working really hard to stop.

Yet somehow, despite his laundry list of unattractive qualities, we all catered to him like he was some sort of royalty.

Don't get me wrong, there were nights I dreamed of ways to silence my fine-feathered nemesis once and for all. Heck, I'd even searched the internet for techniques to waterboard a parrot, but I also had a soft spot for Rudder I could neither explain nor deny with any believability.

So when I stepped inside the pet shop and heard Rudder's succession of snorts, it really didn't come as any surprise that I smiled in response.

For a second.

Maybe two.

"Good morning to you, too, Rudder," I murmured.

"Snort! Snort! S-nort!"

I rolled my eyes and headed straight for the small hallway off the back of the shop. Sure enough, as I approached, I heard Mary Fran humming from inside her inner sanctum (aka closet-sized office).

"'Walking on Sunshine' for the win!"

Mary Fran stuck her head out into the hallway and grinned at me. "Very good. And the artist who sang it?"

"Katrina and the Waves!"

"Impressive."

"You taught me well." I pulled her in for a quick hug and then stepped back for a thorough once over. "You're still sporting the proud mama glow, you know that?"

Mary Fran's smile widened even more. "How can I not?"

"You can't. And you shouldn't." I stepped against the wall to let her pass and then followed her back out to the counter and the pair of stools tucked beneath its interior eave. "So did he sleep with his award?"

"I tried to slip it out of his hand when I looked in on him this morning, but he woke up."

I laughed. "I'd have done the same thing if I won. No doubt, whatsoever."

Mary Fran's smile slipped from her face. "Thank God you didn't."

And, just like that, the lightness of the morning was gone. Although, in all fairness, any lightness I'd felt hadn't started until I walked through the front door. "I still can't believe it, you know?"

"I know. Trust me." Mary Fran scooted my stool around to me and then pulled out her own, stopping short of sitting on it like I did. "I tried to put it out of my mind for Sam's sake, but once the party was over and we were back home, I found my thoughts going back to that awful, *awful* moment."

"I know. Me, too." And it was true. Of the roughly four hours I was in my bed, I'd slept maybe forty-five minutes, and that was being generous. Still, I wasn't sure I was ready to go down that unsettling road again just yet, so I changed the subject. To Rudder, of all things...

"Has he had his morning kiwi yet?" I asked, waving my hand in Rudder's general direction.

"Mor-morning! Morn-ing ki-wi!"

"Yes," Mary Fran said to me before widening her glance to include Rudder. "And he knows he has."

"Mor-morning! Morn-ing ki-wi!"

I laughed and snorted.

"Snort! Snort! S-nort!"

Dropping my head onto the top of the counter, I groaned. Loudly. "And to think I actually missed him a little this morning."

Mary Fran's gasp alerted me to the words I hadn't intended to ever say aloud, and I bolted upright on my stool. "You didn't hear that!"

"Oh yes, I did."

"Yes, yes I did!"

This time when I groaned, it echoed around the store. "Ugh!"

"Your secret is safe with me," Mary Fran said, laughing.

"Safe! Safe with me!"

I shot a death glare at Rudder and then turned an exasperated sigh on my clearly amused friend. "He could drive a person to drink, you know that?"

"I know. You've mentioned it before."

"Because it's true." I slipped off my stool, crossed to the small refrigerator behind the counter, and extracted the Tupperware container of kiwi normally reserved for Rudder and his far sweeter (read: less annoying) counterpart, Baboo. When Rudder began pecking at the side of his cage in anticipation, I simply pulled out a single piece of his favorite fruit, returned the container to the fridge, and then slowly placed the kiwi onto my tongue. "Mmmm...yummy, yummy kiwi."

"Now who's being a pill?" Mary Fran asked through lips that were most definitely twitching.

I closed my mouth, chewed the rest of my kiwi, and then swallowed dramatically. "He started it."

"Snort! Snort! S-nort!"

Mary Fran held up her hands, crossing guard style. "Enough, you two. Enough."

I lowered my head in shame (not really, but I made it look good) and returned to my stool. "So when's Drew coming home?"

Mary Fran's smile was back and I was glad. Especially considering the reason—a reason that, prior to January, had been on par with hell freezing over. "Friday."

"Your glow is back."

"I know."

"I'm happy for you, you know."

"I know that, too," she said. "And I also know I have you to thank for it."

"Yes, yes you do." I allowed myself a moment of mental back patting and then leaned against the edge of the counter. "That's the thing with someone who's really smitten, as my grandfather says. It drips off them."

Mary Fran lowered herself onto her own stool and eyed me closely. "Then I'm guessing you saw it dripping off him last night. At both the award show *and* your party."

"Him?" I echoed with a squeak.

"Your grandfather."

I wanted to protest, to tell her she was seeing things that weren't really there, but to do so would be akin to delusion, and I wasn't the delusional type. Most days, anyway.

I stood and wandered around the store, stopping every few steps to peer into the cat cages, Max's hamster condo, and at a half dozen goldfish that would likely end up in someone's toilet within the next few months. "As much as I loved and miss my grandmother, I'm not opposed to my grandfather finding someone to live out his remaining days with, I'm really not. But Ms. Rapple? Seriously? I-I just don't get what he sees in her."

"He doesn't see her the way we do."

I made a fish face against the outside of the glass tank and when the fish didn't respond, I shrugged and turned back to Mary Fran. "You mean he doesn't see her as a mean, nasty shrew who has nothing nice to say to anyone, ever?"

"She says nice things to your grandfather." Mary Fran patted me back over to my stool, but when I didn't heed the invitation, she joined me over by the bin of cat toys I felt a sudden need to organize. She let me arrange and rearrange for a few moments and then, when I tried to move on to the bin of dog toys, she grabbed my hand and held on until I looked at her. "She's making him happy, Tobi."

I tried to speak, but all that came out on the first three attempts was an odd raspy noise and an audible swallow.

"And, quite frankly, he's softening her in return."

"Did you say *softening*?"

Mary Fran nodded.

"We're still talking about Rapple, aren't we?"

Again, Mary Fran nodded.

And again, I swallowed.

"Did you not see the way she encouraged him to eat his vegetables last night? Or the way she gently rubbed his back when he could barely sit still in the moments leading up to your category?" Mary Fran gently tugged me back toward the pair of stools but stopped short of pushing me onto mine. "She calmed him with her voice, with her touch. And it was...*sweet.*"

I tried to keep my bottom lip from hitting the floor, but the only reason it didn't was because, well, lips can't hit floors unless one is sprawled out on the ground—which I wasn't.

Yet.

"You do realize you just called Ms. Rapple sweet, yes?"

Mary Fran shifted from foot to foot. "I said her *behavior* toward your grandfather was sweet. She's got a long way to go until I call *her* sweet."

I felt my shoulders relax ever so slightly at her answer. "I think it's an act. I mean, we're talking about Rapple, no?"

"People have been known to change, Tobi."

"Name one."

"You."

I drew back so fast I nearly fell off the back of my stool. "How have I changed?"

"For starters, you're kicking butt with your company."

"That's not me *changing*, Mary Fran. That's just things working out. With a lot of hard work."

"There's the fact that you allowed yourself to give Andy a shot despite all the hurt caused by what's-his-name."

"Nick. And while we're on the subject, might I remind you that you, too, talked a good game about never getting involved with another man again?"

"Oh, I remember. Still pinch myself, on occasion. But I never said you're the only one making changes."

I knew a slippery slope when I saw one.

"So..." I cast about for yet another new topic of conversation, but, in the end, I took us back to the point of my first veer-off. "Did you happen to watch the news last night when you got home from the party?"

Mary Fran looked as if she was about to protest my steer-job, but, in the end, she let it go and for that I was grateful. There would be time to figure out this Grandpa Stu/Ms. Rapple thing later. Or, with any luck, maybe I'd bide my time long enough, my grandfather would come to his senses, and all would be back to normal in my little world.

"No, no news for me," she finally said. "Once Sam and his award went to bed, I called Drew and then went straight to sleep. Why?"

"They think what happened to Deidre last night was intentional."

"Oh. That. Yeah, I know. I read it in this morning's paper." Mary Fran swept her hand, and my attention, toward the paper folded neatly beside the shop's register. "Though, honestly, the picture they ran of her makes it hard to imagine anyone having any sort of ax to grind with her, you know?"

I leaned across the counter, grabbed hold of the paper, and peered down at the professional photograph of the mother of two. "If Grandpa Stu's theory is correct, Deidre wasn't the target. The *winner*—whoever it turned out to be—was."

"But who would do that?"

"Someone who was angry they weren't nominated?" I offered as convincingly as I could.

"Like?"

"Cassie Turner, for one."

"Cass—wait. Why does that name sound familiar?"

I unfolded the paper and swept my gaze across the front page article and the rest of its accompanying photographs. "She won my category *last* year."

"Right, right, right… And she's the one who handed Deidre her award this year, right?"

I nodded without looking up.

"Do you think there could be any truth to that theory?" Mary Fran asked.

"I don't know, maybe. I mean, Cassie *is* known for being a bit of a competitive diva, but that said, I'm pretty sure she's friends with Ben Gibbens."

"Ben Gibbens?"

"One of my fellow nominees."

"So…"

"If she was targeting the category and he'd won, he'd be the one dead right now." It was a thought that had come to me during the night, but this was the first time I'd voiced it aloud. Not that it mattered, really.

"Could she have known who the winner was in advance?"

"I don't think so, but I can't say for sure." I allowed my gaze to travel to the bottom of the page and last year's picture of Cassie standing on the platform at the top of the spiral stairs, her ad displayed on the screen behind her head. "I know it would be a tragedy no matter who this had happened to, but I can't help but feel like it wasn't supposed to be Deidre at all."

When Mary Fran said nothing, I looked up to find her staring at me. "What are you saying?"

"It wasn't Deidre's ad that was starting to play when she fell. It was Lexa's."

"M-maybe the tech guys made a mistake and ran the wrong one."

"Maybe. In fact, that's what Andy thinks, too. But it's also possible that—" I stopped, took in Cassie's high-wattage smile, and shivered.

"Possible that, what?" Mary Fran prodded.

I lifted my gaze back to my friend and went for broke. "Maybe Cassie *deliberately* read the wrong name."

~Chapter Six~

I'm not much of a cook. Never have been. If a meal didn't come from a box (hello, Cocoa Puffs), my freezer, or one of about a half dozen eateries that offered delivery, I didn't eat. Unless, of course, my grandfather was in town and it happened to be a Sunday.

Which he was and it was.

Sunday night dinner was a tradition that began long before I was born. It was my grandmother's way of keeping tabs on everyone. The fact that my grandmother had also been an amazing cook pretty much guaranteed the success of her plan. By the time I came along, the weekly gathering had grown to include games, an occasional theme, and close friends interspersed around the table alongside blood relations.

So while I'd be lying if I didn't admit a certain sadness at not seeing my parents (they had tickets to a show), my siblings (transplanted to other parts of the country), and my late grandmother (currently cringing at my lack of prowess in the kitchen, no doubt) assembled around the folding banquet table Carter had managed to secure from the theater, I was also pretty stoked about having all of my friends in one place for the second time in as many days. The only thing that could make it any better (other than the ability to raise my grandmother from the dead), would be the subtraction of one person and one oversized rat that doubled as said person's dog.

"So what are you subjecting us to this time, Sunshine?" Carter asked from his spot next to my chair.

I rolled my eyes at the laughter that spread around the table and plunked the first of a half-dozen or so platters down in front of my own personal doubting Thomas. "I'll have you know, my grandmother made this very same roast when I was a kid and it was always a hit, isn't that right, Grandpa?"

My grandfather leaned in close, sniffed, and then looked up at me, his *I-love-you-no-matter-what* face letting me know I'd missed an ingredient (or five). "I'm sure it will be delicious, Sugar Lump."

"If not, I saw an unopened box of Cocoa Puffs in the pantry a little while ago and—" At my answering sputter, Sam laughed and then amended his suggestion. "Okay, so there's an *opened* box of Cocoa Puffs we can pass around if necessary."

"Ha. Ha. Everyone's a comic." I returned to the kitchen, grabbed the bowl of mashed potatoes and the bowl of stuffing, and carried them back to the table and the empty spots on either side of the roast.

Curling her upper lip, Ms. Rapple lifted her fork from the table and poked at the contents of each bowl. But just as she was obviously revving up for one of her cutting remarks, she glanced at my grandfather seated to her left and...smiled.

This time when I rolled my eyes, it was mirrored by both Mary Fran (who sees everything) and Carter. But that wasn't enough for me. Oh no...

"Is there a problem, Ms. Rapple?" I challenged, earning myself a flash of surprise from my clearly smitten (and therefore blind to the reality of McPhearson Road's resident nut job) grandfather.

"Of course not, Tobi. Everything looks"—Ms. Rapple stopped, cleared her throat, shifted in her seat, and smiled at my grandfather—"delicious."

I reared back to challenge the sincerity in her words, but let it go as Andy rose from the table and ushered me into the kitchen with an offer to help shuttle in the rest of my attempts at cooking. Still, the second my feet hit the chipped linoleum denoting the start of my rental unit's kitchen, I balled my hands into fists and released a frustrated groan.

Andy leaned against the kitchen sink and motioned me over for a power hug. "Let it go, Tobi. It's just one dinner and there's enough of us here we can talk around her if necessary. Don't let her presence ruin a really cool idea."

He was right and I knew it. But still, I had to have my say. Because, well, I'm not exactly a fan of silence. "Her presence shouldn't even be an issue because she shouldn't be here. This is supposed to be for family and friends. She qualifies as neither."

"She was there last night, to cheer you on."

I stepped out of his embrace and made a face. "She wasn't there to cheer me on. She was there because my grandfather invited her and she has the hots for him."

Bookending my shoulders with his hands, Andy waited until my gaze met his. When it did, he gave me the smile that generally turned my legs to mush. But even the addition of his dimples didn't work this time. I was aggravated. Plain and simple.

"I hate to be the bearer of bad news, sweetheart, but your grandfather has the hots for her, too."

I shuddered so hard all conversation in the other room stopped for a moment. When it resumed, I marched over to my cabinet, reached inside the Cocoa Puff box I'd opened for sustenance while I was cooking, and pulled out a gorilla-sized handful. "I don't get it. What does he see in her? She's mean-spirited, her breath is questionable, and she bears an uncanny resemblance to the beast currently sitting under the table—uninvited, I might add."

"Apparently your grandfather sees something very different when he looks at Ms. Rapple."

"Does Medicare cover eye transplants on wiry bald grandfathers?" I groused. And when I say groused, I mean *groused*.

Andy waited as I shoved the last few puffs into my mouth and then pulled me close once again, his breath against the top of my head a comfort. "I know she's not who you would have picked for your grandfather."

"I wouldn't pick Rapple for the delivery guy who dropped my pizza on the sidewalk last week, either."

The sound of a throat being cleared in the general vicinity of the kitchen doorway made me jump back in time to see my grandfather's hooded eyes gazing back at me. "I thought I'd check and see if you needed any help, Sugar Lump."

I looked from Andy, to my grandfather, and back again as my heartbeat rose into my ears.

Uh oh.

"Grandpa, I—"

He stepped all the way into the kitchen, pointed at a bowl of green beans on the table, and then hooked his thumb in the direction from which he'd come. "I'll take these out to the table before Carter starts lecturing everyone on the importance of greenery at all meals."

I looked to Andy for help, but his eyes were cast down at the floor. Mine joined his until my grandfather (and the beans) were en route back to the living room.

"Please tell me you don't think he heard me," I whispered.

Andy's answer came via his silence and a squeeze of my left hand.

"Crap." I raked my hand through my hair only to realize, as I did, that I'd completely screwed up the braid I'd let Carter do when I returned from the pet shop that afternoon. Great. Now *Carter* would be irritated, too.

"Come on, Tobi, let's just get everything else out to the table and keep things light. With any luck, by the time we've eaten and played a few rounds of whatever themed charades Carter has up his sleeve, your grandfather will have forgotten everything."

I think I managed a placating smile.

And I know I grabbed the basket of rolls and pointed Andy toward the butter.

But as I followed him back out to the table, I knew the chance of my grandfather forgetting what I'd said was slim to none for two simple reasons. One, my grandfather forgot nothing. Ever. And two, the sadness in his eyes as I returned to my seat and encouraged everyone to dig in for dinner was impossible to ignore no matter how hard I tried.

Still, I tried…

I talked about my meeting the next day with a potential client—a microbrewery out in St. Charles County.

I prompted Mary Fran to share some of the more funny stories about Rudder and the rest of the pet store gang.

I quizzed everyone on their feelings about the last episode of the newest, yet incredibly addicting, reality TV show, *Suburban Warrior*.

And I encouraged Carter (with the help of a few effective under-the-table kicks) to do what he did best—entertain.

Occasionally, when I snuck a peek at my grandfather, I saw him nod at something that was said. A few times, he even spoke when addressed. But the mischievous sparkle that was as much a part of my grandfather as his love for me was noticeably absent. And it was my fault.

Somehow we made it through dinner and dessert. But it was while eating the chocolate cake I'd purchased from Tara's Tasty Treats that I gave into my guilt and slumped back against my chair.

"Still thinking about what you said earlier?" Mary Fran asked. "About Cassie?"

Realizing she was talking to me, I forced myself to focus just as Carter snapped-to on my left.

"When she first came out, I was mesmerized by her hair. But then, when she turned, it was all I could do not to stand up, march on to that stage, and smack her upside the head for that one ombré strand that just threw it all off." Carter set his coffee cup down on the table and made himself breathe. "I mean, why? *Why!*"

Andy pushed his own cup into the center of the table and reached for a cookie from the tray Mary Fran had brought. "Cassie is the one who handed out the last award, right?"

"Yes, that's the one." Mary Fran, too, took a cookie and shook it at me. "Tell them what you came up with while we were talking at the pet shop this morning."

Grateful for the opportunity to step away from my guilt, I seized on the conversational gem I'd been handed—a gem that would surely appeal to my magnifying-glass-packing grandfather.

"Okay." I pushed my empty dessert plate off to the side and, with the help of the elbows I probably shouldn't have on the table in the first place, rested my chin atop my hands. "So there are two reasons Lexa's ad might have started to play on that screen at the top of the spiral stairs. Either the tech crew responsible for running the videos last night pressed the wrong one... Or they pressed the right one and the wrong winner was called."

Sure enough, I saw my grandfather's eyebrow cock upward.

Phew...

Sam set down his glass of milk at the far end of the table. "Wait. Each presenter comes out carrying a sealed envelope with the winner's name in it, right?"

"Yes."

"So then the only way the wrong name could be called is if the wrong name was put in the envelope—from like a miscount or something, right?"

I used the index finger of my free hand to dab up a chocolate smear from my plate and then licked it off with my overeager tongue. "That would be *one* way, sure, but it's not the *only* way the wrong name could be said."

When I verified all eyes (including my grandfather's) were on me, I filled in the blank with the same realization I'd shared with Mary Fran at the pet shop. "The presenter—which in this case was Cassie—could've simply called a different name than what was on her card."

No one said anything for what had to be a good thirty seconds but, eventually, Carter spoke, his eyes round with intrigue. "So you think Ms. Ombré-Strand read the victim's name even though the real winner was the other woman?"

"It's certainly a possibility."

"But I thought we were looking at the *category* as the target," my grandfather said, pushing his chair back from the table, and heading toward the same piece of paper he'd jotted notes on after the party at my agency.

"It's certainly a possibility, but I can't shake the feeling that it's not."

"Think this idea that Cassie made it so Deidre was on the platform when it collapsed is a theory you should raise with the police?" Andy asked, as he, too, pushed his chair back. But unlike my grandfather, Andy didn't stand.

He merely hiked his left ankle onto his right knee and tented his fingers beneath his chin. "It certainly seems an avenue worth exploring."

My grandfather looked up from his notes, his eyes finding and then abandoning mine before doing the same with Ms. Rapple. I looked at Ms. Rapple to gauge her reaction, but her attention was focused on Gertie, her brows furrowed in something that looked a lot like worry. Before I could inquire though, Carter took a turn with my latest supposition.

"If Ms. Ombré Strand—"

"Cassie. Cassie Turner," I corrected.

Carter swept his hand in my general direction. "Semantics. Anyway, if Ms. Ombré Strand called Deidre's name in error just to get her up on that platform, there would have to be something pretty big there between them. Because if she was just angry she hadn't been nominated and she was railing against that, she wouldn't have cared who was on the platform when it gave way. But if you're right, and she intentionally changed the real winner to Deidre, there had to be a reason. Something big. Something that would drive a seemingly successful person in their own right to retaliate against someone else via murder."

"Carter's right," my grandfather said.

Carter grinned at Sam. "That has a nice ring to it, don't you think?"

But I was focused on my grandfather and the fact that while he was finally looking me straight in the eye, it felt different. Hollow, even.

I shivered.

"Do you remember hearing any scuttlebutt about the two of them?" Mary Fran stood, gathered up everyone's dessert plate, and handed the stack to Sam. When he took the hint and carried them into the kitchen, she moved on to the forks and spoons, handing that pile to Carter. "Any sort of run-in, bad blood, salacious rumors, et cetera?"

"About *Deidre*? No. She wasn't the type."

"You sure of that, Tobi?"

The sound of my name—my given name—on my grandfather's tongue caught me by surprise. I couldn't remember the last time he'd called me Tobi, instead of Sugar Lump. I just knew I didn't like it one little bit.

"Am I 100 percent sure? No. But I'm up for changing that if you are."

Andy held his hands up in the air. "Whoa. Whoa. Whoa. Do I need to remind the two of you what the job of the police is?"

I met and held my grandfather's gaze. "No. But I could have been on that platform just as easily as Deidre. And while I can't say I knew her super well, I know she didn't deserve to die the way that she did."

~Chapter Seven~

I'd always considered myself a punctual person, usually arriving wherever it was I needed to be a full five to ten minutes before anyone else. But compared to JoAnna, I was a complete slacker.

So I wasn't too surprised when, at ten minutes to nine, I stepped inside my agency to find my secretary not only at her desk, but also typing at her usual one hundred-words-per-minute pace. And that's without coffee....

"Good morning, Tobi," JoAnna said, her fingers slowing to ninety-nine-words-per-minute as she smiled at me around her desktop computer. "I stopped at Central West End Perks and picked you up a medium hot chocolate with whipped cream, and at Tara's for one of those chocolate donuts you love so much. They're both on your desk, along with a copy of the program from Saturday night in the event you didn't think to keep one."

She shifted her attention back to the screen, her fingers picking up speed as she did. But less than five seconds later, she stopped and made a face at me. "What? What's with that look?"

"I should be used to you by now. It's been a year. But yet you still surprise me." I reached for the pair of sticky notes in my otherwise empty tray behind her desk and shuffled through them to find a good morning call from Andy, and a call from Ben Gibbens, my former co-worker and fellow nominee. "Ben called?"

JoAnna craned her neck around my body in order to see the note and then nodded. "He left a message shortly after noon yesterday."

"On a Sunday?" I looked back at the note and the phone number it contained. "Did he say what he wanted in his message?"

"Just that he'd like you to call when you get a chance."

"Hmmm..."

"He was one of the other nominees for your award, wasn't he?" JoAnna asked.

"For *Deidre's* award...yes." I shuffled Andy's message into the top position and tapped the two-note pile against the palm of my opposite hand. "Hey, I don't know if I said it Saturday night, but thank you for the party for Sam and me. I know I was more than a little distracted and I'm sorry about that. You did an amazing job and it was really nice for Sam to feel special."

"It was for both of you, remember? And there's no need to apologize for anything that night. I probably shouldn't have insisted we even *have* the party after what happened, but I just didn't want the evening to end there. You and Sam worked too hard for that." JoAnna pressed a button on her computer, stood, and after a quick trek in and out of my office, handed me the hot chocolate and donut she'd purchased. "Sit."

I sat.

"So how are you doing? Really?"

I set my still warm to-go cup on the little table next to my chair and took a bite of my donut while I considered the various answers I could give. But just as JoAnna was ridiculously punctual and organized and on-task at all times, she was also a bird dog when it came to getting the answers she wanted.

It was why I hired her.

And it was also why I knew it was best just to give her what she wanted.

"I'm rattled, frankly." I took a bigger bite of the unexpected breakfast treat and chased it down with a few sips of my hot chocolate. "I only knew her from industry things, but she was always the one who registered in my head as being nice...sweet...genuine. If we were at a conference, we tended to gravitate toward seats in the general vicinity of one another."

"Did you talk?"

"A little. I knew she was married and that she'd put her career on hold until her kids were both of school age. And I know that she wasn't in to the backstabbing and other crap that seems to be becoming more the norm in our industry these days. In fact, when I think back, she seemed to keep to herself most of the time."

JoAnna perched against the front edge of her desk, her eyes clouded with a worry I knew was for me. "That could have been you up there when that platform gave way, Tobi."

"It could've, I guess. But..." I looked at my donut and contemplated a third bite, but as appealing as it had looked when she first handed it to me, my desire for more was gone. "Grandpa Stu thinks *the category* was targeted more than a single person. Like maybe someone was pissed off that they weren't nominated."

"Which makes the notion that it could have been you even harder to push away, doesn't it?"

Shrugging, I took the napkin she held in my direction and, laying it atop my lap, set my donut down. "Then there's the theory that *Deidre* was, in fact, the target."

"But that would mean her winning wasn't a surprise."

"If she won at all."

JoAnna's gasp brought her back into my field of vision. "You think that other ad starting to play wasn't a mistake?"

"You noticed that?" Wait. Of course JoAnna noticed. She noticed everything. I scooped up the donut, offered the rest of it to JoAnna, and, when she refused, wrapped it inside my napkin for a possible snack after my first appointment. "Hey, you'll be pleased to know I didn't kill anyone with my cooking last night. In fact, I'm pretty sure I overheard Sam asking his mom why I have a reputation for being a bad cook as they were heading home after dinner."

JoAnna opened her mouth for what I'd be willing to bet was a protest of my intentional topic change but, after studying me like a scientist might study a test rat for any sign of problems, she humored me and played along. "I'm sorry I couldn't join you. Maybe the next time Stu is in town?"

"He wants to help me solve Deidre's murder."

"Help you?"

"Uh huh."

"But that would mean you're actually planning on *getting involved*," JoAnna said.

"I'm already involved. At least on some level."

"And Stu is okay with this?"

"You know my grandfather and his love of a good mystery."

"I do, but that doesn't hold a candle to his love for you."

I sank back against my chair and released the sigh I had been holding in until that moment. "I don't think he's too happy with me right now."

"Who? Stu?"

I think I nodded. I know my hot cocoa sloshed around inside my cup. But that could have been from the way my hand was trembling. All I knew for sure was my eyes were stinging as JoAnna's index finger guided my chin upward. "Talk to me, Tobi."

"He heard me bitching about Rapple to Andy."

"Oh, Tobi…"

"I can't stand that woman, JoAnna. She's nasty for the sake of being nasty. Has been since the day I moved in—to *good people* like Carter and Mary Fran. And now I'm supposed to forget all that and jump up and down over the fact my grandfather has taken leave of his senses and has a thing for the old biddy?"

"Maybe she's changed?"

I laughed. "Rapple? Changed? No. She's simply putting on the charm for a man. We all know the type. They eat, sleep, and breathe insincerity. And sorry, but I don't want my grandfather involved with someone like that."

"If that's true, I can understand that."

"If that's true?" I echoed in disbelief. "C'mon, JoAnna, you've met Rapple. Heck, you've seen her in action more than a few times. The way she's constantly taking mean spirited jabs at Carter? The way she nitpicks everything Mary Fran says? The way she glares at me and tries to boss me around like I'm some sort of child? The way she ridicules all of us to her *dog*?"

"Oh I've witnessed all of that. I'm just not sure if she's that way because of an innate bent toward cruelty or because of something else—something far more basic."

I flung myself forward and out of my chair, my hand now trembling from anger more than anything else. "More basic than just plain mean?"

"Yes."

"Such as?"

"Loneliness. A lack of friends. Take your pick."

"If Rapple is lonely and has no friends, it's her own fault."

JoAnna gave a halfhearted shrug and then made her way back around her desk to her chair. "The part you need to remember in all of this is that your grandfather apparently sees a different side of her. And if the way he was with her at both the awards dinner and back here at the party afterward was any indication, he likes that side *a lot*."

Like a balloon that's been pricked with a pin, I felt the fight leave my body. "Oh God, please don't say that. We're talking about Rapple, remember?"

"Did you happen to notice the way she was with him? The way she looked at him and after him the whole night? If you did, then you have to know she's pretty smitten with him."

"Maybe she thinks he has money."

"Money? C'mon Tobi, you're being silly now. He lives in an assisted living facility and doesn't even own a car."

I couldn't argue, so I stayed silent.

"Maybe, just maybe he brings out the best in her. And maybe, just maybe, if you give her a chance, you'll realize there's more to this woman than what she's shown you these past few years."

"I'm not giving her anything, least of all a chance," I murmured like the petulant child I was being at that moment.

"And you can certainly take that route if you so choose. But if you love your grandfather the way I know you do, you need to accept that he seems to enjoy her company right now. And whatever this is or isn't may only last a few weeks...or a few months...or even a few years. You can't know that yet. But you do know that your grandfather is a smart cookie. And if he thinks there's something special about this woman, you need to accept that. You owe him that."

More than anything I wanted to argue until the cows came home, but I couldn't. JoAnna was right. My grandfather had stood beside me, championing me and my choices my entire life.

"Ugh!!! I know you're right JoAnna, I really do. I just..."

"You just need to find a way to trust him, Tobi."

"I never stopped. Not ever."

"Then trust his choice in friends. Even if it's Ms. Rapple."

"I'll try...to try." I took one more deep breath and then smiled at my secretary-turned-personal lifesaver. "Thank you, JoAnna. For everything. Always."

"Anytime." JoAnna lowered herself back into position behind her computer but stopped short of returning her hands to the keyboard. "I'll let you know when Mr. Brogan from Brogan's Microbrewery arrives. In the meantime, is there anything you need me to do beyond the usual?"

"Can you see if any funeral arrangements have been made for Deidre Ryan and send some flowers over from us? And while you're at it, maybe see if someone is setting up some sort of scholarship fund for her kids that I can donate to?" I started to turn toward my office but stopped as yet another idea hit. "And if you have a few moments, could you compile a list of the campaigns Deidre has worked on?"

"Of course." JoAnna plucked a pen from the wooden holder to the left of her computer and jotted herself a reminder. "Are you looking for anything in particular?"

"I don't know. I guess I'm hoping I'll know it when I see it."

~Chapter Eight~

I was just finishing up with my post-meeting notes on the microbrewery when JoAnna knocked on my door with a look that got my immediate attention. "Please tell me you didn't overhear Eric calling another ad agency on his way out the door."

"Of course not. Quite the contrary, in fact; he was whistling when he waved good-bye. Which leads me to believe you've just added another client to the stable."

Tossing my pen onto my notes, I slumped back against my chair, the relief over another successful meeting merging with my lack of sleep and making me wish I was back in preschool with its mandatory nap-time. "Let's hope you're right. The more padding of the bottom line we have, the better."

JoAnna stepped all the way into my office, her favorite notepad in her hand. "Deidre's viewing is scheduled from four to six and again from seven to nine tomorrow night, with a funeral mass being held at St. Mary's the following day at eleven. Tobias Ad Agency will have a floral arrangement at the funeral home, and the director of the home said he'd get back to me on whether anyone is setting up a scholarship fund for her children or not."

"If there's not, maybe we should." I pushed my notes off to the side of my desk and reached for the rest of my chocolate donut, inhaling it in three bites while JoAnna shook her head in amusement. "What? I didn't finish it for breakfast."

"I didn't say anything."

"No, but your eyes did." I wiped the corners of my mouth with the napkin that had housed my donut over the past two hours and then balled it up and tossed it into the wastebasket next to my feet.

"And what, exactly, did they say?"

"That my food choices leave much to be desired."

"My *eyes* said that?" JoAnna challenged.

"Yup."

"I bought you that donut, remember?"

"But you intended it for breakfast."

JoAnna rolled her eyes and gestured toward my phone. "Did you call him?"

"Him?"

"Your former colleague, Ben."

I sat up, shifted through my pile of notes, and plucked out the message. "Nope, but I will now."

JoAnna came over to my desk, worked her organizing magic, and, when my meeting notes were in one pile and my to-do notes in another, she stepped back, hooking her thumb over her shoulder as she did. "Think you can hold off on calling him back just a little longer?"

If it was possible to feel one's ears perk, mine were perking. "Is this about that list? Of Deidre's campaigns?"

"There's a lot there so it's taking a while, but, no, this isn't about her past campaigns."

"But it's about her?"

JoAnna's gaze dropped to her wristwatch before returning to me and motioning me to follow.

Shrugging, I accompanied her out of my office and down the hallway, my gaze immediately gravitating toward the series of shadow boxes that were starting to fill up the wall quite nicely. Each box represented another client, another campaign. I loved the sight of them all for vastly different reasons, but my favorite was, without a doubt, the one representing Zander Closet Company. It had been a gift from Andy that I would treasure for the rest of my life. That glass-fronted box with the miniature skeleton hanging from the rod and the gold plate displaying my slogan for Zander Closet Company: *When we're done, even your skeletons will have a place*, had said so much about him. He listened, he cared, and he got me.

The rest of the boxes had come from JoAnna who had liked Andy's line of thinking so much she'd decided to keep it going. Now, I had shadow boxes representing my work on New Town, Pizza Adventure, Salonquility, Peter Piper's Children's Boutique, and, hopefully soon, Brogan's Microbrewery.

JoAnna veered into the extra room that doubled as my pitch room for new clients, tripled as my place to view my competitors' campaigns via the tiny television in the corner of the room, and quadrupled as Grandpa Stu's investigation command center when he was in town and needed access to a computer and an assistant (aka JoAnna).

"We only have a few seconds." After grabbing the remote off the conference table, JoAnna aimed it at the television. "I'm sure it'll be the lead in."

"Lead in?"

JoAnna nodded, motioned me over to one of the conference table chairs, and then took the one next to it. "I went to Channel Five's website a little while ago to see if they had any information pertaining to scholarships for Deidre's children."

"Okay..."

"They didn't have anything. What they did have, however, was a teaser for the noon news show."

"Snow in April?" I joked.

The familiar opening music for the station's newscast muted my laughter as a familiar face filled the screen. Only this time, instead of a tuxedo and the same cheesy proud-of-himself grin he'd worn for his master of ceremony duties on Saturday night, Carl Brinkman wore his standard suit jacket and the same serious expression he wore at the start of each and every newscast he anchored. "Did he get demoted because of all those bad jokes the other night? Is that why he's anchoring the noon news instead of—"

"Shhhh."

"Good afternoon, everyone, I'm Carl Brinkman, sitting in for Alicia Haldiman. As many of you know, I was serving as Master of Ceremonies for the annual St. Louis Advertising Awards on Saturday night when tragedy struck a young St. Louis area mother. Deidre Ryan, of The Whitestone Advertising Agency, had only recently returned to full-time employment and was being recognized for her work on the St. Louis Public Library's annual reading campaign when the platform on which she was standing, after receiving her field's highest honor, gave way beneath her feet, sending her to her death in what was quickly ruled a deliberate act. Today, police are working hard to find her killer, while those behind the scenes of the award show are asking the same questions the rest of us are asking."

Mavis Callahan appeared on the screen, the footage obviously shot the night of the awards. "I-I don't understand. It wasn't supposed to be this way," Mavis moaned in a voice choked with emotion before the image on the screen moved to an on-air female reporter standing outside Callahan Advertising in downtown St. Louis. The box at the bottom of the screen said it was live.

"For those not familiar with the St. Louis Advertising community, Mavis Callahan has been involved in the annual award show since the very beginning. And when her husband, Shamus Callahan died, she made sure to keep it running, year after year, in his honor. Yet today, many inside the Callahan Foundation are likely wishing she hadn't."

The image changed again as footage, shot earlier that morning, played on the screen. I watched, along with JoAnna, as employee after employee was stopped on their way into work to share their "feelings" on what had transpired at the annual award show over the weekend. A few of those interviewed used words like "shocked' and "saddened." Another simply swiped at her eyes, said something about being glad Shamus Callahan hadn't been around to witness the awful tragedy, and then hurried inside the building, head down.

Eventually, the reporter appeared back on the screen just long enough to send it back to Carl in the newsroom. When she did, I turned to JoAnna. "And why did we need to see that?"

JoAnna pointed the remote at the screen and powered off the television set. "I thought maybe they'd have something new that would negate your need to get involved. Instead, they simply exploited that poor woman."

"You mean Mavis?"

Nodding, JoAnna wrapped the fingers of her left hand around the tiny locket affixed to the thin gold chain around her neck and slid it back and forth. "It's just that seeing that woman in such pain gets to me."

I don't know what I was expecting her to say, but that wasn't it. "I don't understand."

"She's older than me, of course. Probably a good *twenty years* older. But I remember my mom coming back from her friend's house one day, talking about poor Mavis Callahan. And that's how she said it—*poor Mavis Callahan.*"

My stomach registered its hunger once again, prompting me to cover it with what I hoped was a muting hand. "You mean because of Shamus's affair back in the day? Trust me, I wrestle with that all the time, especially having been philandered on, myself. But his campaigns were amazing and you almost forget about that bad side when you think back on his legacy."

"No small thanks to Mavis."

"What are you talking about?"

"It's because of that woman's grace in handling his indiscretion that so many people are able to look past the skeletons in Shamus Callahan's closet."

I waited to see if her unintentional nod to my campaign for Zander Closet Company would register, but when it didn't I moved on. "I have to admit, I was taken by her obvious affection for Kevin's children at the award show. So much so, I didn't even really think about them only being her grandchildren by way of that same affair."

"Yet another example of Mavis Callahan's grace. Not only did she *stay* with Shamus after she found out, she also welcomed the child born from that affair into her home when his mother—aka the mistress—died of cancer a few years later."

"I can't imagine it, but it sure seems as if they've forged a real mother/son relationship. A relationship that now extends to his children, as well." I allowed myself a momentary smile at the memory of the Callahan matriarch fawning over her granddaughter and then turned my attention back to a still frowning JoAnna. "What? What's with that face?"

"I don't think many people paid attention to what that man"—JoAnna pointed at the now darkened television screen—"said on Saturday night, but Mavis was an artist when she met Shamus Callahan."

My stomach gurgled its awareness of the lunch hour, but I did my best to ignore it in favor of providing the pair of ears it seemed JoAnna needed at that moment.

"My mom knew Mavis from church. Said Mavis was incredibly talented, yet pushed it all aside to be the good, supportive wife of a man who ended up humiliating her in such a public way." JoAnna rose to her feet and made her way around the conference table, her steps aimless. "You know that award you wanted so badly? The one I'm certain you'll have one day?"

"How could I forget? I've dreamed about it for years."

And I was this close....

"I don't mean the category, Tobi. I mean the actual award—the trophy."

"The Golden Storyboard." I heard the wistful tone of my voice and felt the answering guilt as my thoughts traveled back to Saturday night and that look on Deidre's face just before she fell. "Carl said Mavis designed it."

"She did. According to my mom, Shamus *asked* Mavis to make it something special—something worthy of such talent. And she did that on top of helping him get that inaugural award show up and off the ground."

"Well, she did an amazing job on both fronts. The award show is still going strong now, forty-one years later. And in terms of the Golden Storyboard, it is *the* coveted award by everyone in my field."

I followed JoAnna around the room with my eyes, watching as she stopped to neaten the computer area (it didn't need it), place the remote on top of the television (it was fine on the table where she'd left it), and push in every chair around the conference table (with the exception of the one I was sitting in, although she tried). I considered pulling the boss card and making her sit, but I knew she'd get to whatever was bothering her in time.

And I was right.

"Do you know why Shamus Callahan started that award show in the first place?"

Based on the way she was setting the questions up, I suspected my answer was inadequate, but I gave it anyway. "Because he thought it would be fun?"

JoAnna made a face. "More like because he was trying to lavish his mistress with attention and praise."

Like a bloodhound who'd just hit on a scent, I sat up tall. "Wait. Kevin's mother was in the business?"

"That she was."

Whoa. How I'd missed that salacious tidbit was beyond me. Then again, when it came to work, I was pretty focused. And workplace gossip had never held much appeal for me. "Anyone I would have heard of?"

"Theresa Kinney."

My mouth dropped open. Literally.

When it finally returned to its normal position, I leaned forward. "Theresa Kinney...as in the first person to ever win Best Overall? For"—I stopped, snapped my fingers in an effort to help my brain along, and then pointed at JoAnna as I struck memory gold—"MoDot, right?"

"I guess. I don't know."

"I looked it up—along with all the other winning campaigns since then—when I was nominated. You know, so I could get a feel for the pioneers before me." I dropped my hand back down to the table as I recalled the hours I'd spent happily slogging through old advertising campaigns at the Callahan Foundation's offices downtown. I was a dweeb and I knew it. So, too, did JoAnna. "Just about every one of the winning campaigns hit it out of the ballpark in terms of creativity and memorability. Except—"

I braced my hands on the edge of the table, pushed back my chair, and stood, my thoughts rewinding to the moment I'd walked into my ex-fiancé's apartment and found him in bed with a waitress from our favorite restaurant—the one where we'd gotten engaged, in fact. At the time, and in the months that followed my heartbreaking humiliation, I'd actually managed to convince myself they didn't come any slimier than Nick.

"Wait. So you're telling me he had Mavis—*his wife*—help plan an award show he started solely because of his pregnant mistress?"

"Actually, I'm telling you he had Mavis design the award he made sure the floozy got."

Wow.

I took a moment to process what I was hearing, my mind's eye taking me back, again and again, to the sight of Mavis, smiling at her granddaughter at the Callahan table on Saturday night. Sure, I'd known the granddaughter was Kevin's child. And yes, I'd known Kevin was the product of an affair Mavis's husband had decades earlier. But I'd never known the sordid details. And now that I did, I couldn't help but feel both pity and awe for Mavis Callahan.

Repeating my amazement via another *Wow* (aloud this time), I pushed in my own chair and then watched as JoAnna swooped in and made its distance from the table match those of all the other chairs. "So she remained married, accepted a child that wasn't hers, raised said child when the floozy died, *and* continued to be one of the powers-that-be behind the very same award show she so blindly supported while Shamus made a public mockery of their marriage? What a prince."

"Hence the reason I hate seeing her having to deal with this latest mess now, too. It's too much." JoAnna stopped, brushed her hands against one another as if dislodging crumbs or freeing them of dirt, and then squared her shoulders with an audible inhale. "I'm sorry. I didn't mean to go off on such a tangent. Especially when you look as if you could eat a horse right now. Should I head across the street and grab you a sandwich, or would you rather I call something in? Like maybe a Stromboli or maybe some Chinese?"

"A sandwich sounds good."

"Chips?"

"Nah, let's go with pretzels, instead." I trailed her out of the conference room and into the hallway, flicking off the overhead light as I did. "Can I see that list of Deidre's campaigns?"

"It's far from complete, let me tell you."

I stepped around the corner and joined her by her desk as she retrieved her purse from its normal work-hours resting place. "I take it there were a lot of distractions while I was in my meeting with Eric Brogan?"

"No, it's just that she was part of a lot more—"

My cell phone rang from inside my office, cutting our conversation short. "Hold on a second. I'll be right back with my lunch money."

I jogged into my office, recovered both my phone and my wallet from my purse, and took the call en route back to JoAnna's desk. "Hey, Mary Fran. Is everything okay?"

It's not the way I'd normally answer a call, but Mary Fran rarely called me during the work day. My radar was on alert.

"Actually no. Ms. Rapple called me in hysterics a few minutes ago and—"

A cold chill made its way down my spine. "Did something happen to my grandfather?"

"No! It's Gertie."

"Gertie?" Wedging the phone between my ear and my shoulder, I used my now-free hand to open my wallet, pluck out a twenty, and hand it to JoAnna, mouthing what I hoped was a clear *get yourself something too,* as I did. "Why, what's wrong? Did our resident rat-dog rip a hole in one of her little sweaters while tearing through my shrubs or something?"

JoAnna's disapproving eye wasn't wasted on me, so I did the only thing I could at that moment: I turned away.

"She said Gertie hasn't moved all morning. Hasn't picked up her head, hasn't left her little bed, hasn't eaten a thing."

"That doesn't sound good."

"No, it doesn't."

"So why did she call you? Shouldn't she call a vet?"

"She's on a fixed income, Tobi. You know that."

"Snort! Snort! S-nort!"

Rudder.

I rolled my eyes at the bird's never-ending association with my name and sunk onto the chair across from JoAnna's desk. "I know, but she's always so nasty to you."

"Lately, she's been nicer."

"Lately?"

"Since...well...you know."

I did know. And I didn't like it, not one little bit. Still, JoAnna had made some valid points earlier and I didn't like feeling as if I'd caused my grandfather any pain. "Do you know if my grandfather was with her when she called?"

"No, and I think that was only adding to the hysterics," Mary Fran said. "You know how she is with that dog. He's her whole world—or, was, until...well...you know."

I closed my eyes, counted to ten in my head, and then slowly opened them to find JoAnna still standing by her desk with my twenty in her hand.

Aware of the hunger pains building to a crescendo at the thought of the sandwich that had yet to be ordered, I closed my eyes again in the hopes that would let me focus on Mary Fran for just a few more minutes. "So you want to go over and see what's going on?"

"I do."

"When?"

"Now. *If* you're free and can maybe man the store for a few minutes? Say thirty at most? That'll give me time to assess what's going on and advise Ms. Rapple on what's the best thing to do."

Before I could respond one way or the other, Mary Fran continued. "Everyone has been fed—including Rudder, so it's really just about being here if a customer comes. Maybe ringing up an order or two."

"You want me to man the pet shop for thirty minutes." I opened my eyes yet again, this time fixing them on JoAnna. "Mary Fran needs me at the—"

"Pet shop. I know. I got that part."

"Do we have anything scheduled for the next little bit? Any meetings or phone calls?" I was virtually positive we didn't, but I guess I was hoping JoAnna had dropped the ball on something and my sudden inquiry would niggle it back into place.

"Nope. Your afternoon is wiiiide open." JoAnna folded my twenty in half and slipped it into the front pocket of her dress slacks, my stomach gurgling in protest.

Bye-bye sandwich...

Bye-bye pretzels...

I turned my attention on JoAnna's candy jar and allowed myself a silent sigh. "Okay, Mary Fran, I'm on my way."

"Ms. Rapple and I thank you."

~Chapter Nine~

Mary Fran was gone less than half a second when Rudder started in, rocking back and forth on his little metal perch, letting loose a string of snorts designed to make me give him a kiwi in the interest of shutting him up.

I knew it.

Had lived it many times.

Yet unlike all those times before, I found myself opening the mini refrigerator, extracting the Tupperware of kiwi from inside, and carrying it over to the counter. No, I hadn't forgotten the whole don't-reward-bad-behavior mindset I religiously followed where my fine feathered nemesis was concerned.

Quite the contrary, in fact.

Instead, I set the container on the counter, popped open the lid, and tossed back a half dozen pieces of kiwi, much to Rudder's vocal displeasure.

"Snort! Snort! S-nort!"

"Keep snorting, buddy and I'll eat it all. I swear I will." I rooted through the container, found another five or six big and juicy pieces and inhaled those as well. "Wow. I. Am. Absolutely. Positively. Starving. With a capital S."

"Snort! Snort! S-nort!"

I knew I was being a stinker, but really, I couldn't help myself. Something about imagining a sandwich (and pretzels) and then having to put it on hold for an undetermined amount of time had driven me to the brink of insanity. Rudder just had a way of pushing me all the way over at times.

Piece by piece I ate my way through the container until there were just two bites left. I considered eating them as well, but when I looked back at Rudder and noted that his rage had transitioned to something that looked a lot more like heartbreak, I brought them over to him and stuck them between the slats of his cage. "Peace offering?"

He gobbled up the fruit and then turned his back to me.

"I'm sorry!" I protested. "You have no idea how hungry I am."

My pleas fell on deaf ears.

"The second Mary Fran gets back, I'll head over to that fruit stand across from Fletcher's and get you some fresh kiwi. I promise."

He kept his back to me but I was pretty sure I saw his posture soften a smidge.

"And when I get back from doing that, I'll give you a great big piece of kiwi before I put it in the fridge, okay?"

"Snort! Snort! S-nort!"

Not the response I wanted, but I'd take it.

I moved on to Baboo's cage, told him he looked handsome today, and then made my way back to the counter and my purse. While not the ideal place to conduct business, I didn't see any harm in utilizing the lack of customers to return Ben's phone call.

He picked up on the second ring. "This is Ben."

"Hey, Ben, it's Tobi—Tobi Tobias."

"Snort! Snort! S-nort!"

I shot Rudder a glare to end all glares and hoped he got the message to pipe down. Just in case he didn't, which was more likely than not, I did my best to shield the lower half of the phone with my free hand. "You left a message on my agency's voicemail yesterday and we just—"

"We need to talk," he whispered, his tone showing signs of...*nervousness*?

Knowing what I knew about the living hell it was being in the employ of John Beckler, I felt my intended arm's-length demeanor falling by the wayside. "Look, if you need a reference, I think I saw enough of your work ethic during our overlap time to be able to write something up for you if that'll help."

Instead of the relief and appreciation I would have expected to hear in response to my offer, I heard only silence. But before I could fully switch gears from empathetic to resolute, his whispered voice returned in my ear. "It's not that."

"Okay..." Wedging the phone between my shoulder and my cheek once again, I braced my hands atop the counter and pulled myself up until I was sitting in the same spot Sam favored whenever he was in the store and not busy with tasks. "So what do you want to talk about?"

"Not now. Not here."

"Are you okay?" I asked while the part of me that hated surprises began sifting through the possibilities.

He'd caught John Beckler, one of my former bosses, doing something unethical, stupid, illegal, or all of the above and wanted me to be the first to know.

He was considering staging a coup to overthrow said former boss and needed to pick my brain.

He got an inside line on a client Beckler was wooing and wanted to give me a heads-up so I could throw my hat in the ring.

I took advantage of the continued silence to really consider my thoughts and realized they made no sense. While our time at Beckler had overlapped for only about six months, Ben and I really hadn't traveled in the same circles. He'd been John's handpicked intern and, as a result, I'd kept a wary distance.

"Could we meet somewhere after work?" he finally said, his voice still hushed and difficult to hear against the various pet store sounds that never fully ever went away. "Preferably somewhere away from here."

Hmmm... The plot thickens.

"Can I at least know what this is regarding?"

"Saturday night."

I felt the inexplicable chill start at the base of my neck and spread down my spine. "You mean the award show and what happened to Deidre?"

"Will five-thirty work for you?" he asked.

"Uhhh...yeah...sure." I took a moment to slow my breath and, hopefully, my heartbeat. "Where?"

"There's a little Italian place off Brentwood Boulevard, north of the mall. Red and white awning."

I opened my mouth to suggest something closer and less out of the way, but before I could even utter the first word, he was gone. I pulled the phone from my cheek and checked the screen.

Yup: *Call Ended.*

"Huh. Weird."

"Huh! Huh-Weird! Huh! Huh-Weird!"

It was on the tip of my tongue to lecture Rudder on the rudeness of listening in on a person's phone call, but when I really thought about what he'd said (and, more importantly what he hadn't said), I couldn't help but smile. "It is, isn't it, big guy?"

"Biggg! Biggg-guy!"

The string of bells mounted above the front door jingled, stealing my attention from Rudder and sending it to the front of the store.

"I'm back, Tobi!"

"Snort! Snort! S-nort!"

So much for progress.

I stuck my tongue out at Rudder and then jumped off the counter and onto my feet. "How'd it go? How's Gertie?"

Mary Fran tossed her purse onto the counter next to mine and slumped back against the display of dog food. "Honestly? Not good."

"Regular not good, or *really* not good?"

"My inclination is the latter, I'm afraid. But I brought them to the best vet in the area and told the secretary to call me and let me know what's going on as soon as they know. If it's bad, I'll close the shop early and drive out so I'm there when they give her the bad news."

"You mean…" I let the rest of my sentence trail off to that place where all stupid questions should go to die before they're ever fully asked. Still, I couldn't just let it go. "You think Gertie might…*die*?"

"Depending on what's wrong, there's a chance they might have to put her down, yes."

"Wow. I just always assumed that dog would be around for years— digging up every bulb I try to plant, killing every bush with her high octane pee, and waking me up every Saturday morning with her obnoxious bark that I will swear to this day is intentional." I looked across the store at Rudder and tried to imagine how I might feel if I walked into the store one day and his cage was suddenly empty.

The answering lump in my throat told me everything I needed to know.

"Does Rapple know? That it's not looking good?"

"I'm not sure, but I didn't feel right pressing her about it, either. You know how she is about that dog, and she's already out of her mind with worry as it is. Why freak her out even more unless—or until—it's necessary." Mary Fran stopped, looked at me oddly, and then reached around me for the empty kiwi container. "Um, Tobi? This was full when I left."

"Snort! Snort! S-nort!"

I snarled at Rudder and then batted my eyes as angelically as possible at my friend. "I know that."

"I also told you he had his lunch before you got here."

"I know that, too."

Mary Fran's brows furrowed with worry as she turned and made her way over to Rudder's cage. "You know he can get sick if overfed."

"He didn't eat it." I looked at the empty container now back on the counter and heard my stomach gurgle hungrily in response. "*I* did."

"You ate all of the kiwi?" Mary Fran turned, hands on hips, and stared at me.

"Well, technically, I gave him the last piece. But I have to say, he was rather ungrateful when I did."

Mary Fran nodding knowingly at Rudder before looking back at me. "I take it you didn't have lunch?"

"JoAnna was getting ready to head out to the lunch place across the street for me when you called."

Raking her hands through the ends of her ponytail, Mary Fran sank back against the counter to my left. "I'm sorry, Tobi, I—"

"Snort! Snort! S-nort!"

Mary Fran laughed.

I didn't.

Fortunately she continued where she left off rather than at the start of her sentence because, if she had, I might have had to throttle a certain bird. "I didn't know you hadn't eaten. I just know what that dog means to Ms. Rapple and I didn't want her to wait any longer than necessary. Think about it, until this thing with your grandfather started up, *Gertie* was all she had. It's like her version of my Sam."

"Your Sam and now your Drew," I corrected.

Mary Fran's face lit up. "Yeah... Drew is pretty incredible."

"Said the woman who had sworn off men for the rest of her life." I stuck out my chest, flat as it was, and added a *ta-da* in true Superman style, belting out the next few words in song-like fashion. "I...saved...the...day!"

"I'm not sure Rudder would agree," Mary Fran responded, pointing at the empty kiwi container.

I dropped my head, nodded, and then snatched my purse off the counter. "I know. I know. Give me ten minutes, and I'll be back with some fresh kiwi for the king."

"No. He can wait until after school. I'll have Sam stop by the stand and restock my supply." Mary Fran closed the gap between us and planted a kiss on my cheek. "Go get some lunch and enjoy the rest of your day."

There was no denying the way my stomach responded to the word lunch, but there was also no ignoring the way that all stopped when I recalled the reason for my delayed lunch in the first place. "Hey, if things go bad with Gertie, and you need to go back to the vet to be with Rapple, call me, okay?"

"Am I picking up a note of concern in your voice?" Mary Fran teased.

I wished I could play it off, but we both knew I was full of hooey. So I switched gears and hoped for the best. "I guess an upside to my grandfather liking her so much is that she'll have someone to help her through the grief should the unthinkable happen."

"That's assuming he'd actually return her calls so she could tell him." I stared at my friend. "Excuse me?"

"I told you. Grandpa Stu doesn't know about Gertie yet."

"Yeah, but that was when you first called. I assumed by now that..." I let the rest of my sentence go as Mary Fran shook her head.

"Maybe he went somewhere with Carter."

"Carter is at work," Mary Fran countered. "Ms. Rapple said so."

"Maybe my grandfather went *with* him."

Mary Fran dug at a nonexistent speck on the counter before dropping her hand to her side and sighing. "After I left Ms. Rapple and Gertie at the vet, I swung by your place on my way back here."

"And?"

"I knocked. Three times, actually. But your grandfather didn't come to the door."

"It's like I said. Maybe he's with Carter... Or maybe, he's yakking it up with Jack Fletcher down at the newsstand. I swear, when those two start trading jokes and riddles and other assorted fascinations, large chunks of time can just up and disappear. I've seen it. Many times."

"No, I'm pretty sure he was inside and just chose not to come to the door."

"Maybe he thought you were a solicitor?"

"No, because after I knocked, I called into him that Gertie was sick and Ms. Rapple really needed him by her side."

Weird.

"Why are you so sure he was inside?"

"Because I turned and looked back at your front window as I was getting in my car."

"And you saw him?" I asked.

"I saw the curtain slide back into place real fast like he was trying to stay out of sight."

It made no sense.

It also meant I needed to push my sandwich off even longer.

"Okay, thanks. I'll see if I can figure out what's going on." I crossed to the pet shop's front door and then looked back at Mary Fran. "Other than an unexpected meeting that's come up for me at five-thirty, I should be around if you need me."

~Chapter Ten~

More than anything, I wanted to steer my new car in the direction of my office and the lunch I knew would be mine no more than ten minutes later. But I couldn't. Not without feeling intense guilt—which I hated.

Instead I turned toward home and called JoAnna on the way. She, being the poster child of efficiency, picked up at the start of the second ring.

"Good afternoon, Tobias Advertising Agency, how may I help you?"

"I honestly can't imagine a time when I won't get a kick out of hearing you say that," I said, stopping at the first of three stop signs between the pet store and home. "It has such a nice ring to it, don't you think?"

I could hear JoAnna's smile through my car's speakers. "It does, indeed. And I've been saying it with greater frequency over the past few months."

Owning my own agency had been my dream since I was a little girl. But four years of college (and business classes) had brought a little realism to my life and I realized that working for someone else's agency was far more likely.

That is until I spent a few years working for John Beckler and realized mini-me had been right all along. After a dicey six months, Tobias Advertising Agency had begun to gain some traction. So much so, JoAnna had gotten all her paychecks, the utilities had remained on at both the office and my home, and I no longer had to borrow wheels to get where I needed to go.

"Tobi? Are you still there?"

"Yeah. Sorry. You caught me reminiscing."

"*Good* reminiscing?"

"The best kind." At the second stop sign I stopped, looked both ways, and then turned left. "I just wanted to let you know that I'm all done at the pet shop and I'll be heading back to the office in about twenty minutes or so. I just need to stop out at the house real quick to check on Grandpa Stu."

"So what happened with Martha's dog?"

It always took me a minute for my brain to catch up when someone referred to my next door neighbor by her first name, and today was no exception. So, after a second or two of cluelessness, I was back in the game. "Apparently she's not in good shape, although Mary Fran isn't exactly sure what's wrong. She took Rapple and Gertie out to some vet Mary Fran thinks is the be-all-that-ends-all and dropped them off for testing and stuff like that."

I took the opportunity afforded by the third and final stop sign to check my glove box for anything resembling a piece of candy (or maybe a small package of snack crackers), but there was nothing. "Anyway, Mary Fran seems to think there's a chance Gertie might not make it."

Audible tsking filled my car's pristine cabin and brought me back to the task at hand and the reason I was pulling up to the curb in front of my house at two o'clock in the afternoon. "So that's why I'm stopping at home for a second—to make sure my grandfather is up to speed on what's going on."

"Wow."

I cut the engine, pulled my key ring from the ignition, sent the call to my cell phone, and exited my car in favor of my front walkway. "Wow what?"

"You really took our earlier conversation to heart, didn't you?"

"Earlier conversation?"

"Yes. About respecting Stu's feelings for Martha. I think your grandfather is going to be pleased."

I briefly considered telling JoAnna she was giving me far too much credit, but I knew if I did, the conversation would go much longer than I wanted it to go. Besides, the sooner I got in and out here, the sooner I could get there and fed. "Well I'm here, so I'll see you in a few, okay?"

"Should I order your sandwich now?"

"I'll call you as I'm leaving, if that's okay. That way it's fresh in the event traffic builds up on Euclid."

"If you get delayed, you might just want to consider making it dinner, instead," JoAnna suggested.

My stomach lodged its protest of my secretary's words via a rumble that was so loud there was no chance JoAnna hadn't heard. Her laugh just served as confirmation I chose not to dwell upon. "Actually, I have dinner plans—odd ones, but dinner plans nonetheless."

"Odd ones?"

I told her about the call to Ben and the cagey way he'd acted even before suggesting we meet at some no-name restaurant on Brentwood Boulevard. JoAnna, of course, wanted to know more specifics in case she needed to send out a search party if I didn't return (I swear, sometimes I think she's on my mom's payroll), so I gave her what I knew.

"Oh! I know that place. It's called Vinny's, although I'm not sure there's actually any sort of signage on the building."

"A restaurant with no sign? Huh... Maybe you should get me two sandwiches when I call, since I obviously won't be ordering anything."

JoAnna sucked in a breath that echoed inside my ear. "No! You have to order something. The food is incredible. In fact, you should get the chicken marsala—it's divine."

"I'm finding it hard to believe you with the description of this place."

"Have I steered you wrong yet, Tobi? About anything?"

I tried to think of a time, but I came up empty. "No."

"Get the marsala tonight, and I'll get your sandwich when you call. In the meantime, I probably should get back to the task at hand."

I started to hang up but stopped. "Hey, before you go, did you happen to get that list of Deidre's campaigns together for me?"

"That's what I'm working on now. You didn't tell me how prolific she was."

"What do you mean?"

"I mean Deidre Ryan has been part of a lot of campaigns over the years."

In lieu of a chair, I wandered over to the lone tree in my front yard and leaned against its trunk. "How? She's only been with Whitestone since the fall, when her youngest started full-time kindergarten."

"Most of these aren't for Whitestone."

"Who then?"

"Ross Jackson."

A squirrel who, only seconds earlier had been running across the grass oblivious to my presence, stopped dead in his tracks at my answering gasp. "*Ross Jackson*? Seriously?" Then, before she could answer, I spat out, "When?"

"Over a three year time period that ended about seven and a half years ago."

"Seven and a half...wait." I pushed off the tree and made my way back to the front walkway. "That actually makes sense. She probably left Ross Jackson when she had her first—"

"Tobi? I hate to cut you off, but there's a call coming in on the other line and I should probably get that." I slid my phone into the front pocket of my purse as I stepped onto my porch and headed straight for the first of my two front doors—one I shared with Carter (which was unlocked), and the other that was specifically for my apartment. With practiced fingers, I picked through the keys on my ring and inserted the correct one into the lock.

"Grandpa Stu? I'm—"

I stopped on the two-by-two piece of linoleum that doubled as my entryway and took in my grandfather in his most ratty pair of sweat pants and a flannel shirt I was pretty sure hadn't been washed since last worn. He sat in the center of my couch, his eyes directed at the TV even though it wasn't on. "Grandpa Stu?"

"Is it five fifteen, already?" he asked without so much as a glance in my direction.

I stepped all the way into my living room, soaking up all the non-wardrobe parts of my lifelong partner in crime—like the shadows around his eyes and the paler than normal coloring of his unsmiling face. The look certainly fit the wooden, almost lifeless tone of his voice, but none of it fit my Grandpa Stu.

"No. It's only a little after two."

"Something happen at the office?" he asked.

Still holding my keys, I sat down on the couch and turned so I was facing him. "No. Nothing like that. I came to check on you. To make sure everything is okay."

"Everything's fine. Peachy, even."

"Then why are you sitting here…dressed like that…watching nothing?"

"Why? Did I miss a Grandpa-Do list or something? Because I didn't see one in its usual place."

"Grandpa, why are you acting like this?"

Slowly, he moved his gaze to me. "Like what?"

"I don't know…almost sad."

He shrugged. "I get sad sometimes. It's hard being without your grandmother. Has been since the second she took her last breath."

I lurched forward and buried my face in his shoulder while I worked to get my sudden, yet all too familiar surge of emotions under control. When I was sure I could speak without crying, I sat back up. "I miss her, too, Grandpa. All the time. But she'd be the first person to say she doesn't want you sitting around, being sad. You know that."

He said nothing for a few moments and then, just as I was trying to figure out something else to say, his shoulders rose and fell beneath his misbuttoned flannel shirt.

And that was it. No smile. No nod. No attempt at a real reply.

So I took another road entirely. "How come you didn't answer the door when Mary Fran knocked a little while ago?"

Again, my words were met with a shrug.

"Something is wrong with Gertie, Grandpa Stu. Mary Fran thinks it could be bad. She thought maybe you'd want to know so you could lend some moral support to Ms. Rapple."

Yup, got another shrug. But this time, it came after he cast his eyes down at his lap and his jaw tightened a smidge.

Hmmm...

Trouble in paradise?

I tried to stifle the smile I felt forming lest he choose that exact moment to engage me in eye contact, but it was hard. The notion of our time together going back to being just about the two of us (and friends of my choosing, of course) would be an answer to my prayers.

"Anything new on the murder?"

The sound of his voice startled me back to the present and I set my backpack on the floor at my feet. "No, nothing—wait! Yes. When JoAnna got in this morning, there was a voicemail on the office phone from Ben Gibbens, one of my fellow nominees."

Intrigue pulled his eyes up to mine as he waited for me to continue. Since I finally had his attention, even if it was grudgingly, I acquiesced.

"So I called him back a little while ago and he was very weird— whispering, and being rather cryptic. Asked me to meet him today at five thirty...at some restaurant north of the mall. Back booth."

Granted, Ben hadn't specified a table location, but in the interest of pulling my grandfather from his funk, I took a few liberties—sue me. I let him process the update and waited for him to invite himself along. But the request never came.

"I-I wish we had access to one of those wire things the cops put on their witnesses on those shows you love. Then you could hear everything Ben says."

I waited for the widened eyes and the rush to go with me back to the office so he could research how one might go about securing such technology in the next two hours or so, but it, too, never came.

The ensuing silence was broken only by Grandpa Stu's index finger pointing toward my feet. Sure enough, I heard my phone vibrating from inside my backpack and sent up a mental prayer of thanks for the welcomed distraction. I dug my hand inside my bag and pulled out my phone, the sight of Mary Fran's name kicking off an *uh-oh* bell in my head.

"Is it Gertie?" I asked in lieu of a more standard greeting.

I stole a glance at my grandfather while I waited for Mary Fran's answer, but other than a quick shift of his body, there didn't appear to be a discernable reaction.

"I checked in with Ms. Rapple via text about ten minutes ago, but Gertie was still in the back having tests done."

"Oh. Okay."

"I'm actually calling to see if you're planning on going to Deirdre's viewing tomorrow night, since you kinda knew her and all."

Now, I normally prided myself on the ability to shift gears at a moment's notice, but this was a shift I hadn't seen coming and I'm sure my initial *uhhh*, reflected that. Still, I managed to get it together before she did one of her *Earth-to-Tobi* things.

"Yes, I'm planning on going. Why?"

"I was looking through this morning's paper and I came across her obit."

"Okay…"

"I know her husband—Todd. We went to school together."

I tried to focus on what Mary Fran was saying and to make the appropriate *I'm listening* sounds, but my still-slumped-in-the-same-spot grandfather was making it hard to concentrate on much of anything besides, well, *him*.

"It's funny, but the other night, at the award show, I actually thought the guy who kissed her as she stood up looked familiar. But it's been twenty-five years, and he was part of a very different crowd than mine. In fact, he was one of the theater kids. I actually went to the last show senior year with my friend, Carrie, just so we could say we did, and, *wow.…*"

In the interest of keeping my own mood from plummeting any further, I made myself look at something else, which in this case, was my kitchen doorway. "Wow? Wow, why?"

"You know the show, *Into the Woods*, yes?"

"Of course."

"Well, then you know the wolf is a pretty diabolical character, yes?"

"Okay, sure."

"That was the role Todd played. And, Tobi, when I tell you he nailed it, I mean he *nailed it*."

I waited for more since I wasn't grasping the problem, but when she said nothing, I helped her along with another *okay*.

"I'd always seen him as this wimpy kind of kid who had a crush on pretty much every girl in our class that was completely out of his league. But wimpy kids can't pull that kind of role off, not like that, anyway." Mary Fran took a sip of something and then continued. "So afterward, when the cast came out to the hallway after the show, I told him he was pretty amazing. He thanked me and then said something like, *it's the quiet ones you have to watch out for, eh*? Carrie found it funny and laughed. But I found it a little unsettling, quite frankly."

"Unsettling? Why?"

"I don't know."

I wasn't sure why she was telling me all of this, but considering the alternative had me continuing to try to make conversation with Grandpa Funk, I decided not to look a gift horse in the mouth.

"Anyway, the obit says they have two children together and that they live out in Chesterfield."

I nodded along even though she couldn't see me. That didn't seem to matter as she kept right on talking.

"He was one of the ones who didn't show to our reunion in January, but he sent a nice note. Said he *had* to take the wife on a cruise, but hoped he could make it for our thirtieth."

"Had to?"

"That's what he said and, yeah, I found it to be an odd word choice as well, but, considering where I was with men at that point, I wasn't surprised." Mary Fran took another sip of whatever she was drinking, offered some sort of soothing reply to Baboo, and then sighed. "Anyway, this is all a long way of saying I'd like to go with you to the viewing—preferably the one from seven to nine, although I'll make the four to six work if need be. Sam can always cover the store for an hour or so if necessary."

"Really? You want to go?"

"I kind of feel like I should. Since I know Todd and all."

I considered calling her on the curiosity I knew was truly driving the train, but I kept it to myself. Because even if some measure of that was accurate, I also knew Mary Fran's heart, and I knew the fact that his kids were now motherless pulled at her heartstrings.

"Sure, we can go together. Unless you think you'd rather go with one of your old high school chums, or even Drew if he's back by then."

"He's not back until Friday night. And no, I'd rather just go with you, if that's okay."

"Of course."

"Cool. Thanks, Tobi."

"Snort! Snort! S-nort!"

I rolled my eyes toward the ceiling in conjunction with Mary Fran's laugh. "I really hate that bird, sometimes."

"No you don't." Mary Fran said something to Rudder to make him stop, and then turned her attention back to me. "Anyway, thanks again for earlier with the store, and again now for letting me tag along tomorrow."

"Not a problem. We'll talk later."

When the call was over, I tossed my phone back into my bag, tried to engage my grandfather with a smile, but when he failed to respond, I slid my backpack onto my shoulder and stood. "Well, I better get back to the office. I've got a little more work to do before I wrap up in time for this dinner with Ben. But it's an Italian place, so if you'd like me to bring you back something, I'd be happy to—"

"I've been taking care of myself for a long time now, Tobi. I'll be fine. Go."

~Chapter Eleven~

To say the next two hours were a blur would be an understatement. But somehow, despite the round of calls I made to my various clients, the check-in call with Mary Fran for an update on Gertie (there was none), and the planning session JoAnna and I had regarding prospective clients, I managed to eat (okay, *inhale*) my sandwich and pretzels.

So while I wouldn't say I was completely satiated yet, I wasn't as grumpy as I could have been when Andy's name showed up on my caller ID. Still, I took a deep breath, smiled at myself in the rearview mirror, and hoped the attempt infused itself into my voice as I accepted the call.

"Hi, Andy!"

"You sound mighty chipper this evening. Good day at work or just glad it's quitting time?"

I glanced into my side mirror and jumped into the left lane, my patience for highway buffoonery not exactly high. "Work was...fine. Gina and Dom are beside themselves with how well things are going out at Pizza Adventure. So much so, they're getting serious about finishing off two more destination rooms."

"Oh? What do they have in mind this time?"

"Gina said it was a surprise."

"How can you help them advertise the change if they don't tell you what they're adding?"

I passed a trio of cars and then slid into the middle lane. "No, she just wants to tell me what they're thinking during our next face to face meeting. On Thursday morning."

"I'm thrilled they're doing so well, though it's really no surprise. Not only is their concept incredible, but the pizza is the best I've ever had."

I let up on the gas just a little as I exited at Brentwood Boulevard and stopped at the traffic light at the bottom of the ramp. "I'll be sure to tell Dom you said that. He'll be pleased beyond belief."

"Oh, I know he will. He glows every time I tell him that when you and I are heading out the door and he comes out to say good-bye."

I drummed my fingers on top of the steering wheel as I waited for the light to change. "I've never heard you tell him that."

"That's because while I am, Gina is pinching your cheeks and giving you the high sign about how perfect she thinks I am for you."

I laughed. Not because of what sounded like an inflated ego on Andy's part, but rather because of the truth in his words. Gina did have a habit of pinching my cheeks and she was a huge proponent of my relationship with Andy.

The light turned green and I turned right. I passed the mall on my left, a slew of shops and restaurants on my right, and continued north. "I also spoke to Esi at Salonquility and she's thrilled with the increase in traffic they've been seeing since our campaign finally got started."

"Happy customers—always a good thing."

"Indeed." The first of the three remaining traffic lights between me and my final destination turned red and I stopped once again. "You still at the office?"

"I'm heading out the door as we speak, which is why I'm calling. Can I take you to dinner and a movie tonight? Or, better yet, I can pick you up and we can go back to my place and order in a pizza and watch a movie on TV. With popcorn and treats, of course."

"Actually, I have plans for dinner, but the rest sounds perfect." The light turned green and I lurched forward with all the other commuters and shoppers only to stop at the second light. "I don't know how you handle these lights on a daily basis, I really don't. They're maddening."

"Lights? What lights?"

"On Brentwood."

"Wait. Where are you?"

"One traffic light shy of your office. Which in some towns might mean I'm a few seconds away. But on this road, make it ten minutes." I felt the grumpiness seeping back in and mentally chastised myself for it. "Sorry. It's been a long day."

"What are you doing around here?"

"Meeting Ben Gibbens for dinner at some place about a mile or so up the road. JoAnna says it's good, but the fact it doesn't have a name anywhere on the building gives me pause."

"You're going to Vinny's?"

Traffic light number two turned green and again I moved forward only to stop for the third time. "You've heard of it?"

"The food is amazing." He cleared his throat quickly. "So who is Ben and should I be jealous?"

"He was one of my fellow nominees for the award and no, you shouldn't be jealous. Of him, or anyone else."

"Ahh, so that's why the name rang a bell."

"That and the fact you may have heard his name or even met him when you and Gary were originally working with John Beckler. Ben works for John."

"Hmmm, the plot thickens."

The final light turned green and I happily stepped on the gas. "Meaning?"

"You hate Beckler. Yet you're having dinner with one of his people?"

"I'm having dinner with Ben as my fellow nominee, not as one of John's people." Though even as I said it, I had to wonder if I was right. Because really, I had no idea why Ben had called me, why he acted so cagey on the phone, why he wanted to see me, and why it had to be in a restaurant that, despite glowing praise from both Andy and JoAnna, was rather out of the way compared to the half dozen or so popular eateries I'd already passed. "I don't know why he wants to talk to me, but he was pretty insistent."

"Sounds weird."

"I know. But if nothing else, JoAnna said the Marsala is fantastic and—"

"She's right. And, I'll be honest, I'm kind of kicking myself that I haven't thought to take you there yet."

I glanced to my left and smiled at the edge of the office building where Zander Closet Company was housed, my mind filling in the visual with an image of Andy standing beside his car, phone in hand, talking to me. For a brief moment, I thought about making a U-turn at the next possible opportunity and stealing a quick hug, but if I did that, I'd be late. And the sooner I got to my meeting with Ben, the sooner I could find out what he wanted and be on my way to Andy's.

Instead, I continued north, passing under 170 before moving into the right lane and slowing as the landmarks JoAnna had described on my way out of the office began to appear exactly as she'd said—red brick building, alleyway, jewelry store, vacant storefront, and the red and white awning that was my signal to turn right into the next parking lot. "I'm here, I think."

"Red and white awning?" Andy asked.

"Yup."

"There's a lot just beyond it. Park in there."

"I know. I'm already in it."

"There's an entrance to the restaurant in back, but the hostess stand is up front so it's better to go in under the awning."

I parked, got out of my car, and tossed my keys into my bag. "It's scary, sometimes, how much you and JoAnna sound alike."

It was Andy's turn to laugh, the sound tickling my ear and making me wish I'd thrown caution to the wind on being late and actually made the U-turn. "I'll take that as a compliment, since JoAnna is pretty much Super Woman."

I crossed to the top of the parking lot, stepped onto the sidewalk, and made my way over to the door beneath the awning—a door that truly had no name or marking, anywhere. "And you're sure this is a restaurant?"

"I'll wait while you open the door."

Switching the phone to my left hand, I tugged on the door with my right, my nose immediately lifting to capture the glorious smell of sauce...and warm bread...and—

"Oh. My. Gosh."

"Welcome to Vinny's, Tobi." His laugh was back. "Anyway, enjoy the food. Good luck with the meeting."

"Thanks." I let the door close behind me and stepped over to the empty hostess stand to wait. "Hey, before you go, can I ask you a favor?"

"Of course."

"If you're not too busy, is there any way you could stop by my place and check on my grandfather?"

"Sure. Is he sick or something?"

"He's not sick, but something isn't right." I saw the hostess heading in my direction and gave her a no-rush wave. "I guess I'm hoping maybe you could cheer him up or, if not, figure out what's going on?"

"I'm on the case."

"Thank you, Andy."

I closed out of the call, slipped the phone into my bag, and smiled as the hostess welcomed me to Vinny's and asked if I was dining alone. "Actually, I'm meeting *him*." I pointed to Ben and, at the hostess's nod, made my way back to the table.

Ben looked up as I approached, and while I knew we weren't necessarily friends per se, I was still surprised to see a lack of anything resembling a smile. Instead, his Adam's apple moved with a swallow and his gaze darted forward toward the front door and then around at the handful of booths and tables scattered around the tiny dining area. When he was done with his once-over of our surroundings, he motioned for me to take the bench seat on the other side of the table.

"Thanks." I tossed my bag onto the bench first and then slid in behind it, breathing in the tantalizing aromas of my surroundings as I did. "This place smells amazing."

The words were no sooner out of my mouth when our waiter—a young twenty-something who introduced himself as Vinny Junior—placed a basket of what my nose knew was fresh bread from the oven even before my hands moved the red and white checked cloth out of the way for visual confirmation. Vinny Junior took our drink orders and said he'd be back for our dinner order in a moment.

"I'm not eating anything," Ben informed me as the waiter left. "I've gotta get home to my wife. But you should stay and eat something."

"Considering you picked a restaurant to meet in, maybe I should." I heard the sarcasm lacing its way through my tone but really, who cares? It was the truth.

"It's the only place I could think to meet," Ben said, splaying his hands after yet another quick inspection of the dining area.

"You mean besides my office, your office, or one of the millions of establishments between the two?" Then, without waiting for an answer, I propped my elbows on the edge of the table and leaned forward. "Before we get started, I feel the need to get a few things on the record in the event John is behind this unexpected meeting somehow. I'm doing great. *My agency* is doing great. Signing New Town out from under John was really quite the coup. And now that I think about it, I never did get around to sending him a thank-you note for that."

Yes, I was moving from sarcasm to mildly bitchy, but I was starting to get irritated. And honestly, sending a seemingly nice guy like Ben in to do a little nosing around had John Beckler written all over it. The fact that I'd failed to really consider it as a reason behind this clandestine meeting spoke to how fried my brain was after Deidre's fall.

Ben leaned back against the booth, his lips twitching with the first semblance of a smile I'd seen since arriving. "Wow. He really got under your skin, didn't he?"

I don't know what kind of response I was expecting, but that wasn't it. Before I could come back with something, he was back at it again. "I'd heard through the grapevine how awful he was to you, but I figured it was a sort of office legend. But now, after"—he rolled his hands in the air—"*that*, I'm becoming a believer."

"People still talk about me at Beckler?" I asked while simultaneously plucking a piece of bread from the basket, slathering some butter on it, and moaning in pleasure over the first bite.

"All the time. You're the one they stupidly let get away."

"*Stupidly*? People really say that?"

"All the time." Ben, too, took a piece of bread. "In fact, there were a few reps who actually went out and celebrated your signing of New Town."

I stared at him over the remaining bite of my own piece. "You can't be serious. Beckler losing that account could've meant layoffs for you guys."

"You're right. But they still celebrated."

At a loss for what to say at that moment, I simply gave into the goofy grin I could no longer hold back and stuck my hand in the bread basket once again. "Wow."

Silence filled the space between us for a few moments before Ben pulled in an audible breath. "I didn't ask you here to spy for John. I do my job, I get my paycheck, and I keep my eyes open for the first opportunity I have to work for someone else—heck, *anyone else* most days."

I took the glass Vinny Junior set in front of me, raised it in a makeshift toast, and then lowered it back down to the table as I placed my order for Marsala. As previously stated, Ben ordered nothing.

When Vinny Junior returned to the kitchen, Ben leaned forward. "Look, I've been feeling really lousy since Saturday night. Like guilt, almost. And I know it makes no sense—heck, I should be *thrilled* I didn't win, but yet I can't shake this guilt that's been pressing down on me since… well…you know."

"I know. I'm feeling it a little, too. JoAnna, my secretary, she calls it survivor's guilt. And I'm guessing she's right on account of the fact she's always right. About everything."

Ben shrugged and then, with seemingly aimless hands, picked up his napkin-rolled utensils only to set them back down in their original spot. "Okay, so you get it."

"I do."

Nodding, he relaxed against the back of the booth. "So, what's your read on Deidre having won, anyway?"

"I thought her campaign was great."

He bobbed his head slightly to the left and then slightly to the right before lifting his gaze to mine. "But did you really think she was gonna *win*?"

I wasn't really sure what to make of his question so I didn't say anything. I was well aware of the egos in my line of work, but something about those egos juxtaposed against what happened to Deidre made me uncomfortable.

"Look, I'm not saying she didn't deserve to be nominated, because she did. If you've read *Bitch Pitch* even a few times, you know she worked her tail off. I'm just—"

"*Bitch Pitch*? As in that blog that exposes some of the behind-the-scenes crap that goes on at all the local agencies?"

"You read it?" he asked.

"Sometimes. When I'm bored."

Ben cracked the faintest hint of a smile. "Scintillating reading, wasn't it? Gonna miss that start to my Monday morning each week." He pitched forward, lowered his voice to its original near-whisper and added, "Can you imagine being on the other side of a bathroom stall and listening to Maggie Jenkins listing all her attributes to herself in the mirror? I'm not sure how Deidre kept from laughing."

The Greek he might as well have been speaking to that point, suddenly rescinded as my head caught up with his mouth. "Wait. You think the masked exec behind *Bitch Pitch* worked at Whitestone with Deidre?"

"Uh, you could say that."

Something about his tone connected the final wire in my brain. "Nooooo."

He nodded and leaned back against the booth once again. "Yup. Deidre Ryan was *Bitch Pitch*."

"Noooo." I knew I was repeating myself but I was still in shock.

"I only know because a few weeks ago, *Bitch Pitch* mentioned being at a park the previous day when some unleashed dog started terrorizing the kids on the playground. And, it just so happens, I was running along a nearby trail at that same time. I spotted Deidre trying to shoo the dog away from the swing set where her kids were playing."

"Wow."

Ben took a sip of his soda and set the glass back down with a soft thud. "I know, right? I always pictured the person behind *Bitch Pitch* being more, well, bitchy."

So had I.

"Anyway, to get back to what I was asking before, were you as surprised as I was that she actually won."

I made a mental note to go back and read some of my favorite *Bitch Pitch* posts the next chance I had, but I wasn't sure that would help. Never in a million years would I have thought that the quiet, unassuming woman I'd sat beside at a conference or two was the face behind one of the most biting, eye-opening, and occasionally entertaining exposé blogs I'd ever read.

"Tobi?"

I met Ben's quizzical eyes and forced myself to focus on the change in conversation. "The only thing I was aware of when Deidre's name was called was the momentary disappointment that it wasn't me. I'm guessing you felt the same, yes?"

Ben waved at my words. "Maybe for a split second, sure. But I knew I wasn't going to win, just as I knew you weren't going to win."

"Gee, thanks."

"I didn't think *Deidre* was going to win, either."

"Meaning, what?" I asked. "You expected Lexa to get it?"

"Didn't you?"

I settled back against my own side of the booth, my mind's eye instantly filling in the TV, print, and radio spots Lexa had created. "I know her campaign was very well received by the public, but I don't think it did much for MetroLink."

"It didn't. The message got lost in the fluff."

"Which is why it makes sense that a panel of judges who are versed in the true reason behind advertising didn't give Lexa the..." My mouth stopped moving as the memory of Deidre's face, in the seconds before her death, mocked my words.

If Ben noticed my veer off-point though, he didn't let on. Instead, he broke off a piece of his bread and balled it between his fingers. "I didn't say I thought Lexa's was better, Tobi. I just said I expected her to win."

"Why?" I ran my index finger along the top edge of my water glass as I waited for him to explain his point and then get to the one that had me sitting across the table from him instead of being with Andy.

"You do realize who Lexa works for, yes?"

"Of course, Ben," I finally said in lieu of the words I really wanted to utter. "I'm very aware of who Lexa works for. So what's your point? You think she was going to win because she's with Callahan? Because if that's where you're going with this, Ben, you're wrong. There have been *tons* of Callahan nominees for Best Overall over the years, and plenty haven't won. Case in point, Tom Jergen last year. He lost to Cassie Turner from Ross Jackson. Hell, I'm pretty sure that Ross Jackson has dominated that award the last ten years."

"Just because someone hasn't worked for Callahan doesn't mean they weren't involved with the foundation as a volunteer or a donor." He looked at me funny. "Tell me this isn't the first time you're hearing this."

Not wanting to cop to my naiveté, I went the devil's advocate route, instead. "And you're saying a volunteer would have a leg up over an employee? Because I'm pretty sure Cassie doesn't volunteer with the foundation."

"Maybe last year was an anomaly. Or maybe since Tom was *male*..."

Ahhh...

The male who can't handle being bested by a woman.

How refreshing.

"Maybe, just maybe, last year's panel of judges simply felt Cassie's campaign was better because it was...well, *better*."

"Maybe. Or maybe it's the method someone like that chooses to use in order to get to the top of the ladder." He threw his shoulders back, cast a dramatic and knowing gaze down at his chest, and then looked back at me and batted his eyelashes.

I finally got it. He was referring to Cassie's reputation of using her personal assets to land clients and get promotions. A trick that was as old as time, really. Was it frustrating to compete with that? Sure. But was he seriously going to negate the accomplishments of all females based on a few bad apples?

"Look Ben, I've made it this far without engaging in gossip and backstabbing. And honestly, I'm not about to start now. So, to that end, I'm going to choose to believe that talent, and talent alone, put the four of us up for that award."

"You really believe that?" he asked. "Even when you know, as well as I do, that Lexa's campaign wasn't even worthy of a nomination?"

Vinny Junior appeared at the table again, this time holding my plate of Chicken Marsala. I watched him set it down in front of me and then grabbed my fork, my stomach refusing to wait any longer than necessary for this meal. "Until I'm given irrefutable proof to the contrary, yes. After all, Lexa didn't win. *Deidre* did."

I hoped I sounded convincing.

But I wasn't so sure.

~Chapter Twelve~

I wasn't even fully seated behind the steering wheel when I grabbed my laptop case off the passenger side floor and powered up my computer. The restrained, mature side of my personality knew I should just wait until I got home, but the rest of me simply couldn't.

Deidre Ryan had been behind *Bitch Pitch*.

Deidre. Ryan.

The sweet, unassuming woman who came across as being above the deplorable antics of our colleagues.

I wanted to believe Ben was completely off base, but I'd always suspected the masked blogger worked at Whitestone. It wasn't that she'd shared an inordinate amount of stories about Whitestone ad execs, but there had been some—enough to ping my personal radar on occasion.

When my computer was fully booted, I typed in the blog's URL and watched as the familiar page appeared on my screen. Slowly, I scrolled through the entries until I reached the one Ben had referenced. A few words in, I remembered having read it when it was posted, but, because of the lack of salacious dirt I hadn't paid it much due.

I scrolled down some more, chuckling all over again at some of the funnier posts over the past few months, including one I'd read over the phone to Carter as it had been a blatant slam of my former boss. Carter had laughed along with me, commenting on the cleverness of the descriptive words used to describe a man I held in such little regard. Again, I giggled at mention of the "blow hard" who had the same appeal as a "Christmas fruit cake."

Eventually, I moved on, scrolling down through the once-a-week entries. I clicked one from September titled "When Talent Comes Back and Scores." Amusing at the time, I found myself looking at the piece in a very different way now that I knew the identity of its author. Now, references to the "pair of boobs" that "bested me last time" had me wondering what campaign Deidre had lost in the past, and what campaign she'd just landed that left her feeling as if she'd "settled a score."

I read through the post one more time and then, as I tried to scroll down some more, realized "When Talent Comes Back and Scores" had been *Bitch Pitch's* inaugural entry.

Hmmm…

I was mulling over what to do next when my phone beeped to indicate a text message. A quick peek at the screen made me shut down my computer, slip it back into its case, and start my car once and for all. Soon, I was heading west on Highway 40, my smile growing bigger with each passing mile.

Sometimes, when I looked back over the past twelve months, the changes in my life were so monumental I felt the need to pinch myself just to be sure I wasn't dreaming. So I pinched. And, sure enough, I wasn't dreaming.…

Yes, I'd quit Beckler and Stanley.

Yes, I'd put all my cards on the table when I opened my own agency.

Yes, I'd been on the brink of losing everything when I failed to sign any clients for the first six months.

Yes, I'd pulled myself up by the bootstraps thanks to Zander Closet Company.

Yes, I'd signed some pretty impressive clients since then.

Yes, I'd been nominated for the biggest award in the local advertising community.

And yes, after having my heart smashed to smithereens by my ex fiancé, I had finally found the kind of guy that made me smile from the inside, out.

I was at the top of my game as my grandfather would say, and I liked it.

Yet somehow, despite all the positives surrounding me, an unease I couldn't ignore was beginning to pick up momentum. And while most people would likely trace it to the horror of watching a woman tumble to her death, I knew its origins preceded that tragedy. By mere seconds.

The few times I'd let myself revisit the confusion on Deidre's face in the seconds leading up to her death, I'd quickly seized the reason that made the most sense: the tech crew had started to run the wrong ad. Period. After all, mistakes happened. And if the crew wasn't privy to the winner prior to Cassie's reveal, all four ad campaigns must have been ready to roll. Really, the notion someone in the tech booth had pressed the wrong button wasn't that far out of the realm of possibility, was it?

Mistakes happened.

Every day.

I knew this.

So why did that moment keep resurrecting itself in my thoughts—more so than the sound of the rope snapping, the horror of watching Deidre plummet to the ground, and the heart pounding chaos that ensued? Was it because I wasn't as naïve as I liked to think I was? That, like Ben, I was shocked by the fact Lexa hadn't won the coveted award? Or was it because, on some level, I knew she had?

In hindsight, I couldn't help but wish I'd asked Ben whether he noticed the video snafu at the award show, but as always, hindsight was twenty/twenty. Besides, I didn't need confirmation from Ben or anyone else about that moment right before Deidre fell. I saw the screen. I saw the ad that started to play just as Deidre stepped onto the platform.

But what did it mean, really? If Lexa's ad had, in fact, been played by mistake, that simply shored up my theory that Deidre was the target. And now that Ben had clued me into a side of Deidre I hadn't known, I had to consider the very real possibility that others may have known about Deidre's extracurricular activity, too. The fact that said activity often involved humiliating the very people who were seated in the audience when Deidre fell to her death kinda had my spidey senses tingling anew.

I considered calling JoAnna to share what I'd discovered but opted to wait. I wanted and needed this time with Andy. I didn't want to talk about Deidre, or the fall, or the way the sounds associated with her fall were making it so I couldn't sleep at night. I just wanted to be with him—to talk about anything *but* Deidre Ryan. Because here's the drill: spending time with Andy calmed me. And if there was one thing I knew about myself, it's that a calm-me was also a better-thinking-me.

Exit by exit I made my way out to Andy's neck of the woods, the post-dinner hour making the normally commuter-clogged thoroughfare more manageable. Still, I pressed down on the accelerator all the way to Andy's exit. A few minutes later, I turned right onto Andy's road, parked in front of his townhouse, and made my way up to his front door, the promise of his smile making me take his front steps two at a time.

Half a knock later, I got my smile.

And a hug.

And a really, really nice kiss.

When the welcome party was over, he ushered me into his living room and over to his couch. "Can I get you anything? A drink? Some chips? Pretzels? Cocoa Puffs?"

I aborted my sit just before my backside hit the couch cushion. "You have Cocoa Puffs?"

His answering smile and its accompanying dimples weakened my knees enough that I completed my sit. "*You* love them, yes?"

I nodded.

"And *I* love *you*, yes?"

I blinked back the tears I knew were only seconds away and nodded again.

"So of course I'd have Cocoa Puffs on my shelf. What kind of boyfriend would I be if I didn't?" He leaned over, planted a kiss on the top of my head, and then stepped back. "Cocoa Puffs then?"

"I'm actually still full from the Marsala you and JoAnna both suggested I order at Vinny's."

He shrugged and then dropped onto the cushion next to me. "Awesome, wasn't it?"

"Oh. My. Gosh. It was incredible." I leaned forward so he could slip his arm around my shoulders and then rested the side of my face against his chest. "The only thing I don't understand is how and why I didn't know about this place until today."

"Trust me, I've been asking myself that same thing."

I took advantage of the break in conversation and overall noise of any kind to simply listen to the steady beat of his heart against my ear, the rhythmic sound incredibly soothing after a day with its fair share of stress. Eventually, when I felt like maybe I'd been quiet for too long, I peeked up at Andy. "I have to say, as amazing as that dinner was, this—right here… with you, is exactly what I needed."

"You mean I trump food?"

I moved my head in a weighing gesture and, when I got the laugh I was seeking, I buried my cheek back against his chest. "Yes, you trump food. And that *includes* Cocoa Puffs."

When his laugh receded, I made myself sit up so I could see his face. "So? Did you get anything?"

His eyebrow lifted in confusion. "Get anything?"

"From my grandfather. You know, on why he was acting so…*weird* earlier today."

Andy let his head drop back against the couch, his gaze leaving mine in favor of the ceiling. "I never saw him."

I reached out, patted his arm. "Hey, no worries. It was a lot to ask as you were heading out the door after a busy day at work. I probably shouldn't have even asked—"

"No"—he lowered his chin until he was looking at me again—"I don't mean I didn't go. I did. But by the time I was done talking to Ms. Rapple, your lights were off and I didn't want to chance waking your grandfather if he'd gone to bed early."

"Gone to bed?" I turned my head and noted the time on Andy's DVD player. "Andy, it's only seven thirty now. So best case, you were at my house at what? Six thirty, six forty-five?"

"I was on the highway heading back here at six twenty."

"There's no way Grandpa Stu was in bed at that time. He's a veritable night owl." I stopped, swallowed, and tried to rein in the disapproving tone I heard in my own ears. "I-I thought you knew that."

He fisted his hand to his lips and exhaled. "I do. And trust me, I thought it was weird. But when I took into account what you'd said, about him being quiet and all earlier today, I thought maybe he was napping or he went somewhere with Carter."

"Was Carter's car there?" I asked.

Andy's shoulders rose in a halfhearted shrug. "I guess I was more affected by my conversation with Ms. Rapple than I realized because I didn't even think to look." He stopped my sudden fidgeting with his hand and squeezed. "I'm sorry, Tobi."

I slowly reclaimed my spot in the crook of his arm. "So what was so engaging about your conversation with..." I suddenly sat back upright. "Wait. How's Gertie?"

"The vet is keeping her overnight for observation and, potentially, more testing come morning. And Martha, well, she's absolutely lost right now."

"*Martha?*" I knew I was looking at Andy as if he'd grown a second head, but I couldn't help myself. First, my grandfather, and now, Andy? What was I missing?

"You didn't see her, Tobi. She was utterly lost when she got out of that cab. Her eyes were puffy from crying, her hands were chalk white from the way she was squeezing them so tight, and her voice was so strained it was hard to make out much of what she was saying when I met her on the front walkway." He rested his head back once again, his eyes cast toward the ceiling even though it was clear to me he wasn't actually seeing it. "Did you know that Martha's mother gave Gertie to Martha not a month before she succumbed to cancer?"

I waited for more, keenly aware of a tightness forming at the base of my throat. But when it became apparent *he* was waiting for *me*, I shook my head and added something resembling an audible no.

"Since Martha never married, her mother didn't want to leave her with no one. So this dying woman had her live-in nurse bundle her up and take her out to an animal shelter so she could find her daughter a family."

"A family?"

Andy scrubbed his face with his left hand and then let it drop back down to his lap. "I've never known that, you know? That not-having-anyone thing. My parents are still alive, Gary and I get along well enough, I'm tight with my cousin, Blake, and his wife, Peggy, and now I have you. I can't imagine being left with...no one."

The tightness expanded all the way up my throat, making it tough to speak, but if Andy noticed, it didn't slow him down. "I can't imagine having a good day at work and not being able to share it with you on the phone. Or having a particularly grueling day with a client and not being able to blow off some steam with Gary."

I knew what he meant. My parents were out in western St. Charles County—far enough to have my own life, but not too far to go running home for a hug if I really needed one. My Grandpa Stu was never more than a phone call away (assuming, of course, he wasn't sleeping on my couch). My siblings, while busy and living on opposite ends of the country, were also semi-easy to locate. And beyond blood, I had Carter, Mary Fran, and Sam within a stone's throw pretty much twenty-four/seven.

Swallowing around the guilt, I reached past Andy for a throw pillow and pulled it against my chest. "Rapple has...*no one*?"

"Other than Gertie? No. Which is why she comes across so different to us when she's around your grandfather. Because she is."

I paused in my pillow-futzing. "Meaning?"

"The Martha we see out on the sidewalk most days—the one who snaps at Carter, keeps tabs on you, harasses Mary Fran, and grills me every time I step foot on your property—is lonely, sad, hurt, and maybe even a little desperate for human contact, no matter the form. The Martha we see with Stu? She's happy, content, hopeful, and, thus, a very different person."

My face must have reflected my thoughts because Andy met my eyes and then pulled back ever so slightly. "Why are you looking at me like that?"

"Looking at you like what?"

"Like this." He scrunched his forehead.

"Maybe because you *look* like Andy Zander...and you *smell* like Andy Zander... But you *sound* just like JoAnna."

"Meaning?"

"She said the same basic thing about Rapple this morning, when I was telling her how my grandfather walked in on me bitching about her to you last night."

He resituated himself in his spot and then scratched at a patch of skin just below his ear. "I really thought he was hurt by that, but it looks like I was wrong."

"Oh?"

"Martha said she left a message for him today about Gertie acting funny, and then another one an hour or so later when Mary Fran dropped her off at the vet, and then again when the vet decided to keep Gertie and Martha needed a ride home. But he never answered her calls."

"Maybe he was out," I suggested even though I knew how lame I sounded.

My grandfather hated to let calls go unanswered. He claimed it was the ringing that bothered him, but I knew better. Grandpa Stu loved to talk. It didn't matter if it was someone he knew, a phone solicitor hell-bent on selling him something he didn't need or want, or a wrong number. If it had a mouth, he'd say, it had a pair of ears, too. But even more than unanswered calls, he hated the message indicator beep on my home answering machine. If it was beeping when we returned from a store or a walk, he made a beeline for my bedside table just so he could press play, listen to the message, and get rid of the beep.

Which was a long way of getting to the reality looming large in my brain at that moment: Grandpa Stu knew about Gertie.

"Do you think there's a chance she simply didn't tell him something was wrong?"

Andy's left eyebrow shot up in a classic *are-you-kidding-me* lift.

"Okay. Okay." I held my hands up in surrender. "You're right. Stupid question."

He pulled my hand off the edging on the throw pillow and held it close. "It's not that. It's just if you'd seen how devastated she was out on the sidewalk this evening, you'd know there was no way she could have kept that out of her voice for anyone or any reason."

"So then why didn't he call her back? Or try to track her down at the vet?" I pushed off the couch and wandered around Andy's living room, the built-in shelves and the treasures they held little more than a blur in my peripheral vision as I revisited my earlier conversation with my grandfather. Granted, he'd said very little, but what he had said could certainly explain all of this. "My grandparents were grade school sweethearts, did you know that?"

A quick glance back at Andy revealed the sweet smile I loved. "I knew they went back a long way, but I didn't realize it started when they were little."

"Miss Appleton's first grade class, to be exact." I loved the sound of the words on my tongue almost as much as I'd loved hearing them in my formative years. In fact, as much as I'd loved the storybooks my grandparents had both read to me upon my repeated requests, the story I'd loved more than any other hadn't come with pictures. Instead, through my grandfather's animated re-telling (and my grandmother's answering smiles, chuckles, addendums, and blushing), I'd *felt* their story in a completely different way. Now, when I shared the story the way it had been shared with me over the years, it was as if *I* were in that first grade classroom...or with them on the playground...or walking beside them on their way home. And the smile my grandparents both wore during the telling became mine, as well. "He said she was the *purtiest* thing he'd ever laid eyes on, and he knew he was going to marry her."

Andy's laugh stopped my forward motion and brought my attention, albeit briefly, back on him. "In first grade?"

"He married her, didn't he?" Then, without waiting for his nod, I lowered myself to the hearth and hugged my knees to my chest. "He never left her side after that first sighting, with the exception, of course, of the time they spent with their families. They played together on the playground, walked to and from school together every day, and helped each other with their studies—although my grandfather says Grandma did most of the actual helping on account of her being pretty *and* smart."

"Did they date other people along the way? You know, as they got older and into actual dating ages?"

I was shaking my head before he'd finished his questions. "Nope. They found their other half and they didn't see any sense in wasting time."

"Wow."

"They were that way my whole life—until my grandmother slipped away in her sleep. In his arms." I tried to keep the shake of emotion from my voice but the moment I saw Andy rise to his feet and head in my direction, I knew I'd been unsuccessful. Still, I had more to tell and for whatever reason, I needed to tell it. "Until that moment, I'd never seen my grandfather without a smile. But now that she's gone, it's like the candlelight that burned behind his eyes—a light that was directly connected to his lips—simply doesn't exist anymore."

I closed my eyes at the memory of my grandfather standing over my grandmother's grave, a dozen wildflowers clutched in his hand. I'd never seen someone look so lost before and just the memory of it made my heart ache all over again.

"He went away for a little while after that. Didn't tell anyone where he was going, just that he'd be back. And as he walked out the door, he told me not to worry. And I didn't. Because Grandpa Stu told me not to."

"How long was he gone?"

"A month."

"And you didn't worry?"

"I missed him something fierce, but I didn't worry. He'd told me he'd be back and he always kept his word." I took a deep breath and leaned my head against Andy's shoulder. "I'll never forget the moment he walked back in my parents' front door. My best friend was back. He was and is different now, but he's still my Grandpa Stu."

"Was and is different *how*?"

"It's hard to explain. He just is. He's still wonderful, he's still funny, he's still all the things I love about him, but yet there's something that's not quite the same. Like a puzzle where you have all the pieces but one— the picture is still there, you know what it is, yet it's not entirely whole."

"Have you seen the missing piece at all since your grandmother passed? Even for just a moment or two?"

I allowed my mind to travel back to a time when my grandmother was still alive—the way Grandpa Stu's smile almost blinded, the way he hummed almost non-stop, and the way he liked to tease her until her cheeks turned red.

Yet now that Andy was asking, I *had* seen my grandfather's smile approach its former wattage a few times. I'd also been lulled into more than a few impromptu games of Name That Tune around the house since he came for his latest visit. And as nauseating as it was to watch, I'd also caught him teasing—

I jerked my head up off his shoulder so hard and so fast I would have toppled off the hearth if not for Andy's quick movement and fast hands.

"What's wrong?" he asked, holding me steady.

"I..." I smacked my hand over my mouth in an attempt to hold back my scream, but it did nothing to stem the whole body shudder that followed.

"Tobi?"

"Oh my God."

"What? What did I miss?"

Slowly, I slid my hand down my chin. "I don't understand. How could..." My thoughts petered off only to return in a slightly different spot. *Rapple*? *Really*? But *how*...

He caught my hand just as I let go of my chin and held it until my thoughts were in sync with my eyes. "Tobi, what's going on? Where'd you go just now?"

"My grandfather. He..." I stopped, swallowed, and then made myself continue, my stomach protesting my every thought with an appropriate flip and a counteracting flop. "I-I think he's...*in love* again."

I saw the confusion in Andy's face, even wished I could still be there myself, but I couldn't. Not any longer.

Yup, it all made sense now.

The increase in visits...

The humming...

His sudden curiosity in attire that matched....

I closed my eyes against the images of upcoming Christmases with my grandfather in his favorite pair of red flannel pajamas sitting next to a flannel-pajama-wearing Ms. Rapple, Thanksgivings with the two of them side by side as we shared the things we were thankful for that year, my future children running to the door to see Great Grandpa Stu and—

Great Grandma Rapple?

I allowed myself a tiny shudder for old times' sake and then, as much as I hated to do it, I brought Andy up to speed on my breath-hitching new reality. "Grandpa Stu. He's in love with Rapple."

~Chapter Thirteen~

It was nearly ten o'clock when I made my way up my front walkway. I was pretty sure, as I pulled up, that I saw the curtain in my living room window move, but if it had, it had been quick. Still, knowing my grandfather the way I did, there was no way in hell he was asleep.

First, there was the fact that I was still out. And although I was a week shy of my thirtieth birthday and had been living on my own for quite some time, if I was out and my grandfather was visiting, he waited up until he knew I was home, safe and sound.

Second, my grandfather was a late night TV junkie. Granted, he invariably nodded off halfway through the host's monologue, but when I'd suggest he call it a night for real, he'd pop his eyes open and look at me as if I'd lost my mind.

And last but not least, my grandfather had a glass of milk and a single chocolate chip cookie every night at eleven o'clock. No one knew how or why that was a thing with him, but it was.

We needed to talk.

I knew this.

I also knew I needed to apologize for the things he'd overheard me saying about Ms. Rapple last night—things that had obviously hurt him deeply based on his behavior today. Then again, if my suspicions about my grandfather's feelings for the old biddy were correct, why would he dodge her calls?

Could it be that they'd had a fight? That he'd already wised up?

One could hope, and hope I most certainly did. The fact that I added a fair amount of finger crossing and silent praying was an additional *for-good-measure* kind of thing.

"Hey, Tobes."

I stopped mid-step and looked up at Sam's bedroom window. Sure enough, the sixteen-year-old's screen was open and he was hanging out the window, waving at me.

"Don't you have school tomorrow?" I called out.

"Nope. This is my spring break, remember?"

"I guess I forgot that. Sorry."

He waved off my apology and then pointed toward the front door he and his mom shared with Ms. Rapple. Like the two-story house I shared with Carter, the outer door led to a vestibule and a pair of interior doors—one for the downstairs apartment (Rapple's), and one for the upstairs apartment (Mary Fran and Sam's). "I developed my pictures from the award show the other night and I'd love to show them to you if you have a few minutes."

I looked back at my own house and tried to see into my living room.

A quick flicker of blue around the edges of the curtain I'd hung to keep Ms. Rapple's prying eyes out let me know the television set was on. Which, extrapolating a step further, meant this whole notion of my grandfather having gone to bed early was, in fact, a crock. But even if I tiptoed up the stairs and stealthily let myself inside before he could feign sleep, I knew the likelihood I'd be dealing with the same bleh mood as earlier was high.

Unless I got creative and made it so his curiosity would get the better of him.

"Why don't you bring them over to my place?" I asked, glancing back at Sam. "That way Grandpa Stu can see them, too."

"My mom knocked on your door earlier to see if he wanted to come over for her famous meatloaf, but he wasn't home."

I considered correcting Sam's assumption, but let it go in favor of waving him over to my place. "I have chocolate chip cookies."

"Did you say *cookies*?"

"Yup."

Sam pulled his head back inside his room and slid his window closed. Two and half minutes later, he met me on the walkway with a bulging white envelope in his hand and a sheepish grin on his face. "We're out of cookies at my house."

"Hmmm… Might that be because you consider a single-serving to be six cookies?"

"*Eight*, actually. And yeah, that's probably a factor."

Laughing, I led him up the steps and across the front porch I shared with Carter. As we walked, I pointed at the envelope. "I take it those are the pictures?"

He nodded. "I kinda feel bad wanting to remember Saturday night after what happened to that lady."

I looked back at Sam while simultaneously slipping my house key into the front door. "What happened to Deidre Ryan is awful. There's no getting around that, Sam. But I don't want you to ever forget your accomplishment that night. Because that was—*is*—huge."

Sam's face flushed red with the praise. "Thanks to you."

"I didn't take those pictures."

"I took them *because* of you."

I turned the key and pushed. "And that's because of *your* talent."

"Yeah but—"

"Give it up, Sam. I give you work because you're talented. You won that award because you're talented. Stop selling yourself short and just own it, kiddo."

This time, the increased color in his cheeks was followed by a smile that spread like wildfire across his mouth. I matched it with one of my own and then led the way into my living room. Sure enough, the television was on, my grandfather was on the couch, and his eyes were wide open.

"Hey, Grandpa. I'm glad you're still awake. Sam has the pictures he took the other night at the award show and I figured you'd want to see them, too."

Sam stepped around me to extend his hand to my grandfather, but his face fell as the gesture was returned with a straight up handshake rather than with the handshake-elbow-thump-pinky-hook routine they'd come up with within moments of their first ever meeting. After an awkward beat or two of silence, Sam looked at me, wide-eyed.

I wanted to offer an explanation, something that would help Sam make sense of the perceived snub, but until I understood it myself, I wasn't sure what to say. Instead, I clapped my hands and then hooked my thumb in the direction of the kitchen. "I promised Sam some of those chocolate chip cookies I bought the other day, Grandpa. You want some, too?"

His answering shrug wasn't necessarily the level of enthusiasm I was aiming for, but at least it was something. Still, I could feel the questions firing away in Sam's head as he filed into the kitchen between me and my abnormally taciturn grandfather. Halfway into the kitchen, they veered off (as per standard operating procedure) in favor of my two-person Formica tabletop while I ventured over to the cabinet tasked with housing my Cocoa Puffs, my cookies, my pretzels, and my set of four Bugs Bunny melamine bowls and matching snack plates.

I grabbed the cookies and three snack plates and carried them over to the table while Sam set up the folding chair I kept in the corner for those times when my two-person table needed to accommodate a third. When the chair was at the table and I'd poured a glass of milk for all, I plopped onto my chair and tapped my finger on the envelope now serving as a resting place for Sam's non-cookie-holding hand.

"So let's see 'em."

Shoving the rest of his second cookie into his mouth, Sam reached into the envelope and pulled out a stack of pictures that, even from my sideways angle, I could see were crystal clear and exactly what I'd expect to see from the award-winning photographer.

"Ese irst—"

I held up my own cookie-holding hand and laughed. "Chew and swallow. We'll wait."

He chewed, he swallowed, and then did the same with one more cookie before wiping his hand off on his jeans and turning the stack so Grandpa Stu and I could see the top photo. "These first half dozen or so are of Mom helping me with my tie."

"Which, I will point out, would have gone a little easier if you weren't trying to document the moment in the mirror at the same time." I blinked off the misty haze that made me feel all mom-like for about thirty seconds and, instead, reached for another cookie and dunked it in my glass. "That said, these are really cute pictures."

Sam groaned at the word *cute* and moved on to the next set of pictures in his stack. "I shot this one of Andy as he was walking up the sidewalk to pick you up. Mom says you can tell how crazy he is about you."

I stopped dunking and stared at the picture, Andy's smile a near carbon copy of the one I see in the mirror when I know he'll be showing up at any minute. And even though it was just a photograph, I could sense anticipation in his step.

"Best feeling in the world right there," Grandpa Stu said, tapping the picture. "Makes you feel like you're king of the world—at least your own little corner of it, anyway."

Snapping my head to the left, I couldn't help but stare at my grandfather. Yes, I was shocked he'd said something with multiple syllables, let alone multiple words, but even more than that was the wistful tone in which he'd said them—a tone I'd come to associate with memories of my grandmother. But before I could offer a comforting word, he rolled his hand at Sam in a keep going gesture.

Sam obliged and moved on to the next picture—this one of me, Andy, Grandpa Stu, Rapple, and Gertie standing in front of the maple tree in my front yard. Andy and I were laughing thanks to Carter who'd positioned himself just over Sam's shoulder as the picture was being taken. Even Rapple, who was never amused by anything Carter-related, was smiling. And my grandfather, he was looking down at Rapple and—

"You look like Andy in this picture, sir."

I looked up at Sam and waited for him to explain his odd comment. When he didn't, I added in my best quizzical brow.

"Look." Sam pulled the last picture out from the bottom of the pile—the one of Andy coming up my walkway—and held it next to the one on top. "See the expression on Andy's face? Now look at Grandpa Stu."

I did as Sam asked and instantly felt my mouth go dry.

Sam was right. The expression Andy had worn just moments before seeing me was the same one my grandfather donned as he looked down at Rapple. The same anticipation, the same excitement, the same—

"Makes you feel like you're king of the world—at least your own little corner of it, anyway."

I swallowed, sans cookie, and slowly slid my gaze to my grandfather. He, too, was looking at the picture, only instead of the crimson hue I knew my cheeks were sporting, his face was pale and his eyes sad.

"This next one my mom wants framed even though I didn't take it." I followed my grandfather's focus back to the stack of pictures in front of me—a stack now topped by the picture of my crew at the award show.

Mary Fran.

Sam.

Carter.

JoAnna.

Andy.

Me.

Grandpa Stu.

And Rapple.

I took a moment to study each person, their place in my life and in my heart resurrecting the earlier mist and making it a lot harder to blink away. Mary Fran had been stunning in her black cocktail dress, but it was the smile of pride she had for her son, seated next to her, that jettisoned her beauty to a whole different level. Sam looked dapper in his suit and tie, his excitement over being there as a nominee plastered all over his face. Carter glowed as he always did, and JoAnna's quiet yet pleased-as-punch presence was on full display. Andy had pulled me close just as the picture was snapped and the joy I saw on my face warmed me down to my toes. And, once again, Rapple was smiling a real smile and so, too, was my grandfather. Only his smile wasn't aimed at the camera. No, his encompassed Ms. Rapple on his immediate left, and me one spot beyond.

"And here, the ceremony is starting." Sam's voice pulled me out of my head and focused me on the stack of photos once again—the top picture now of Carl Brinkman, the local news anchor-turned-master of ceremony as he welcomed the crowd.

My grandfather cleared his throat and leaned forward, his breath skirting the side of my face. "Little did that fella know his promise of an eventful evening would be such an understatement, eh?"

"Truth." Sam shuffled the picture to the bottom of the stack to reveal the show's first presenter as she walked out to the podium with a Golden Briefcase in one hand and the famous white envelope with gold, sparkly edges in the other. "I think this one was for"—he leaned in for a closer look, only to tap the tip of his finger on the envelope's gold lettering—"yup, Best Fifteen Second Spot."

Sam moved on to the next picture and the beaming forty-something winner as he accepted the award from the presenter and victoriously held it over his head. "Mom loves this shot. Says I need to track down an address for this guy so he can have it. I told her they take pictures of all the winners backstage with their award, but she thinks this is better than a staged one."

"I agree with your mom." I watched as he moved on to the next award and yet another action shot of a winner's face as she accepted her award. "I suspect everyone who won that night would love one of your pictures. In fact, if you want, I'll have JoAnna compile a list of all the winners and their agency's address so you can send the appropriate winner their picture."

"And include one of them cards of yours with each picture." Grandpa Stu helped himself to two cookies but handed one to Sam.

"One of *my* business cards?" Sam asked. "Why?"

I took the stack of pictures from Sam's hand so he could enjoy his cookie. "Grandpa Stu is right. Your award put you on their radar, kiddo. Your card will tell them how to find you."

"But I work for *you*, Tobes."

"When I have a job I need you to shoot, yes. But that doesn't mean you can't take jobs from other people, too, Sam. You have a college education to be saving for, yes?"

He tried to play it off, but I could see the smile tugging at the corners of his lips. "You really think other people would hire me to do the kind of stuff I do for you?"

I handed him his glass of milk, waited for him to gulp it down, and then took the empty glass from his hand. "You still don't get it, do you?"

"Get what?"

"Just how good your photography really is."

At his sheepish shrug, I moved on to another photo and the award I suspected came next. Sure enough, the presenter for Best Photograph in a Print Ad stood at the podium with the Golden Briefcase in one hand, and the sparkly gold trimmed envelope in the other. A peek at the envelope confirmed the category. I slid the picture to the bottom of the stack and then held the next image in front of Sam—his enthusiasm as he accepted his award plain to see despite Carter's shaky picture-taking hand. "Do you see this? You getting this award? This isn't an award everyone gets simply for showing up, Sam. There are thousands of pictures taken for advertising agencies in the metro St. Louis area every year. Pictures that are used in print campaigns for magazines, newspapers, and signage. And out of all those pictures, yours was one of only four that were nominated for this award. And you, my friend, won. Against professional photographers— people who have been doing what you do for far longer than you've even been alive. Yet *you*"—I shook the picture at him—"my just turned sixteen-year-old friend, *won*."

Sam looked from me, to the picture, and back again. But before he could say anything (or grab another cookie), I hooked my finger under his chin and held his gaze steady with mine. "Trust me, Sam, people will most definitely want to hire you to do what you do for me."

I sat back so as to keep my face from getting in the way of Sam and Grandpa Stu's cookie high-fiving, and continued moving through the pile of pictures, smiling at the winners as they stepped onto the stage, and laughing at the little pictorial asides Sam took of our tablemates along the way.

Eventually I came to my category and the moment Cassie Turner appeared from backstage in her form-fitting gown with her blond hair cascading across her shoulders in long flowing waves. In her left hand was the most coveted award of the evening—the Golden Storyboard. Even now, a full forty-eight hours after witnessing the moment firsthand (and losing), I still felt my palms moistening in anticipation.

"Your campaign was better than all the rest of them, Tobes."

I lifted my gaze to Sam and rewarded his sweet loyalty with the smile it deserved. "Thanks, Sam. But I'm okay. Did I *want* to win? Of course. I've been wanting that since the moment I learned these awards existed. But I just need to work harder, dig deeper, give the judges a campaign that'll blow them away next time."

Sam's nod told me he understood. That he got that kind of drive.

My grandfather's nod told me he was proud.

"And I will," I added as much for myself as Sam or my grandfather. "Because as cool as it is to be *one* of the best... I want to be *the* best."

I allowed myself another moment or two to study the trophy and then shifted my gaze to Cassie's other hand—the hand holding the plain white envelope.

Confused, I pulled the picture closer, confirmed the plain edges, and then looked at the words scrawled across the front in a thick black ink: Best Overall Ad Campaign. "Do you see this?"

Sam pulled his cookie out of my milk glass and leaned in for a closer look. "See what?"

I pointed. "This envelope."

"Yeah, what about it?"

"It's different than all the rest of them."

"So is the trophy," Sam reminded.

"But the trophy has always been different for this particular category. The envelope hasn't."

My grandfather shifted in his seat next to mine. "What are you saying, Sugar Lump?"

"The winner's name is always in an envelope trimmed in this gold-sparkly stuff. I know because the first time I went to this thing a few years ago, I saw that gold stuff catch the light as the first presenter came out onto the stage and I vowed right then and there that my name would be in one of those envelopes one day."

"Okay..."

I tapped the envelope in the picture. "This one. In Cassie's hand. It's not trimmed in anything. It's a basic white envelope. And the category isn't written in gold, either, see?"

"Looks like it was written in a regular black marker to me." Sam placed the entire cookie in his mouth and, after a quick chew or two, swallowed it virtually whole. "The kind mom uses around the store all the time."

"Exactly." I set the picture in question down on the table and pulled out ones depicting each of the night's presenters. When I was sure I had them all, I set them down around Cassie's picture and waited.

"Maybe they ran out of envelopes." Sam pointed toward his empty glass and, at my nod, headed for the refrigerator for seconds of milk. "I mean, when I can't find a pen that works, I grab the next best thing—pencil, marker, a tube of my mom's lipstick, whatever."

"But this is special."

"Are you sure they've always done that with the gold? For this category?" my grandfather asked, his voice still void of its usual pep.

It was a valid question. Especially since my memory of the whole gold-sparkly envelope thing was specific to the first presenter of the first show I'd attended as an industry professional. Which meant I'd kind of just assumed the gold-edged thing was standard operating procedure for the award night. Still, it seemed weird they'd only do it for some categories and not others.

"Tobi?"

I looked at my grandfather and shrugged. "I think so. I don't know why they wouldn't."

"We could check."

I slid my focus on to Sam. "How? By calling past presenters? I think I'd look like a psycho if I started asking them about gold sparkly-edged envelopes—"

"No, we can check on the computer." Sam gulped down his second serving of milk and then pointed toward the living room. "Can I use your laptop real quick?"

"Yeah, sure." I flipped through the last few shots from the award ceremony—Cassie opening the envelope, my face as I waited to hear whether I'd won, Deidre's joy as she accepted the Golden Storyboard, Deidre walking up the stairs with tears running down her eyes, Deidre on the platform looking back at the screen, and then finally Deidre as she looked back toward the crowd, her brow furrowed.

"Is that what you were talking about?"

I glanced up at my grandfather. "What?"

"That expression." I followed Grandpa Stu's finger back to the picture that had unknowingly captured the last second or two of Deidre Ryan's life. "It's like you said. She looks confused."

I started to nod but stopped as my focus shifted to the screen just beyond her head—a screen depicting a father and son decked out in Cardinals gear. "And I think she was confused because that ad playing right there"—I pointed at the picture's background—"wasn't hers. It was Lexa's."

"Tobes, come here... You were right," Sam called from the living room.

"I'll be right there." I waited for my grandfather to soak up the image frozen on the screen behind Deidre's head and then gathered up the pictures I'd displayed across the table, keeping Deidre's last shot on top.

"Seriously, Tobes, you need to come check this out."

I set the pile of pictures to the side, tossed the empty cookie sleeve into the trash, and led the way into the living room. Sam was seated in the center of the couch with my laptop on his lap.

Once we were seated on either side of him, Sam pointed at a picture on the screen. "You were right about the gold sparkly edged envelopes being a thing. See?" He leaned back so Grandpa and I could both get a better view. "They were definitely used for the big category as recently as last year when Cassie Turner won. And this one, here"—he clicked on an open tab at the bottom of the screen to reveal the image of yet another winner of the prestigious Best Overall award—"is from like three years ago."

Sure enough, the envelope containing the winner's name in both images Sam unearthed were just like the ones depicted in each and every one of the pictures he, himself, had taken on Saturday night.

Except the one for this year's winner of Best Overall Campaign.

For the first time in years—if not ever—that one envelope was different than it had ever been before.

Now, two days later, the winner was dead, her plummet to the stage below being ruled a homicide.

Coincidence?

Perhaps.

But I didn't buy it. Not by a long shot.

And judging by the way my grandfather reached into the front pocket of his flannel shirt for his trusty notebook and his magnifying glass, I wasn't the only skeptic in the room.

~Chapter Fourteen~

If I were an outsider with even a passing knowledge of my life, I would think something was really wrong with me. It would be the only sensible reason for why I was poised to walk out my front door a full hour earlier than normal.

Don't get me wrong, I'm not immune to the pull of getting to work early. I am, after all, a workaholic when it comes to my agency. But I live next door to a woman who sets her watch by her dog's need to pee and, for whatever reason, seven-thirty (rain or shine) is that time (hence the reason I never leave before eight at the absolute earliest).

Which brings me back to the must-be-something-wrong-with-me thing.

It's seven thirty.

In the morning.

My backpack is hoisted onto my left shoulder.

My key ring is in my right hand.

A paper cup filled with Cocoa Puffs is in my left hand.

And my ear is cocked toward the front left window, waiting for the stomach churning sounds that mean Rapple is moving about on my front lawn. After a moment or two of nothing, I relaxed my pose just enough to afford a view of my grandfather sprawled across my pull-out couch.

His weathered face, pillowed by his age-spotted hands, looked sad even in his sleep, and I made a mental note to push the issue with him the next time we were alone. On the floor, no more than an arm's length from his body, was his trusty magnifying glass and his favorite notebook. Even without moving any closer, I could tell he, too, had spent some of those final pre-sleep moments working through what we know/don't know about Deidre's death. I also knew, without seeing his notes, that he, too, had probably determined Cassie Turner to be our next step. And as I stood there, taking it all in, I found my throat starting to constrict and my eyes starting to mist at the realization that yet another visit with Grandpa Stu was rapidly drawing to a close.

I took a step toward the couch and the cheek I wanted to kiss, but stopped as a familiar sound wafted through my slightly opened front window and greeted me with a less than pleasant reminder as to why I was standing where I was in the first place.

Rapple was loose.

Or, rather, Rapple was out and about as she always was at this time.

I mustered a fortifying breath, squared my shoulders, pulled open my front door, and made myself step out into the vestibule I shared with Carter. If Carter were awake, he'd check me for a fever. Since he wasn't, I checked myself and then continued through the outer door and onto my front porch.

Sure enough, there, not more than five feet from my minuscule patch of landscaping, was my next door neighbor, sporting one of the trillion hideous housecoats (this one in turquoise) that had become her uniform in life. Why my lawn had become Gertie's personal toilet was still beyond me, even now, two years after taking up residency in the ground floor apartment.

Carter's theory was that our lawn gave the old biddy a better vantage point of the neighborhood thanks to the placement of our lone front tree in relation to the one in front of the house she shared with Mary Fran and Sam.

Sam's theory centered on the movement-monitoring band she wore around her wrist. By having Gertie pee in my yard, Rapple gained an extra twenty steps (round trip), he surmised.

But honestly, I'm confident my theory was the most accurate: the un-peed-upon plants in front of her house looked superior to the not so fortunate plants in my yard.

Welcome to 46 McPhearson Road—home (I mean, *front lawn*) of the criminally insane.

I forced myself over to the porch steps even as I visually perused my daffodils and snowball bushes for any sign of turquoise. When my search turned up nothing, I lifted my gaze to Rapple. And that's when I remembered Gertie wasn't here. She'd spent the night at the vet's, undergoing more tests.

Why it had taken me this long to realize a) I'd heard no barking, b) Rapple wasn't gesturing toward the lone remaining, still-green side of my snowball bush (hence, my theory), and c) said still-green side wasn't jiggling, was beyond me. But now that my brain had finally caught up with the reality bus, I was noticing all sorts of things.

Like the fact Rapple's eyes were puffy and red-rimmed...

Like the fact she was literally carrying a box of tissues in her hand...

Like the fact that the area around my dead and dying plants was littered with balled up (*ewww*) tissues...

Like the fact that—

"Oh, Tobi. I was wanting to knock on your door this morning but I didn't want to wake you if you were still sleeping."

I took advantage of the sniffles that followed to rein in my desired (and oh so sarcastic) retort about Gertie's morning barkathons having set my internal alarm clock a long time ago. Instead, after a few deep breaths, I made myself step all the way off the porch and reach (trust me, I know) for the woman's trembling (non tissue-holding) hand.

"Mary Fran told me about Gertie. Is there any word yet?"

Ms. Rapple swiped her current tissue across her nostrils and, yup, tossed it onto the ground at my feet. I considered lambasting her for littering but, when I looked at her—really looked at her (sans shudder, believe it or not)—empathy overtook irritation in short order.

"N-no. N-not yet. They s-s-said they'd c-call at"—Rapple hiccupped a few times and then returned to her sniffle-laden sentence—"eight."

I spread my hands to indicate my lawn and did my best not to fixate on the tissues. "I'm so used to seeing you out here with Gertie that I almost forgot she wasn't here."

"I-I'm hoping that by f-following her n-normal routines, she-she'll feel me somehow. And-and f-fight this."

"Mary Fran said something about her being fine one minute and lethargic the next?"

More sniffling eventually gave way to a tortured nod and a voice with more rasp than usual. "I noticed her acting a little odd at your house on Sunday night, but thought she was just reacting to the unpleasant smells associated with your cooking. But then lethargy set in Monday morning. I looked everywhere, thinking she got into something she shouldn't have, but I couldn't find anything."

"I'm sorry Rap—I mean, *Ms.* Rapple. If there's anything I can do for you, let me know, okay?" I heard the words as they left my mouth. Even considered reaching into my backpack for my handheld mirror just to be sure I hadn't succumbed to one of those stupid zombie apocalypse things. But I refrained. I was, after all, trying to take JoAnna's advice—to trust my grandfather. Assuming of course, their *thing* wasn't already over.

Please, God.

Please...

I started to launch into a full-blown mental prayer, when I suddenly stopped, the memory of my grandfather's sad face as he slept slapping me upside the head.

"C-could you drop me off at-at the v-vet on your way to w-work?" Rapple asked, between sniffles.

"I thought they were going to call you at eight." I reached around to the outer side pocket of my backpack and consulted my phone for the time. "You still have another fifteen minutes until then."

Ms. Rapple pulled out another tissue, dabbed at her eyes, wiped the line of snot from her nose, and added it to the growing pile at my feet. "I need to see her, Tobi. I need her to know I'm still here. That I'll be by her side no matter what happens."

And then, before I could find even so much as a word to say, she burst into the kind of tears that tore at my heart. "I-I c-can't l-lose her, T-tobi. She's my o-only r-real friend. The one who sees past the p-prickles."

Prickles?

Did Rapple just admit she was prickly?

I was still trying to wrap my head around what I was hearing when the woman's voice dropped to a near whisper. "I-I'm n-not a likeable p-person, T-tobi. Y-you know that. C-carter knows that. Mary Fran and Sam know that. Even your Andy knows that. The o-only per-person who d-didn't, was S-stu."

The tears continued, only now they weren't just Rapple's.

Stealing my hand back, I reached into her tissue box, dabbed at my own cheeks, and with a shrug I'd need to examine later, threw it into the pile with Rapple's. "*I...I...*like you...Ms. Rapple."

I diverted my eyes from my neighbor just long enough to peek at the second floor window behind me. A lack of movement in the area of Carter's blinds let me know my secret was safe.

"No you don't."

I turned back to Rapple. "Um...yes...I...do."

Her free hand found her hip and, in a flash, I heard Carter's voice in my head.

"Incoming! Incoming! Hit the deck!"

She raised her hip hold with a glare when I laughed. But just as I was gearing up for the biting comment that was sure to follow, the woman's whole body deflated like a pricked balloon. "I don't know what happened. One minute everything was great and the next, he shut me out."

"I don't think Gertie is shutting you out, Ms. Rapple. She's just not feeling well, that's all—"

The sniffles were back. So, too, were the tissues.

"I'm not talking about Gertie. I'm talking about Stu."

I wanted to cover my ears and beg her to refrain from talking about my grandfather, but thanks to JoAnna, I couldn't.

Even without the pile of tissues at my feet and scattered around my plants, I could tell Rapple was miserable. I saw it in her re-puffed eyes. I heard it in the sniffle/hiccup combination that had been nearly constant since I stepped outside. And I felt it in my chest every time a fresh round of tears re-started the combination.

It was a misery that was achingly familiar even though my grandfather's rendition was slightly different. With him, the eyes were droopy—lacking any desire for contact, and showing no signs of their normal mischievous spark. With him, there was no sniffle/hiccup combination. Instead there was almost complete silence. And while the feeling in my chest in response to his misery was far more acute, there was no denying the underlying truth.

Rapple was heartbroken without my grandfather.

And, like it or not, Grandpa Stu was showing some signs of being heartbroken without Rapple.

It wasn't what I wanted. Not by a long shot. But if I'd learned anything in my almost thirty years of existence, it was that things didn't always go as I hoped. When it didn't, it always stunk in the immediate. But eventually, in most of those cases, the happenstance I'd thought was akin to the demise of the world ended up being not so bad. Or, in some cases, way, *way* better.

Like when Nick broke my heart by fooling around with that waitress. At the time, I thought my world was caving in. But now, with Andy in my life, I realized that one horrific moment may have been one of the best things that ever happened to me.

I shook the odd correlation from my head and forced myself to focus on the still sniffling woman standing no more than two feet in front of me. "Ever since I was a little girl, my grandfather has always told me to take things one step at a time. He says it's less overwhelming that way. And from what I've seen so far, he's right. So we're going to take his advice now and focus on Gertie, first. We're going to find out how she's doing and what they've found, and deal with that. Then, when you have those answers, you can try to figure out this thing between you and"—I hooked my thumb over my shoulder, in the direction of the house—"him, okay?"

~Chapter Fifteen~

I was halfway through the donut I'd snuck out of the vet's office when JoAnna breezed into my office, her eyes wide with an apology she didn't need to make yet I knew was coming anyway.

"Oh, Tobi, I'm so sorry. The dentist got to talking and the next thing I knew it was nine-thirty."

"The search party was scheduled for nine-thirty-one so you're fine." I held out what was left of my breakfast and offered to break it in half. Thankfully, the offer was shaken off. But in doing so, I couldn't miss the fact that her worry hadn't abated. At. All. "JoAnna, please. You told me yesterday that you might be late this morning, so I wasn't surprised. And… *news flash*… I'm capable of answering the phone if it rings, you know. Which, by the way, it didn't."

JoAnna's stance softened a smidge. "No calls yet?"

"Nope. Although there was one voicemail that came in on my cell while I was turning on the lights."

"And?"

"It was just Carter. Wanting to tell me about a-a hallucination he apparently had."

"What kind of hallucination?"

I broke off a scrap of my donut and rolled it between my thumb and index finger. "He, um, said he thought he overheard me out on our front yard…um…telling Rapple that I…like her."

"Ha!"

I stopped rolling. "So no harm no foul if I don't call him back and correct him?"

"Correct him about what?"

I looked down at the flattened donut morsel between my fingers, shrugged, and popped it into my mouth. "It doesn't matter. So how'd the dentist go? Any issues?"

"None, thank heavens." JoAnna backed into the chair across from mine and flopped down, the expression on her face quickly transitioning from worry, to surprise, to disdain. "Since when do you pick a donut that looks like *that*?"

I noted the lift to both her left nostril and her left eyebrow and then followed the aforementioned disdain to my right hand. "What's wrong with it?"

"There's not so much as a shred of chocolate on it anywhere, unless you licked it off already."

"I don't lick off chocolate!"

Her nostril relaxed enough to allow her right eyebrow to join her left.

"Okay, so I lick sometimes...sue me." I looked down at the remaining bite or two in my hand and then tossed it onto my calendar book. "You're right. It's a lousy donut."

"I can tell that from here. What I *can't* tell is why you ordered it in the first place."

"I didn't order it. I hijacked it." I pushed my chair back from my desk and began foraging through my drawers. I passed over the lifesavers, briefly considered the pretzels, and finally settled on a tiny handful of M&Ms. "The staff at Gertie's vet apparently doesn't do chocolate for breakfast. Or, if they do, they plowed through them before we got there."

"Why were you at Gertie's vet?"

"Because Rapple asked if I'd take her out there this morning." I arranged my M&Ms by color across my palm and systematically ate my way through the piles until I had one of each color left. "So I took her."

When JoAnna said nothing, I looked up to find her watching me with a mixture of amusement and I'm not sure what else. "What? Don't you dare tell me you don't do the same thing when you eat M&Ms. *Everyone* does. I'm pretty sure it's wired into our brains from birth."

"I *don't* do that."

"Liar." I extended my palm across the top of my desk. "What's your order?"

"My order?" JoAnna asked.

"When you have one of each left—green, blue, orange, red, brown, and yellow—what order do you eat them in? Favorite to least favorite, or least favorite to favorite?"

"How is Gertie? Any improvement?"

I considered calling her on her diversionary tactic, but in the interest of getting my chocolate fix, I gave up and popped the orange (I'm a least favorite to favorite gal, myself) into my mouth. "They're waiting on a lab of some sort. So I told Rapple to call me once she knows."

"That was very nice of you."

"If you saw her this morning, you'd understand." I ate the brown, the green, and the blue before contemplating the red and yellow and opting for the red. "So, I have a theory I'd like to run by you if I may."

She held up her finger in the universal wait sign, did a quick yet surprisingly thorough job of organizing the minor mess I'd managed to create across the top of my desk in the thirty minutes I'd been there, and then lowered her hand back to her lap. "Okay, I'm listening."

"You can't help yourself, can you?" I ate the yellow and then stood, my thoughts immediately traveling back to the previous night. "I still need to figure out the why, but I think Cassie Turner had something to do with what happened to Deidre."

"Why on earth would you say that?" JoAnna asked.

"Because the envelope was wrong, for starters, and—"

"Envelope?"

I returned to my desk, woke up my sleeping computer, searched images for the St. Louis Advertising Awards, and, when I found the same handful Sam had shown me the night before, gestured for JoAnna to come around to my side.

When she was in position just over my left shoulder, I pointed at the envelope in each pertinent image. "See? They're always edged in the same sparkly gold glitter stuff, and written on in the same gold sparkly ink."

"It's a nice touch."

"Some of these pictures go back"—I clicked on one that looked older—"years. And while the clothing styles worn by the presenters and the winners have changed over time, that detail hasn't. It's part of the tradition—like the Golden Briefcase and the Golden Storyboard."

"Okay..."

"Even on Saturday night, the envelopes for all of the categories leading up to mine were the way they've always been. Gold sparkly edges. Gold sparkly writing."

When I was sure she'd seen enough of what I wanted her to see, I minimized the screen and turned my attention to the packet of pictures I'd secured in my backpack before Sam headed home the previous night. I extracted the pictures I'd hung on to and held them out to JoAnna.

"Are these from Saturday night?" she asked as she took them from my hand and smiled down at the top one in the pile. "Oh, Tobi, these are wonderful."

"Sam took them, of course."

"This one looks so happy, doesn't he?" She tilted the stack downward so I could see the winner of the Best Fifteen Second Spot award from my seat.

"He does. But look at the envelope."

JoAnna resituated the pile to give herself a better view. "Okay, I see it."

"See the edges? The writing?"

"Sure, it's like the ones you just showed me on the computer."

"Exactly!" I pointed at the pile, and, at her nod, liberated it back from her hands so I could shuffle through the shots to get to the one I wanted her to see. When I found the one of Cassie walking out to the podium, I handed it back. "Now, look at the envelope Cassie is carrying out."

Again, JoAnna did as I asked. Only this time, as she brought the picture close, her brows furrowed. "There's no gold, no sparkle. It's just...plain."

"Exhibit A."

JoAnna studied the picture a bit more and then moved it to the bottom of the pile in favor of the next one—this one depicting the moment Deidre's name was called and Sam (who'd had his camera trained on my face) swung his lens over to her table. The mixture of shock and joy on Deidre's face sagged JoAnna's shoulders. "It's still just so awful."

"Look at the next one."

Again, JoAnna shifted the top picture to the bottom. This time, the image was of Deidre beside the podium, accepting the Golden Storyboard and envelope from Cassie. "Okay..."

"See? Same plain envelope."

"That's what she carried out, Tobi."

"I know that. But why?"

"Maybe they ran out of envelopes and misplaced the pen?" I felt my eyebrow lift, only to have JoAnna wave it back to its normal starting spot. "Scratch that. That's dumb."

I pointed to the pile of pictures. "Now look at the next one—or maybe it's the one after that."

JoAnna moved two ahead and then tilted it back in my direction for confirmation she was on the right one. At my nod, she pulled the picture close. "What am I looking at now?"

"The screen behind Deidre."

"Okay, I see it now. It's proof they started to play the wrong ad. This one is for the Metro Link spot, not the library as it should have been."

I steepled my index fingers under my chin. "Exhibit B."

"I still think the tech crew just made a mistake."

"A valid theory if not for the sudden change in envelope." When it became apparent JoAnna wasn't following my line of thinking, I returned to my feet and the window where I often did my best thinking. "I think there's a chance the tech crew had it right."

"You mean you think the Metro Link ad was the actual winner."

I turned, perched my backside on the windowsill, and settled my hands on their opposing upper arm. "I think *Lexa* was supposed to win that award, not Deidre."

"I don't know why you think that. Your ad was much better than hers," JoAnna protested like the loyal employee and friend she was. "So, too, was Deidre's."

"While it would be lovely to imagine a world where merit is what's rewarded, that's not always the case. Sometimes it's other things if you get my drift."

"I don't. So explain."

"Theresa Kinney."

JoAnna drew back. "Theresa Kinney? Why on earth are you bringing that one up?"

"Why did she win Best Overall that first year?" I countered.

"Because she was sleeping with her boss—her *married* boss, I might add." JoAnna huffed out a breath and then moved around my office neatening papers, picture frames, my umbrella stand, and basically anything and everything she could get her hands on. "The things some women do to get ahead in this world is absolutely mind bog—" She stopped and looked at me. "Wait. Is Lexa Smyth like that?"

"She has that reputation, yes."

"But—"

"The word on the street is that when she was with Ross Jackson, she had a corner office...after only two months."

"Okay..."

"And Cassie had the corner office last year when she won."

"But Lexa isn't with Ross Jackson, anymore. She's with Callahan now, isn't she?"

"She is, but Ross is still a sponsor of the award show. And who knows what Lexa might have going on with one of the judges—who, as you know, represent all of the big agencies, not just Callahan folks."

"Okay, that makes sense." JoAnna gave up on her latest round of cleaning (mostly because everything was clean) and joined me over in the vicinity of the window. "And that's why you think Lexa was supposed to win? Because of the manner in which she climbs to the top?"

"I think she was supposed to win because it was her ad that was starting to play when all hell broke loose."

"And you think Cassie made her own envelope before she came out?"

"I do."

"But if there's anything to what you're saying, don't you think Cassie would have wanted *Lexa* dead, not Deidre?"

"On the surface, yes. But I think there's way more at play here."

"Like what?"

I wasn't sure how to answer JoAnna's question just yet. Right now, I was just operating on a gut feeling that had reared its head in the wee hours of the morning—a gut feeling I needed to explore a little more before I gave it a voice. Still, I didn't want to blow JoAnna off so I grabbed hold of a different bone.

"Deidre Ryan was *Bitch Pitch.*"

JoAnna's inhale echoed across my office. "Noooo…"

"That's what *I* said when Ben told me. But I think he's right. And I think what happened to her could be tied to that somehow. Or"—I shrugged—"I could be reaching for nothing."

Either way, there was no denying there was some hinkyness going on.

The plain envelope was hinky.

The fact that Lexa's ad had started to play as Deidre stepped onto the platform with her award in hand was also hinky.

But the hinkys didn't add up. Not in any way that made any sense. Which meant I still had a lot of work to do to get to a point where I could even begin to figure things out.

"I need to talk to Cassie." I pushed off the windowsill and made my way back to my desk. "I'd also like to see that list you made of Deidre's campaigns."

JoAnna pointed to a folder on the left hand side of my desk—a folder I hadn't noticed until that moment. "It's all there. And it's quite a list."

I grabbed hold of the folder and sank back onto my chair. "And this includes the work she did before she had her kids?"

"It sure does." JoAnna pivoted on her sensible shoes and started toward the hallway. At the door, she stopped and looked back at me. "If you need anything else, you know where to find me."

"I do, JoAnna. And thank you. You're the best."

~Chapter Sixteen~

I'm well aware of the fact that silence has its place.

But there are also times when silence (from a certain bald man) can drive a person (in this particular instance, *me*) nuts.

Sure, I'd gotten a few nods and an occasional grunt or two over the past fifteen minutes, but if I wasn't looking for a wee bit more, I would have taken JoAnna up on her offer to pick me up something to eat on her way back from lunch so I could continue combing through Deidre's lengthier-than-I'd-realized career. Instead, I'd not only called Grandpa Stu and suggested lunch at his favorite sandwich joint, I'd also swung out to the house and picked him up.

I leaned against my side of the two-person table and pointed at his barely touched sandwich. "Is your Reuben not good, Grandpa?"

"It's fine."

"Are you not feeling well?"

"No, I'm fine."

Would you have rather gone somewhere else?"

"No, this is fine."

I stopped my parade of questions and simply stared at my grandfather. "Mom is paying you, isn't she?"

With great effort, he pulled his attention off his plate and fixed it on me. "Paying me? Paying me for what?"

"All those *fines* you just gave me. She always hated it when I gave her that answer growing up. Said I'd know what she was talking about one day." I dug into the second half of my own ham and cheese sandwich and then waved what was left in the space between us. "Though I kind of assumed she meant when I had my own children."

"She did."

I took another bite and then set the sandwich on its wrapper. "So what then? You've taken it upon yourself to give me a taste *now*? *Before* I have kids?"

He looked at me for a long moment before pushing his own sandwich-topped wrapper into the center of the table. "I answered fine to your questions because it fit. The sandwich is fine, this place is fine, and my stomach and whatever else can go wrong at my age is also fine."

"Then why have you been so quiet the past few days? It's not like you, Grandpa, and you know it."

"Maybe I've spent far too much of my life yapping."

"Uh, no..." I pushed my own sandwich out of the way, leaned forward, and patted my grandfather's age-spotted hand. "All those lessons I've learned in life? I couldn't have learned them without you."

"Lessons?"

"Taking things a little at a time... How to work around my lack of a poker face... Where Grandma kept her candy stash... You know, all that stuff."

"All things you'd have figured out on your own, Sugar Lump."

"Not necessarily. And even if I had, learning them on my own would have been a whole lot less fun." I stopped, took a deep breath, and made myself go where I'd sworn I'd never go. "Did you and Rap—I mean, Ms. Rapple, have a fight? Because—"

The vibration of my phone against the table stole the rest of my sentence from my lips and my attention from my grandfather. A glance at the screen, as I rushed to silence the vibration, yielded Mary Fran's name and smiling face. I considered letting her go to voice mail, but picked it up when my grandfather motioned for me to do so.

"Hey, Mary Fran. Is everything okay?"

"Yeah, sure, everything is fine." I shook off the mental image of my mother grinning and tightened my grip on the phone. "I was just calling to double check on tonight and that you're still okay letting me tag along with you?"

Pushing my chair back from the table, I lunged my hand into my backpack and pulled out my day planner, my heart beginning to pound inside my chest as my brain started firing off a host of possibilities I must have forgotten.

Mary Fran's birthday (but it's not).

Sam's birthday (nope, not that, either).

A sleepover at the pet store (please, God, no).

"I mean, I know it probably seems weird for me to want to go when I was never really close to this guy, but she was my age, you know? And their kids are still so little."

And, just like that, I caught up.

Deidre's wake.

Damn.

This time, when I shook my head, it wasn't to dislodge images of my mother or her legendary *I told you so* face. It was to rid my thoughts of the carrot I'd given myself to get through the day—a carrot that looked and felt a lot like Andy did when we were snuggled up on the couch watching movies together.

Damn.

"Tobi? You still there?"

I nodded, only to double back and repeat the gesture in a more phone friendly way. "Yeah. I'm still here. I'd actually forgotten about the wake being tonight until you just said it."

"Oh."

"But now that it's back on my radar—yeah, I'm still going. And yeah, we can still go together if you'd like."

"I would. Thanks."

"So what time is it again?"

"Four to six, and seven to nine. I can do either one if you want, but if we do the four to six one, I need to know so I can either get Sam in here to cover me or put up a closing early sign in the front door."

I searched the wall to my left and the one to my right before finding a clock. "Let's do the later one. I still have some stuff to do at the office after lunch."

"Perfect. What time do you want to meet?"

"It's out in Chesterfield, right?" I asked.

"Yes."

"Let's plan to leave my place at seven. With it being past rush hour, we can be out at the funeral parlor inside thirty minutes. Tops."

When everything was set, I ended the call, set the phone atop my planner, and met my grandfather's curious gaze. "You're coming with us, yes?"

At his raised eyebrow, I filled in the details. "Deidre Ryan's wake is this evening. *Mary Fran* wants to go because she went to school with Deidre's husband. *I* want to go as a show of respect to a colleague and a fellow nominee. And *you*, you can roam around the place seeing if there's anything that can be added to your notebook."

"Think that pretty thing in the blue skirt and high heels will be there, too?"

I tried to conjure up an image of someone in a blue skirt but came up empty. "Pretty thing in a blue skirt and high heels?"

"That one right there." My grandfather lifted his hand off his lap and motioned for me to look over my shoulder.

I surveyed the plethora of tables behind me until I came to one in the back corner. Although my vantage point wasn't ideal thanks to the man with the rather large head seated at a table between here and there, I could pick out the side of a blue skirt and a pair of matching blue high heels.

Swiveling in my seat, I bobbed my head to the right to remove Big Head Man from my sight line. Now that I had, however, I had the blue skirted woman's open laptop to contend with. But as was usually the case when you felt someone looking at you, the woman peeked her eyes over the top of her computer to meet mine.

Cassie Turner.

It took a moment for recognition to dawn on her face, but by the time it did, I was ready with a small wave and a smile. When they were returned, I swiveled back to my original starting place and my grandfather. "When did you spot her?"

"When I was sitting here waiting for you to return with our order."

"Why didn't you say anything?"

"You were talking. I was watching. What difference does it make?"

"So all this time you've been pretty much"—I hemmed, I hawed, I plowed ahead—"incommunicado, you've actually been watching her over my shoulder?"

He drew back as if preparing for an argument, but sank back against his chair, instead. "She hasn't moved since we got here. Hasn't been looking around, neither. Just working on that computer of hers."

"Grandpa, what's wrong?"

"Nothing is wrong, Sugar Lump."

"Are you upset about leaving? Because you can stay past Sunday if you'd like."

His answering laugh held no sign of genuine humor. "You have your own life, Tobi. You have a job, Andy, your friends... You don't need some old coot getting in the way."

It was my turn to prepare for battle, only I had no intention of giving up the way he had. "Getting in the way? Are you kidding me? I feel like I've barely seen you this visit with how busy you've been and all. I-I've missed you, actually, and that's with you *here*—sleeping on my couch every night, instead of in your own place on the other side of the state."

"I've been around the past day or so."

"Geographically, yes. But mentally, no. I need you being sharp. We've got a murder to solve, remember?"

He reached out, ran his finger along the table's edge, scraped at something with his nail, and then returned his hand to his lap. "I remember."

"Then help me figure out who killed Deidre and why. Help me brainstorm possible motives. You love that stuff, Grandpa—"

The vibration of my phone cut me off once again. This time though, a check of the screen revealed a name that caused a visible reaction in my grandfather. I picked it up and held it toward him. "Do you want to take this?"

His only response was to cast his eyes toward the floor.

Interesting...

I pulled the phone back, pressed the button, and held it to my ear. "Do you have news on Gertie?" I asked by way of greeting.

Sniffle.

"Ms. Rapple?"

Sniffle.

Sniffle.

A peek at my grandfather showed that while he was still looking at the floor, he was most definitely listening.

"Do you"—*sniffle, sniffle*—"know how I can reach your grandfather?"

"My grandfather? Sure, he"—I stopped as he sat up, waved his hands, and shook his head with such earnest there was no mistaking the message. Still, I asked Ms. Rapple to hang on while I covered the phone. "Grandpa! She's upset! She wants to talk to you."

"I can't, Sugar Lump." He stopped waving his hands, returning them to his lap with obvious effort. "Trust me. It's better this way."

"How is telling her you won't talk to her better for her?"

"Remember how I used to take off your Band-Aids when you were little?"

I winced at the memory. "Yeah, you ripped them off."

"Got it over quicker, didn't it?"

He had a point, so I nodded.

"Same holds true here. With"—he gestured toward my hand and the covered phone—"*this.*"

"Grandpa, she's upset."

He paused, looked past me toward the table I imagined still housed Cassie, and then pushed back his chair and stood. "I'll be outside in the car when you're done."

And just like that, he was gone, leaving me alone with his uneaten sandwich, a ton of questions, and a sniffling old biddy waiting for me to answer a question I wasn't sure how to answer.

Great…

I grabbed my water glass, downed the rest of its contents with one fortifying gulp, and then brought the phone back to my ear. "Ms. Rapple, I'm sorry, I…uh…just tried my grandfather on my office line and he didn't answer."

I hated having to lie, but I didn't relish stomping on a woman's already broken heart—even when that woman was Ms. Rapple. "But if you tell me what you need, maybe I can help."

There, I'd said it.

I'd offered to help my one and only true non-feathered nemesis in life.

Switching the phone to my left hand, I covered my forehead with the backside of my right hand and tried to gage my temperature. You know, just in case I had developed some sort of plague that was robbing me of my good sense.

When I was pretty sure my delusion wasn't illness-based, I filled in the gap between her sniffles with yet another offer I couldn't quite comprehend was coming out of my mouth. "I-I can come sit with you if that would help."

"C-could y-you just bring us back home?"

"*Us*? You mean Gertie is getting to come back home with you?"

"I c-can't spend another night without her. I just c-can't."

I had more questions, but it was obvious now was not the time. Especially when I was finding it hard to think between Rapple's sniffles and the sight of my grandfather's empty chair and uneaten Reuben.

"Do you need me to come now?"

"I know you're working, Tobi. So I can wait until closer to five if that helps."

I tried to shake off the bizarreness of the moment, but no amount of shaking (or shuddering) changed reality. I was, in fact, talking to Rapple on the phone. And she, in fact, was being accommodating.

I allowed myself one more shudder for old time's sake and then wedged the phone between my face and my shoulder while I wrapped my grandfather's sandwich to go. "I'll be there in thirty minutes. Forty, tops."

"Thank you, Tobi."

I tossed my phone, my planner, and the wrapped sandwich into my backpack and then gathered up the mess left from my lunch and made my way over to the trash bin, which wasn't too far from Cassie's table. The fact an exit to the parking lot (not the right one, but who's counting) happened to be located just beyond her table made stopping by for a quick chat a little less awkward.

Or at least I hoped it did.

"Hi, Cassie."

Cassie's fingers paused atop the keyboard as she looked up at me, the concentration I'd seen on her face as I approached dissipating just a little. "Hey, Tobi."

"Looks like you found a nice quiet place to get some work done, huh?" It was a stupid question but it's all I could come up with on short notice. Though, if Carter were with me, he'd pat me on the shoulder, mutter something about my social skills, and move in with some sort of witty and endearing comment capable of making the mute speak.

"Uh huh."

I looked around for something I could build a conversation around, but short of the trash bin and the elderly couple standing in front of it trying to sort the plastic and the paper into the correct receptacles, there was nothing. Instead, I settled on the only thing we had in common besides our line of work.

"So how are you holding up?"

Her eyebrows darted upward. "Holding up?"

"Yeah, you know, after what happened the other night."

Her face drained of all discernable color as she looked from me, to her computer, and back again. "It was awful, wasn't it? I still can't believe..." Her words trailed off in favor of a deep breath. "Well, I can't believe it, that's all."

"Did you know her well?"

Cassie started to answer, paused, and then looked at me closely. "You mean, *Deidre*?"

I nodded.

"As much as any of us knows anyone from another firm. Which is to say, not really, no. We traveled in different circles and she wasn't anyone I ever had to worry about, you know?"

Actually, I didn't know. Deidre was good at what she did. She might have been quiet and unobtrusive, but she'd put together quite a few eye-catching campaigns over the years. Heck, I'd gone up against her with two different prospective clients over the past few months and I'd only won out once.

But then again, Cassie had always struck me as cocky. So while I was equal parts disgusted and amused by the ease in which she could so easily dismiss a true contender in our field, I shrugged it off in the end.

I could use cockiness to my advantage in landing clients.

I had. And I would.

"Can I ask you a question, Tobi?"

I met Cassie's eye. "Of course. Shoot."

"How long before you think Whitestone will be looking to fill her job?"

"Whitestone?"

Cassie ran her hands through her long hair, releasing a sigh (and dislodging the lone hombre strand that was the bane of Carter's existence) as she did. "Do you think I should wait a full week out of respect, or get my resume in now before anyone else?"

"Whoa." I backed up a step as the meaning behind Cassie's words took root. "You're wanting to submit for Deidre's job?"

I used the time it took for her to nod to rein in my surprise. "Wow. Okay. I always thought you were happy at Ross Jackson."

"I was. And then I simply became good at acting." Cassie grabbed a hold of her to-go cup, shook it enough to rattle what was left of her ice, and then took a quick sip. "I thought it would get better after she left, but then again, I'm not a sloppy seconds kind of gal. Fortunately for me, there's now an opening of equal standing at The Whitestone Agency and I'd like to think I'd be a perfect fit, don't you?"

~Chapter Seventeen~

I was on my way back to my office after dropping Grandpa Sullen Pants off at the house when JoAnna called, her base mode cheerfulness no match for my budding crankiness—a fact she called me out on inside the first minute and a half.

"I take it things with Stu didn't go as you'd hoped?"

"Not. Even. Close." I stopped at the four-way intersection at the end of my road and let a good three or four cars go before I became aware of the car behind me—piloted by a man who'd obviously had enough of my good Samaritanism (aka, zoning time) if the repeated taps on his horn were any indication. I rolled my eyes at him in the rearview mirror (not because he could see it, but because it made me feel good) and turned left. "Why is everyone in such a rush these days, JoAnna?"

"Everyone?"

"Yes. The guy behind me just now at the stop sign...my grandfather...everyone."

I heard JoAnna's chuckle in the background and knew she'd pulled the phone from her mouth in an effort to keep me from hearing, but considering I was the only one in my car at that moment, she hadn't succeeded. Before I could lodge a complaint, her voice returned to the line. "I'd ask if Stu rushed through lunch, but the way you inhale your food makes that question a little silly."

"I don't inhale my food!"

This time she didn't bother to pull the phone away from her mouth. She just laughed. Loudly. "Oh, Tobi."

Now, there were few things JoAnna did that irritated me. But being *Oh Tobi*'d definitely made the list. I suspected that had something to do with the fact they tended to coincide with my mouth uttering something obvious or stupid.

I shook off all flashbacks of my more quickly ingested meals and made myself steady the breath that had become agitated inside the sandwich place. "I was standing there, listening to Cassie possibly admitting culpability in Deidre Ryan's murder when he started texting me every two seconds"—for maximum effect, I modulated my voice to something resembling Grandpa Stu's—"*I'm waiting...are you coming...where are you...I'm going to start walking if you don't*—"

"Wait. Back up. To the part about Cassie."

At the next stop sign I turned right. "You mean the part about her possibly admitting culpability in Deidre Ryan's death? Yeah, I thought that was kind of important, too. But noooo, my grandfather is in a snit he refuses to explain and so, after the fourth text, Cassie said something about it being obvious I was in high demand and she probably should get back to her resume, anyway."

"Did you say her *resume*?"

"Yup, I sure did."

"But I thought you said she was a big shot at Ross Jackson. With a corner office and all."

"I did. And she was. But for whatever reason that's—

"Wait! Maybe this is about what you said earlier. About that woman you were up against being the new shining star for the time she was there."

It took me a minute to switch tracks between the train I was on, and the one JoAnna was driving, but I caught up. "Lexa."

"Maybe being dethroned by Lexa stuck with Cassie even *after* Lexa moved on."

I tucked that notion into the *revisit this later* part of my brain as I pulled to a stop in front of my agency and pulled the keys from the ignition. "I'm here, by the way."

If JoAnna heard me, she didn't let on. Instead, she backed up our conversation one more time. "So what's this about admitting a hand in that poor woman's death?"

"*Possibly* admitting. Possibly."

"Yeah, yeah…"

As tired as I was, I still mustered a grin as I switched our call to my phone and stepped out of my car. "She's going after the new opening at The Whitestone Agency."

"I wasn't aware there was a…" By the time the proverbial bomb exploded in her head, I was in place (and helping myself to a butterscotch candy from her candy jar) when the fallout made its way past her lips. "Good heavens, Tobi! That poor woman's body isn't even in the ground yet!"

I unwrapped the candy but stopped shy of inserting it into my mouth. "So I'm not the only one who finds it fishy?"

"*Fishy*? Try *Appalling*. Beyond that, there are simply no words." JoAnna, now realizing we were no longer speaking via phone, lowered the receiver into place and stared at me across the top of her desk. "I don't understand how someone could even *think* like that. Especially someone who had a bird's eye view of such a tragedy the way we did…the way *Cassie, herself*, did."

I popped the candy onto my tongue and worked it around my mouth while I considered my secretary's words and countered them with the thought that had accompanied me out of the sandwich place and into the parking lot—a thought I'd wanted to share with my grandfather but hadn't because I'd been pissed. "Unless Cassie was prepared in a way no one else was.…"

"Surely someone with Cassie's reputation in this industry could have found a job at another agency without helping her search along in *that* way."

It was a point I hadn't yet gotten to, and one that, if I really thought about it, kind of halted the whole *case closed* proclamation I was itching to make so I could check something off my ever growing to do—

"Oh no."

JoAnna's eyes widened. "What?"

I heard the crinkle of the butterscotch wrapper as I dropped my head into my hand, but it was no match for my groan.

"What's wrong, Tobi?"

"I came back here so I could continue going through that list you made me, but I can't."

"Why not?"

"Because I promised Rapple I'd pick her and Gertie up at the vet now and—"

"So Gertie is okay then?"

Slowly, I lifted my head up, tossed the wrapper into the trash, and hoisted the strap of my backpack up my arm yet again. "Based on what she said about needing to bring the little rat—"

"Tobi!"

"Sorry. Old habits." I pointed at the candy jar and, at JoAnna's eye roll, I helped myself to an assortment of treats to make the trip to the vet and back as bearable as possible. "Anyway, as I was starting to say, based on what Rapple said about needing to bring Gertie home, I get the sense there are still issues. What they are though, I don't know. Yet."

"How did you end up with the job of picking them up?"

"I answered the phone when she called." I started to replace the lid on the candy jar when I spied a small package of Now & Laters midway down the left side and immediately began the kind of search and rescue mission that trained professionals would've envied. "She called hoping to find my grandfather."

JoAnna shook her head at my thievery and then, when I had the desired candy in my clutches, reached over and secured the lid. "Who was there at lunch with you, yes?"

"He was. But he told me to say he wasn't."

"Trouble in paradise?" she asked as she pressed a few buttons on her computer and then turned toward the printer housed on the shelf behind her desk.

"So it seems."

"I would imagine that makes you happy?"

Oh how I wanted to nod. But I couldn't. Not when I couldn't shake the reality that was my grandfather's sudden sadness. Instead, I opened the outer wrapper of my latest candy conquest and shrugged. "I'm not sure how to answer that, so I won't. For now."

I felt rather than saw JoAnna's brow rise in surprise as I retrieved my keys from the top of her desk, but I opted not to react. If I did, I'd never get out of there, and then I'd have an irritated Rapple to deal with on top of everything else. "Anyhoo, in the course of me running interference for Grandpa Stu, she asked if I could pick her and Gertie up. Now I realize I should have checked with you to see if I have any meetings but—"

"You don't."

With the rest of my sentence now rendered useless, I hooked my thumb in the direction of the front door. "I better head out now."

"Take this." JoAnna pulled some pages off the top of the printer, stapled them together, and handed them to me. "That way you can kill two birds with one stone."

I looked down at the first page and the handful of campaigns I'd already culled, and then back up at my secretary. "You're a genius—" The front door opened behind me, ushering in a momentary blast of street noise, and we both turned to find Sam standing there, the smile on his teenage face brighter than ten Christmas trees rolled into one. Tossing his own backpack onto the corner chair, he puffed out his chest in true Superman style and grinned. "I did it! I did it!"

JoAnna covered her mouth from Sam's view and called on my limited lip-reading ability. "Prom?"

I shrugged in response and turned back to Sam. "As much fun as it would be to start a round of twenty questions at this moment, I'm actually heading out for a little bit and I'm already a little behind schedule. Soooo, if you could just tell us who she is and whether she's worthy, that would be great."

The telltale hue of embarrassment appeared on his cheeks only to be chased off with a cough and an emphatic shake of his head. "I got a job, Tobes! Just like you said I would!"

"Oh, Sam, that's wonderful!" JoAnna gushed.

Me, being me, followed up *my* praise with an immediate round of the same game I'd just said I didn't have time for, although in all fairness, my *who-what-when-where* was only four questions rather than the cliché twenty.

Fortunately for me, Sam was sixteen and his brain (and therefore his mouth) answered in rapid fire succession—the Callahan Agency...print work for an upcoming St. Charles area tourism campaign (damn, lost that one)...tomorrow...in St. Charles, of course.

He followed it all up with a triumphant fist pump. "It was just like you said, Tobes. This guy—Kevin Callahan—said I turned heads with the work I did for you and with winning the award and everything and he wants to see what I can do for him and his agency!"

Before I could respond or even puff out my own chest with the pride that was practically bursting out of my pores, Sam caught me up in a hug and spun me around the reception area much to JoAnna's delight. "I did it...I did it..."

When the motion stopped and he released his hold on me, I stepped back and tapped my finger on the tip of his nose. "At the risk of sounding all *I told you so*—which, by the way, I did, thankyouverymuch—I knew this was going to happen, kiddo. Your talent with a camera knows no bounds and it was only a matter of time before it got its due attention."

This time, when his cheeks flamed red, it was because of pride rather than embarrassment and it warmed me from the inside out.

"Tobes, I don't know how to thank you for all of this. For taking me seriously, for giving me a shot, for liking what I do...for all of it."

I felt my throat constricting and did my best to hold it at bay with a few big swallows and a mental reminder of the person who would soon be sitting in the passenger seat of my car. Unfortunately, the latter wasn't as helpful at holding off the urge to cry as I'd hoped and so I accepted the tissue JoAnna held out to me. "You can thank me by knocking this Callahan shoot out of the ballpark, kiddo."

"Oh, I will, Tobes. You can count on that."

~Chapter Eighteen~

We were no more than half a block from my house when Mary Fran reached forward and shut off the radio I'd just turned on, effectively ending the one-person dance party taking place in my back seat.

"Hey!" Carter protested. "That was a good song!"

"That, my dear man, is a matter of opinion."

Carter's rounded eyes met mine in the rearview mirror a split second before his lower lip jutted out in a pout. "I'm crushed, Mary Fran. Simply crushed."

I gave into the laugh I sorely needed and turned left at the end of the road, my general knowledge of the area in which Sommers Funeral Home was located making the need to call on Carter's GPS app moot at this point in the ride. But as good as it felt to rid my head of what had been a fairly crappy day, the knowledge that it was about to get even crappier brought an end to the lightness.

"So, this stuff with Stu… How long before we start waving the flag?"

I headed toward the highway, peeking up at Carter as I did. "Flag?"

"In surrender."

"What do you mean?"

"I'm here instead of him." Carter's focus shifted to the rearview mirror as a whole. "Necessitating the need to go"—he touched his hair—"brown—very temporarily, I might add—and wear...*black*."

"That's an impressive lip curl, my friend." I accelerated up the ramp and onto Highway 40 and immediately jumped into the left lane.

"And that's an impressive attempt to throw us off the scent—although, not impressive enough."

Oh how I wanted to ignore Mary Fran, to turn the radio back on and pray for yet another Boy George ditty that would have Carter dancing and Mary Fran banging her head on the passenger side window in protest. But even if I were successful, it would be a hollow victory. Because the truth was, I relied on these two to help me out of life's trickier moments and this stuff with my grandfather definitely qualified.

So I caved.

"Okay, yes, I'm getting worried. Grandpa Stu is lethargic, monosyllabic, and he hasn't showered in two days."

"Has he resorted to the hunger part yet?"

"Hunger part?"

Carter offered a thumbs up to a man driving a pale yellow Volkswagen Beetle in the middle lane and then settled back against his seat. "Of course. The most effective way to dig in one's heels in protest is to stage a hunger strike."

"What on earth are you talking about, Carter?"

"I mean, I knew he liked her and all, but to take it to this extent?"

I pulled into the middle lane to get around a slow moving vehicle in the left lane and when I was safely back where I wanted to be, I met Carter's eyes again. "Can you speak in English, please? As I have absolutely no idea what you're talking about."

"Think about it, Sunshine. He turned down the opportunity to investigate a murder. And as I was heading out, he pressed these"—Carter held up my grandfather's notebook and magnifying glass—"into my hand."

I felt my stomach begin to churn and forced myself to take a few deep breaths. "No, the part before that…about liking her and all. You're talking about Rapple, right?"

"Who else?"

"I don't think you're right. In fact, today? When I was at lunch with him? She called my phone looking for him and he insisted I not divulge the fact he was with me. Hence the reason I almost ran late for"—I motioned toward the road in front of us—"this thing tonight. *He's* dodging *her*, Carter, not the other way around. Which means whatever this is, it's *his* decision. He's in the driver's seat."

"He might be driving, Sunshine, but only because you're sitting in the backseat with the proverbial gun to his head. And *we're*"—he motioned toward Mary Fran and then over his shoulder in the direction we'd come from—"certainly not protesting."

I looked at Mary Fran. "What the hell is he talking about?"

Mary Fran's upper lip disappeared inside the lower one as she shrugged.

I returned my attention to the occupant in my backseat. "What the hell are you talking about, Carter?"

"You said he heard you the other day, remember?"

I sensed someone's eyes digging into the side of my head and turned to my right in time to register the stare down from a passing driver. Mouthing a sorry, I let him go by and then moved into the middle lane. "Heard me what?"

"Trashing Rapple."

Suddenly, I was back in my apartment, talking to Andy, listening to the sound of my own voice in my head.

"I wouldn't pick Rapple for the delivery guy who dropped my pizza on the sidewalk last week, either."

The memory gave way to a dull roar in my ears. "I was just…"

I let the rest of my sentence fall away as my memory jumped to my grandfather as he'd looked at that moment. He hadn't said anything, hadn't challenged me or chastised me, but I'd seen it in his eyes.

I'd hurt him that day. I knew it then, and I knew it now. Yet in true Tobi form, I fought back the way Grandpa Stu had always taught me to do. "Okay, but if he really liked her that much, why wouldn't he just tell me to stuff it?"

Carter's answering laugh was drowned out by Mary Fran's.

"What?" I protested. "It's a valid question."

"If you were talking about someone other than you in relation to Stu, maybe. But we're not."

"Someone other than me?" I echoed.

Mary Fran sighed, traded eye rolls with Carter, and then shook her finger at me. "Have you seen the way he can power our entire street with his smile when he arrives for a visit to see you? Or heard the way he told everyone within a ten-mile radius about your award nomination? Or listened—*really listened*—to his memories of you growing up and the fun you two always had?"

Before I could truly process what she was saying enough to respond, Carter jumped in from the back seat. "You are the light in his days, the shiniest star in his nights, the whipped cream in his hot chocolate, the cherry on top of his ice cream sundae, the—"

Mary Fran clapped her hands. "Carter, she's got it." Then, leaning across the center console, she narrowed her eyes on me. "You *do* get it, yes?"

I said nothing.

Not because I didn't get the totality of Carter's words, but because I was still trying to figure out what it meant in terms of my grandfather's sudden personality change. I was important to him—I knew that. The feeling was more than mutual. But—

"Oh no..."

"Toot! Toot! The six-fifteen train to reality has just pulled into the station, ladies and gentleman. Next stop—How Do I Fix This."

Mary Fran laughed.

I did not.

"He called it quits with Rapple because of me?"

"You really don't get it, do you?" Carter drawled, pitching forward between the front seats.

"Get what?"

"There's nothing Stu won't do for you. Including putting a lid on his own happiness in favor of yours."

It was official. I felt like a complete heel.

"But hey, cheer up. This means no more night sweats for you and no late night post-nightmare phone calls to me over the image of Rapple as a step-grandmother, right? Because honestly, you kicked off a few doozy nightmares for me, too." Carter pulled a poorly placed quarter out of the appropriate change slot in my center console and resituated it correctly. "Though mine tended to have me Gertie-sitting while the three of you went on a family vacation together."

I stopped myself mid-shudder and tried my best to blink away the moisture I felt building behind my eyes. "I don't know what to say."

"That's okay. Because if Carter is right on the reason Stu didn't come tonight, and the reason he hasn't been answering the door or the phone when you're not home, we're not the ones you need to say it to," Mary Fran said. "Stu is."

I spent the last ten minutes or so of the drive out to Deidre Ryan's viewing in silence—my thoughts walking a well-traveled and much loved road of memories starring me and my grandpa Stu. Only instead of making me smile as they normally did, they only served to stoke a fresh round of self-loathing.

For the most part, Carter and Mary Fran left me alone, their trading of McPhearson Road gossip keeping them busy. But as I pulled off the highway and made my way north toward our destination, Mary Fran released the kind of sigh that simply couldn't be ignored.

So, I took advantage of a red traffic light to take in my friend and the fact that she was fidgeting the side of her slacks. "Mary Fran? You okay?"

"I just keep thinking about Todd, you know? How one minute he's cheering for his wife and her accomplishment and the next...well, you know. It's just"—Mary Fran stopped fidgeting in favor of an agitated finger-pass through her silky smooth hair—"so wrong. I mean, it would be bad enough for that to happen, but to *watch* it happen? I can't even. Can you?"

I followed the car in front of me as the light turned green. "Not really, no."

"I'm not sure I even looked at her table when it happened," Carter interjected from the spot behind Mary Fran's seat where he'd finally settled. "I just remember hearing a woman's screams from that direction."

"That was her mother."

Mary Fran sighed again. "If I'd watched that happen to Sam, I'd have died right there at my spot."

I felt my stomach lurch at the image my friend's words invoked and waved it away. "I can't even think like that."

Silence filled my car for a while, only to be broken by Mary Fran. "So you looked then?"

"Looked?"

"At Deidre's table. When she fell."

Either consciously or unconsciously, I'm not sure which, I tightened my hold on the steering wheel. "Not the second she fell, no. But it's hard not to look toward the source of the loudest screams."

"And?"

I peeked at what I could see of Carter before looking back at the road and the passing street numbers that indicated we were getting close to the funeral home. "They were coming from Deidre's mom. And that's when I noticed her dad was up and out of his chair and running for the stage with someone I'm guessing might have been her brother?"

"Don't you think it was probably Todd?" Mary Fran asked.

"No. Todd was still at the table. I met him on the way in with Andy. The guy I'm talking about looked like a younger version of Deidre's father."

I heard Carter shift to the side and across my back seat. "The husband was still at the table?"

I slowed as the sign for Sommers Funeral Home appeared on our right and signaled my turn for the car behind me. "I only looked for a second, and really, that second was more than enough, but yeah, from what I remember, he didn't move."

"And you didn't find that odd?"

"At the time, I'm not sure what I was thinking about anything."

Mary Fran tugged her visor down and looked at herself in the mirror. "Everyone reacts to trauma differently, Carter. Some react with actions, some react with screams or cries, some are unable to process at all."

I put the car in park, cut the engine, and conducted my own once-over in the rearview mirror while Carter leaned between our seats once again. "Did you study psychology or something in college, Mary Fran?"

"No. But last fall, when Baboo first came to me, I did a little research into stress."

"Baboo is a bird."

Mary Fran stopped primping and popped her visor back into place. "I'm aware of that, Carter. But they cope with stress in much the same way we do. When Preston Hohlbrook was murdered last fall, Baboo's coping mechanism was to retreat into himself, remember?"

Carter and I nodded in unison.

"Well, I suspect Todd was doing the same thing, although, being honest, I wouldn't have guessed that based on the guy he was back in high school."

"You said he was a theater guy, right?" I asked, inserting myself back into the conversation. "And that he was really good at playing a bad guy?"

"Actually, I said he was good at playing diabolical—good, as in scary good."

Carter smacked his hand to his chest. "I didn't know you hung out with theater types in high school, Mary Fran."

"I didn't. Todd just stood out to me as being someone very different on stage. In day to day life he was the wimpy kid."

"Wait. Didn't you say he had crushes on all the popular girls at your school?"

Mary Fran nodded at me. "Funny thing is, he had a girlfriend at the time. A meek little thing named Becky. I always wondered if she noticed the way he'd drop her hand when I'd pass them in the hallway. Or the way he'd slide to the other end of the bleacher when my cheerleading squad took the field. Like he didn't want anyone to know he was with her—especially the girls he saw as being better."

"And you said he didn't go to your reunion in January, right?"

"Right. Because he"—Mary Fran made air quotes—"*had* to go on a cruise with his wife. And I remember wondering at the time whether seeing my name and the names of some of my fellow cheerleaders on the reunion committee played a factor in his word choice."

I paused my hand atop the door handle and made a face. "C'mon, he was married and had kids, Mary Fran. You can't seriously think he was still hung up on girls that barely knew he was alive twenty-five years earlier, can you?"

"I didn't *want* to think that. I still don't. But I'd be lying if I said it didn't go through my head."

"Well, for Deidre's sake, I'm going to hope you were wrong." I looked toward the funeral home and then dropped my hand back to my lap. "Can I bounce something off you two?"

Carter met my gaze in the rearview mirror. "More Stu stuff?"

"No. This is completely unrelated."

"I'm listening...."

"*We're* listening," Mary Fran corrected.

"Eight years ago, Deidre and Cassie worked at the Donovan Agency together. The agency closed its doors a few years ago, but, at the time, they were a decent enough agency. Anyway, Deidre was trying to woo a chain of car detailers that had locations popping up all over the metro area."

"The Finish Boys?" Carter supplied.

I nodded and stayed the course. "Deidre had put together a pitch that the company was all set to go with until about a half second before the buzzer went off—"

"They use buzzers in pitch sessions?"

"No, Mary Fran. It's just a figure of speech." I lifted my finger to the steering wheel and traced it all the way around the edge. When I reached the top again, I continued my train of thought by backing up a few steps. "I guess because Deidre only re-entered the game in the fall, I'd never really given much thought to her career before kids. But I had JoAnna put together a list of her campaigns and it was way more extensive than I realized.

"Anyway, after I dropped off Rapple and Gertie at their place this afternoon, I finally had some time to finish going through the list. That list prompted me to do a little research of my own and that's when I found out that Cassie, who'd only recently come on board with Donovan at the time, somehow managed to steal The Finish Boys campaign out from under Deidre."

"How?" Mary Fran and Carter asked in unison.

I thought back to *Bitch Pitch's* first post and gave the answer I believed Deidre had given in her masked way. "Cassie used a very different kind of wooing."

"A very different kind of wooing? What kind of—"

Mary Fran spun around in her seat to face Carter. "She used her boobs." Then, to me, she added, "I hope Deidre got even."

"She did. She landed the library campaign that earned her the nomination for this year's Best Overall."

"Alongside you, my dear," Carter inserted.

"But instead of Cassie."

Understanding dawned on Carter's face, while Mary Fran's leaned more toward resistance. "Oh, c'mon, Tobi. You can't really think Cassie rigged that platform in the hope that Deidre would win."

"Hope would imply she didn't know whose name was in the envelope."

"Okay... But I thought you said the winners weren't known by anyone but the judges."

"They're not."

Mary Fran stared at me for a full minute before glancing back at Carter. "Is she making sense to you? Because she's not to me."

I answered for Carter. "Cassie would have known whose name was in the envelope if she's the one who put it there."

~Chapter Nineteen~

While I'd only been in a handful of funeral homes in my almost thirty years, each and every one had left me with a few common impressions.

First, there's the lobby and its deafening silence that makes it so the only sound you can hear is the beating of your own heart.

Next, there's that collective hush that greets you as the armchair mourners scattered about try to figure out how you're related to the deceased.

And finally, there's that awful moment when you make eye contact with the grieving, and you know, beyond a shadow of a doubt, that nothing you say or do can even come close to easing their pain.

I knew all of this.

I expected all of this.

Yet I still felt like a rookie as I stepped into the line of people waiting to express their condolences to Deidre Ryan's widower and parents. A quick visual sweep of the room yielded a frightened little boy and girl huddled together in cushioned folding chairs just out of the casket's sightline. Beside them, and talking to them in a quiet, soothing tone was the man I suspected to be Deidre's brother.

I watched them for longer than I should as I moved forward with the line. "They're too young to be dealing with this kind of loss."

I didn't realize I'd voiced that thought aloud until Mary Fran pulled me in for a one arm hug and brought her lips to my ear. "I know. I've been thinking the same thing. I want to do something, but I don't know what."

"JoAnna looked into whether any scholarships have been set up for her kids, but as of yesterday, there wasn't. So maybe that's something we can do."

"It can't bring her back, but it's something." Mary Fran squeezed my shoulder and then released me. "You're next."

I pulled my attention off the kids and fixed it, instead, on the mourner in front of me who was just finishing up with Deidre's father. When she stepped forward to offer her condolences to Deidre's mother, I took the father's hand and held it tightly. "I'm so sorry for your loss."

"Thank you." He took what I suspected was his umpteenth fortifying breath so far that day and forced his lips into some semblance of a smile. "How did you know my daughter?"

"I'm in advertising as well, and Deidre and I would cross paths on occasion at a workshop or conference. She was always very kind and encouraging."

"And what is your name?"

"Tobi. Tobi Tobias. I own my own—"

His smile slipped from his face. "You were up for the same award as my Deidre, weren't you?"

"I was."

The woman to my right made her way on to Todd and, like a well-oiled machine part that knew what was expected, Deidre's father gave my hand a quick squeeze and then released it so I could move on to his wife while he greeted Mary Fran.

When I stepped in front of Deidre's mother, I reached out, encasing the woman's hand inside my own. I expressed my condolences and then answered the same questions her husband had asked before it was time for me to move on again, this time to Deidre's husband, Todd.

"Todd, I am so very sorry for your loss. Deidre was a very—oh. Sorry." I pulled my right hand back, glanced down at the angry red lines traversing his palm, and, instead, extended my left hand to match his. "Deidre was a very sweet woman. And I know I'll miss seeing her smile at the various workshops and industry conferences where our paths often crossed."

His throat moved with a noticeable swallow just before his eyes fluttered closed for half a beat. "Thank you."

I started to say something about possibly starting a scholarship for the kids but stopped when it became apparent his attention was no longer on me but, rather, Mary Fran. For a moment, recognition parted his curtain of grief and I took that as my cue to step over to the casket and pay my respects to Deidre, herself.

And I tried.

I tried to pray like I was supposed to, but at that moment, all I could see was Deidre's eyes as they'd looked just seconds before the fall. And all I could hear was that God awful thud as her body hit the stage. I'd seen the pandemonium as reality dawned on the stunned faces in the crowd. I'd heard Todd's tortured cry as the responding emergency personnel sat back on their heels and quietly shook their heads in defeat. Yet even with all of that, I so wanted to pretend away everything I knew to be true.

But I couldn't.

Deidre was gone. Her kids would grow up without their mother. Her husband would raise their children alone. Her brother would mourn his first-ever friend. And her mom and dad would know the awful pain of outliving their own child.

I knew these things.

Everyone in the room knew these things.

But—

I felt a tap on my shoulder and looked up.

"The line is starting to back up, Tobi," Mary Fran whispered.

I nodded, turned my attention back to Deidre, and dropped my voice to a whisper even Mary Fran would be hard pressed to hear. "I will figure this out, Deidre. You can count on that."

Then, after a silent prayer, I wandered over to the side wall and the first of at least a half dozen photo collages that were displayed on easels around the room. There were pictures of Deidre as a baby, an elementary school student, a scout, a prom date, a high school and college graduate, a new bride, and a mom. And with each new collage, it became more and more difficult to catch my breath until I simply couldn't look at any more pictures. Instead, I continued my trek toward the back of the room, my gaze settling on a familiar face just barely visible behind a wad of tissues. I did a quick sweep of her immediate surroundings to see if her family was nearby, but when I didn't see her stepson, her daughter-in-law, or any of her late husband's loyal employees, I took a seat on a folding chair two over from hers and offered her a fresh tissue from a box perched on a small end table to my left.

"Oh, thank you. I-I just can't stop crying..." Mavis Callahan wiped at a pair of matching tears making their way down her face and then followed it up with a dab of her nose. "I-I can't stop looking at her children. They're not all that much older than my-my"—her already broken voice grew even more hoarse—"Myriam."

I didn't know the Callahans super well, but I knew enough to know Myriam was Mavis's granddaughter—the little girl I'd seen her talking to and coloring with at the Callahan table on Saturday night.

"I can't imagine my precious babies having to face life without Susan. She's such a good, devoted mother who has put aside her own hopes and dreams in favor of helping them discover theirs." Mavis balled the latest tissue inside her fist as her focus left Deidre's children and traveled to the receiving line, her jaw noticeably tightening as it did. But when I tried to see what had brought about the shift, I saw only Deidre's family and a line of mourners that showed no sign of letting up.

"Did you know Deidre well?" Mavis asked, pointing toward the tissue box.

I started to hand her another tissue but when I looked at the growing wad in her hand and the tears still streaming down her face, I opted to give her the whole box, instead. "I knew her enough to say hi when we saw one another at a workshop or conference. And we exchanged congratulation e-mails when we were both nominated for Best Overall this year. As a colleague, I admired her campaigns and her work ethic. And it doesn't take long looking at those"—I gestured toward the line of picture collages—"to know she was aces in her personal life as my Grandpa Stu is fond of saying."

Her eyes widened behind her tissue as she really looked at me for the first time. "She really did seem to have it all, didn't she? She was a wife and mother and still followed her own dreams."

Something about the sudden wistful quality to Mavis's voice made me wonder if perhaps, while contemplating Deidre's life, Shamus Callahan's widow was also pondering her own. The woman's follow-up sigh pretty much validated my suspicion.

Before I could say anything though, a brunette in a simple black dress appeared in our row and knelt in front of Mavis, her cheeks tear-soaked, her hands trembling. "I can't stop looking at her kids. They're still so little and—"

Mavis's eyes widened as she loosened her grip on her tissues and sniffed. "I didn't see you up there just now with Kevin."

"He fell behind. Talking to..." She pinched her eyes closed, firmed her lip, and then opened them to me as she stood. "I'm sorry, I don't think we've met. I'm Susan Callahan, Mavis's daughter in law."

"Good heavens, where are my manners?" Mavis swiped at her cheeks with her tissue and then nodded between the two of us. "Susan, this is Tobi Tobias of Tobias Ad Agency."

I extended my hand and, after a slight hesitation that included a once-over from the top of my blond hair to the tips of my simple sling-back shoes, Susan took it. "I don't think I've seen you around at the usual advertising related affairs."

"I'm more interested in courting clients than other advertising execs." The second the words were past my lips, I felt my blood run cold. Sure, I felt that way. Sure, I'd said those very words to Carter, Mary Fran, my grandfather, and Andy. But someone connected to the industry?

I groaned inwardly.

Lifting my hands to my cheeks, I, too, pinched my eyes closed for a beat. "Um, can we maybe pretend I didn't say that?"

I sat, frozen to my seat, as Susan flashed something resembling a smile in my direction before turning back to Mavis. "Myriam is hoping you'll come by to play tomorrow night after work. She's missed you these past few days and I-I could use a little...time. Maybe take myself out for a coffee."

Mavis looked up sharply. "Is there something wrong?"

"I just... I don't know. I think I just need a little time. To try and figure out what to do."

"What is there to figure out?" Mavis rasped.

Susan looked off to the side, her face, her aura pained. "I don't know, Mavis. I just don't know that I can... I just don't know."

If Mavis was listening to the answer she, herself, had sought, it was hard to tell as, once again, her hand tightened around her tissues in a veritable death grip while simultaneously shifting her focus to the front of the room. But when I tried to follow in true Nosey Nellie fashion, Carter and a puffy-eyed Mary Fran stepped in front of my chair.

"Did you see all those pictures?" Mary Fran asked me after nodding politely at Susan and Mavis. "I was a crying mess before we were even halfway through the first board."

I started to lean around Susan for a tissue but stopped when I felt the weight of Carter's eyes on the side of my face. Sure enough, when I looked up at him, he was staring at me in that *I need to talk to you now* way. Only this time, I was sure it had nothing to do with a sudden and inexplicable need to lecture me about my eating habits (thank you, God).

I responded, in kind, with what felt like my *is everything okay* eyebrow.

Carter raised said eyebrow with an even more intense *I need to talk to you now* expression and a tap of his wristwatch. "Tobi, I'm sorry, but you asked me to remind you about that *stop* we still need to make before we head home, remember?"

"Stop? What stop? I didn't ask you to..." The rest of my sentence faded into the air as the meaning behind Carter's words hit their mark at about the same time the whole *I need to talk to you now* thing was morphing into *oh good God, are you kidding me, Sunshine?*

I cleared my throat, shifted forward in my seat, and stood. "You're right. I forgot about that stop." Then, turning to my right, I extended my hand to first Susan and then Mavis. "I'm sorry we had to see each other again under these circumstances but—"

"Can you believe *that* one faxed in a resume this afternoon?" Mavis mumbled.

Confused, I looked at Susan and, together, we followed Mavis's eyes to the same tall, model-esque blonde I'd seen at the lunch place earlier that day. Before I could process much of anything, including Susan's quiet gasp, a flurry of motion pulled me back in time to see Mavis cover her daughter-in-law's hand with her own and squeeze. "Don't worry. Hell would have to freeze over before I'd let that happen."

"Tobi? We really should go." I felt Carter's arm slide around mine and lock into place, leaving little to no room for a protest in return.

Still, I managed to fire off a few daggers of irritation in his direction as he guided me toward the front of the room with Mary Fran bringing up the rear. Twice I stopped along the way—once to say hello to Ross Jackson, and once to trade sneers with my former boss, John Beckler, but each time Carter permitted me little more than a minute before the forcible guiding (aka pushing) started again.

The second we hit the lobby though, I yanked my arm away and gave him my best huffy breath. "What on earth has gotten into you, Carter?"

Carter surveyed our surroundings in true Carter-esque style and then lowered his voice to a level that mandated a forward lean from both Mary Fran and me. "Those marks. On his hands. You know what those were, right?"

I looked at Mary Fran to see if she had any idea what he was talking about, but her focus had shifted toward an offshoot hallway. A glance in the same direction yielded a pair of familiar faces just as Carter's words hit me with the kind of delayed punch that literally stole the breath from my lungs.

~Chapter Twenty~

One of the best things about Carter McDade, besides his loyalty, his humor, and his very being, is the fact that he seemed to know when I needed to process. If we were in my apartment and I needed to process something, he'd nose around my drafting table looking at whatever campaign I was working on at the time. If we were in his apartment and I needed to process, he'd head for his refrigerator and whatever green vegetable called to him in the way Cocoa Puffs called to me. If we were out and about, he'd busy himself with some good old-fashioned people-watching, sans his usual commentary.

In the car, as we were at that moment, he sat in the back seat, seeing how many drivers he could guilt into waving back at him while I worked through his absolute conviction that the marks on Todd Ryan's hands were rope burns. Mary Fran, however, was an entirely different animal when it came to handling me when I really needed to think. She wanted to talk—wanted to pick apart whatever the problem or issue was until everything was neat and tidy.

She'd done it for months after I caught Nick cheating on me with that waitress from our favorite restaurant. At the time, I'd just wanted to crawl into bed and cover my head while I sobbed. Mary Fran didn't approve of that tactic and, instead, had set me up on the kind of blind dates that still haunted me on occasion, even now.

The problem was, she was dissecting something completely different than I was, and I was finding it hard to focus. I tried, of course, to tune her out, but every time I started to meet with some success, she'd slap her knee or release a huffy breath, or some other equally distracting response to whatever she was revisiting at that particular moment.

So far, she'd talked about a few of Deidre's pictures—like the one that had Deidre's first born wearing the same head cap Sam had worn when he was born…and how the cocker spaniel Deidre had in high school reminded Mary Fran of a cocker spaniel her best friend's grandmother had when she was growing up, and on and on it went. Those comments had been preceded by nostalgic sighs. When she'd talked her way through pretty much every photo collage in the funeral home, she'd moved on to the people who'd been there and how she could pick out (in under two seconds, mind you) who really knew Deidre and who had been there simply to pay their respects—like us. And, from what I could tell while trying hard to concentrate on the verbal slap Carter had given me, it was during her pontificating about the latter camp that the huffy breath came out in all its huffy breath glory.

"I was pretty sure I've seen it all, you know? Restaurants, alleys, hotel lobbies, parking lots, you name it. But at a funeral home? Really?" A second, perhaps even louder huffy breath ended Carter's waveathon (and thus the limited processing I'd been able to do thus far), in its tracks. "Is there no limit to the lengths a cheater will go to make a fool of his wife?"

Carter flung himself forward between the seats, his attention now firmly inside the car, once again. "Okay, sister, what did I miss? And leave nothing— and I do mean, *nothing*—out."

"It was classic. He could barely keep his hands off the bimbo. And she was stirring the pot in true bimbo fashion." Mary Fran tipped the back of her head against the seat rest. "I swear, it's why I can't stand the opposite sex…present company excluded, of course."

"And Drew," I reminded while Carter preened in the back seat. "Because things are still good with him, yes?"

Mary Fran waved off the hint of concern I heard in my voice. "It's still too early to be sure, but he's looking to be a mold breaker. Although, even saying that out loud makes me worried about jinxes and all that stuff. Lord knows, it's happened before, ala Sam's dad, and then again with husband number two.

"But honestly, when I see this kind of crap going on, I'm really tempted to just declare my celibacy and never leave my house."

"Rudder would starve," I pointed out.

"No, you'd feed him."

My laugh echoed around us as I exited the highway and turned in the direction of home. "While I value your unquestionable faith in me, Mary Fran, this is one area where it might be unfounded."

"Please." Mary Fran turned her chin, traded knowing glances with the occupant of my backseat, and then let loose a frustrated groan. "I just want to find the jerk's wife and tell her to take him for everything he's worth and don't look back."

Fortunately for the traffic light we were now waiting at, the process of teeing my hands didn't put us in any real jeopardy. I held the tee as I looked at Carter. "Do you know who she's talking about?"

"No. But the build-up is spectacular, isn't it?"

"That's one word for it." I put my hands back on the steering wheel as I took advantage of the still red light to pin Mary Fran with what I hoped was the visual embodiment of my decreasing patience. "Can you bring me and Carter up to speed without us having to stop at Aunty Annie's craft store to purchase white fabric?"

"Ooooh, clever retort," Carter said. "I see what you're doing there."

Mary Fran stuck out her tongue, chastised me for not moving despite the now green light, and then shifted in her seat so she was facing us rather than the road. "You were right there, Tobi... I know you saw them there... in that little hallway by the bathrooms there at the end. His hand was on her back and he was whispering something in her ear—something that was apparently so funny she had to giggle in that way all bimbos on the prowl giggle around a man."

Carter sunk back against his own seat with all the drama of a thespian rather than the guy who does their hair. "I missed it. I was too busy yacking about—"

"Wait." I maneuvered around a row of parked cars on the right and then stole a glance at my friend. "You're talking about Kevin Callahan and Lexa Smyth?"

Mary Fran shrugged. "Is this Kevin Callahan guy married?"

"He is."

"And this Lexa woman? Is she married?"

"No." I drove through the center of town, past my agency, the deli, the library, and the mini mart, my brain pushing stop once and for all on the processing of Carter's words in favor of Mary Fran's. "But trust me, there wasn't anything there."

"I know what I saw, Tobi."

"And normally, I wouldn't even think of questioning your radar on such matters. It's *almost* impeccable." I shot my palm across the center console lest she try to protest my usage of the word *almost*, and kept on going. "Lexa works for Kevin. That's all."

"How do you explain his hand and her giggle?" Mary Fran challenged.

I slowed at the four way stop and turned left. "His hand was on her back, yes? And he was whispering something to her, yes? I think the back is a pretty innocuous place to put one's hand while trying to whisper something, don't you?"

Mary Fran folded her arms in defiance.

I kept going. "Anyway, on top of all that, this unsuspecting wife you assume he has? That would be Susan Callahan—the brunette who I was talking to when you and Carter came up to me at the end. And the woman sitting two chairs to my right? That was Mavis, aka Kevin's stepmother."

"I swear, Sunshine, every news channel in town seems to have some variation of the same clip from Saturday night with that poor women sobbing." Carter stopped just long enough to let loose a dramatic sigh. "You think they'd respect the fact she lost someone dear to her and—"

"See, now I got the distinct impression this evening, that Mavis didn't really know Deidre. She's just a nice older woman who is clearly heartbroken at what we all witnessed on Saturday night... At a show hosted and sponsored by her family's foundation."

Mary Fran silenced us with a flip of her hand and then narrowed her eyes on my face. "You think cheaters don't flirt with their mistresses in front of their spouses? C'mon, you've seen the chick flicks we've watched. That's part of the thrill for some of these guys."

"For some, maybe. And *mistress*? Really? Don't you think you're jumping the gun just a little here?"

Mary Fran's shoulders returned to their upright position as she jutted out her chin. "No. I know what I saw."

"You saw water cooler chatter without a water cooler. That's all."

"And I suppose you're going to say this Lexa chick isn't the type to hit on a married man?"

If only I could...

"No. I'm not saying that. I'm just saying Kevin's wife and stepmom were there—"

"In another room, Tobi."

I did a rolling stop at the next sign and turned onto the back end of our street. "As I was saying, Susan and Mavis were there, and he has two kids—one of whom is under a year."

"Sam was under a year when *his* father strayed...."

"You're wrong, Mary Fran." I peeked up at my house as we drew close, the flicker of blue coming from my windows letting me know my grandfather was still awake. And while I really wanted to just climb in bed and put an end to a day that had been entirely too long already, Grandpa Stu and I needed to talk.

"So what do you think about what *I* said?" Carter asked as I pulled alongside the curb and shut down the engine. "You know, about the rope burns on the grieving widower's hands?"

I flashed back to the way Todd Ryan's right hand had felt inside mine and the image of the angry red lines that traversed his palm as I pulled back and took his left, instead. "I saw them; I just didn't think much about them."

"Which makes sense if you ignore the fact that the platform that gave out underneath his wife was suspended by ropes and cables."

I stared at Carter in the mirror only to turn around and meet his eyes directly. "Do you realize what you're saying, Carter?"

"Probably the same thing that went through your mind when I mentioned the burns as we were leaving the funeral home."

"You took me by surprise, sure. And I tried to remember the way his hands looked to see if you're right but—"

"They were rope burns, Sunshine."

"Even if you're right—and I'm not conceding a hundred percent that you are—that doesn't mean he killed his wife!"

"True. But it might mean Cassie isn't the only one you need to be looking at for this." Carter opened his door and stepped out onto the road, a move I matched as if on auto pilot. "Or, if you want to keep your focus on her, turn this possibility with the husband over to Stu. It'll give him something to do."

I looked across the roof of my car at Mary Fran, but other than registering the fact she'd exited the car and therefore I could lock it, I didn't really see her. "Why on earth would Todd Ryan want to kill his wife?"

But even as I asked the question, I knew I really didn't need either of my friends to answer. Sadly, I'd learned a thing or two about murder over the past six or seven months and while I could never imagine taking a life myself, I knew there were all sorts of reasons that drove others to do just that.

Revenge.

Jealousy.

Greed.

"But he looked so...so distraught," I muttered as I shut my door and trailed Carter over to the sidewalk and Mary Fran.

"And back in high school, in that show I told you about, he looked like the diabolical wolf." Mary Fran slipped her arm inside mine and walked with me all the way up to the point where she needed to veer right to get to her place. "I'm telling you, Tobi. Todd Ryan could've had a helluva career out in Hollywood. Oscar winning, actually."

~Chapter Twenty-One~

There was so much I wanted to say to my grandfather, things I needed to explain, an apology I needed to offer, and theories I wanted to brainstorm, but as was the case when I had a lot on my plate, I was at a temporary loss on where best to start. So, despite the late hour and my eyes being a wee bit droopy, I'd popped some slice-and-bake cookies into the oven, set the timer, and readied the table for what I hoped would be a lengthy and productive powwow.

Granted, when I suggested making the cookies upon my return home ten minutes ago, he'd balked, giving me some song and dance about him being tired and needing to watch his sugar intake before bed. But since Grandpa Stu was the quintessential night owl, I knew his first reason was bogus, and, since he'd invented eleven-o'clock-cookie-time, I knew the second one was as well.

Which is why, once the smell of freshly baking chocolate chip cookies began to make its presence known in my kitchen, I wasn't the least bit surprised when I heard the telltale sound of his slippers as they left the threadbare fibers my landlord proudly declared a carpet and headed over to my trap (aka my kitchen table).

Without asking, I pulled a pair of glasses from my cabinet, carried them over to the refrigerator, and filled them to the top with milk. When I'd pretty much drained what was left of the gallon I'd picked up the previous day, I set both glasses and a heap of napkins on the table and returned to the oven in time to pull the cookies out in their primo gooey state.

I'd imagine, based on experience, my grandfather sighed at the sight, but considering how loud my own sigh was, I couldn't be sure. "Oooh, these look good."

I yanked open the utensil drawer, located my favorite spatula, transferred the half dozen cookies to their waiting plate, and carried them over to my now seated grandfather. "From a purely aesthetic standpoint, Grandma would be pleased, wouldn't she?"

My grandfather straightened his shoulders and peered down at the cookie, making a grand gesture of judging my efforts. It was a routine I knew well as he'd done the same thing about everything I'd ever created from the time I could remember. Every picture I brought home from pre-school, every test I brought home from grade school, every self-assigned advertising project I'd brought home during high school, every guy I ever dated, and every cake I'd ever baked had gotten the same over the top once-over. And, just as I'd always done, I held my breath, waiting for my Grandpa Stu's reaction even though, at nearly thirty years old, I knew what it would be. It would be what it had always been—pride…in me. It was something I'd been able to count on my whole life, and the thought of one day not having that was more than I could fathom.

Sure enough, as I stood beside the table, waiting with bated breath, he looked up, gave me the smile I'd loved my whole life, and followed it up with two thumbs up and a bite of the very first cookie. When I saw his eyes roll back in his head, I sat in my own chair and helped myself to a cookie, too.

While I munched (and maybe even moaned, a little), I tapped my finger atop the notebook Carter had handed me when we parted at our respective front doors. "Carter asked me to give this back to you and to apologize for his handwriting."

I followed his eyes to his favorite sleuthing book and then pushed the plate of cookies closer to him. He took one but stopped short of taking a bite. "You found something?"

"Carter thinks we did."

"And you don't?"

"I don't know enough about Todd, or about the mechanics behind how that platform Deidre was on was suspended, to really say one way or the other. But I think it's a stretch, that's for sure."

"Who's Todd?"

"Deidre's husband."

My grandfather wedged his second cookie between his lips and, with his now free hand, opened his notebook and flipped through the pages until he came to the one with Carter's serial killer handwriting. I, in turn, waited as he patted the front pocket of his flannel shirt, and then handed him the magnifying glass Carter had given me back, as well.

A second later, his full attention was back on me in the way it always used to be, not the way it had been the last few days. I made a mental note of the change and then motioned toward Carter's note.

"Carter says the marks on Todd's hand were rope burns."

"And you don't agree?"

I broke off a piece of my second cookie and popped it in my own mouth, chasing it down, almost immediately, with a big gulp of milk. "I noticed the marks but I didn't really pay them much mind. Carter is the one who thought it could be a clue."

"If he were involved, that means he killed his own wife," my grandfather murmured as he flipped back a few pages in his book, stopping as he reached a page with his own notations.

"But here's the thing. Remember the newscast that night? Where they interviewed that stagehand guy?"

"Doug."

"Remember what he said that night? He said the suspension cables holding the platform had been loosened. Likely by a screwdriver they found nearby—a screwdriver that had been wiped clean of prints. He made no mention of ropes."

"Not that night, maybe."

"*That* night?" I left my chair to come around and stand behind my grandfather's so I could get a right-side-up view of whatever it was he was reading. Sure enough, he'd written what appeared to be a behind-the-scenes guide for the Callahan Foundation's annual award show for the St. Louis advertising community. "Where'd you get that?"

"From Doug."

"Doug?" I stopped, blew a renegade strand of hair off my forehead, and waved my hands around until my grandfather looked up at me. "You're telling me you talked to the guy on the news? For real?"

He nodded.

Exasperated, I reached over my grandfather, secured the rest of my second cookie, and nibbled it as much for fortification as something to do with my hands that didn't involve grabbing my grandfather by his flannel collar. "I'm listening...."

The silence continued for a few more seconds as my grandfather continued to consult his notebook. When he was done, he tapped the open page. "From what I wrote here, it certainly looks as if the person behind that platform collapse could have come away with rope burns."

The pull of my milk glass led me back to my chair. "Okay, hold on. You're kind of all over the place right now. Can we get back to the stagehand part first and then work our way out from there?"

He looked up at me, but only briefly. "Right. I saw him this morning."

"Where?"

"At Fletcher's."

Fletcher's Newsstand was a staple in my neighborhood. Located at the corner of Euclid and Maryland, the old-fashioned outdoor cart was run by Jack Fletcher, a true gentleman in every sense of the word. Jack had come by the stand honestly after having worked beside his father from the time he was four, counting back change and stacking papers. The pictures that hung from a clothesline beneath the awning told their story to people like me, who hadn't grown up in this part of town.

On the days I opted to walk to work, Fletcher's was a must-stop for me. It wasn't that I had a burning desire to pick up the day's paper, but interacting with Jack was always a great way to start the day. Sometimes, we simply exchanged pleasantries—*have a great day* and *you look nice* sort of stuff. But other days, especially when the sun was shining and there was a window between customers, he'd share a story from his past with me.

My grandfather loved Jack, as well. He said talking to him was like spending time in the barber chair—only instead of sharing tales over the buzz of a razor, they shared them over the ping of silver into the same tin bucket Jack's dad had used when he'd run the stand. The fact that Jack was always asking me about my grandfather whenever he saw me simply proved the feeling was mutual, and I was glad. I liked knowing that my grandfather had a growing cast of people to further connect him to my home. It gave him more reasons to want to come and stay for a while, or, at least, I hoped it did.

"Okay..." I finally said when it became apparent my grandfather was more intent on mulling something in his head than he was in getting me up to speed on things.

"I recognized him from the news before he said a word, and I was ready, with my notebook, the moment Jack started asking him about the accident. Along the way, I asked him how the platform had been erected. And he said exactly what he'd said on the news. You know, about the suspension cables...the fact they were loosened...and finding the screwdriver nearby. But he also said there was some roping, too. As a fail safe."

"Some fail safe."

"It was cut."

"*Cut?*" My fingers, which had been contemplating a third trip to the cookie plate, clamped down on the edges of my two-person table. "Are you serious? He didn't say that on the news that night."

"He said that's because he didn't realize they'd been cut until later that night, when he was walking the scene with the police."

It was a lot to digest. But even as I tried to, another question filtered through my mouth. "But would a person get a rope burn simply by cutting it?"

"I guess that would depend on how it was held, how long it took to cut through it, that sort of thing." My grandfather grew quiet as he pushed his opened notebook off to the side, removed his glasses, and kneaded the bridge of his nose. I could tell he was troubled, but I wasn't sure if it was because of the subject matter at hand or something else.

"There's only two reasons I can figure a man would want to kill the mother of his children—especially a mother he's still married to." I paused, waited until his glasses were back on, and then slid the plate with his final cookie into his reach. "First, he's carrying on an affair and doesn't want to go through the drama of a divorce. Second, he needed money for some reason and he decided to get it via her life insurance policy."

When he said nothing, I continued. "So I guess we have two suspects for your page now. Todd Ryan and Cassie Turner."

"Still thinking Cassie switched the envelopes?"

"It makes sense. Especially when you add in the history between Cassie and Deidre, and the fact that Cassie wants to leave her job at Ross Jackson and Deidre's demise leaves an open desk over at Whitestone."

Intrigue pulled at the corners of his eyes. "When did you find that out?"

"Today." I finished my last sip of milk and eyed my grandfather's last cookie. "I didn't tell you about the job part at the time, because you showed no interest in talking and I was trying to process it all. And the other part—the one that had Deidre landing a campaign Cassie wanted—I put together later on at the office."

"That's a lot of motive," he mumbled.

"I know. I think so, too. But now, with this rope burn stuff, maybe I'm wrong. Maybe it's not Cassie at all."

My grandfather shifted in his seat and then pushed his final cookie back across the table to me.

"You don't want it?" I asked, stunned.

He held out his hand, palm splayed, and shook his head, the same sadness that had hovered around him the past two days beginning to descend across his very being once again. "It's hard for me to imagine a person going to such measures to get out from under a marriage when I'd do just about anything to have mine back."

The lump that always appeared in my throat when my grandfather talked about my grandmother took its place, and I knew the time had come to address the elephant that had been holding court in my apartment ever since I inserted my foot into my mouth on Sunday evening.

"Grandpa, I want you to know how sorry I am about the other night. I know I was being snarky and that it hurt *you*, but you have to know you're the last person on the face of the earth I'd ever want to hurt."

His gaze dropped from my face to the plate and lingered there as he said nothing. I swallowed, shifted in my own seat, and reached forward, past the plate, to cover my grandfather's hand. "I didn't realize you were standing there when I said what I said. And I'm sorry. Truly."

"Thank you, Sugar Lump." He turned his hand beneath mine, squeezed it softly, and then pulled it out so he could steady himself as he stood. "It's getting late and you've had a long day. I think we need to do a little checking on this Todd fella's background. Maybe we'll find something on that Facebook thing that'll give us a better idea of his marriage to Deidre."

He picked up our empty glasses and carried them to the sink. "If you want, I can do that while you look into the leggy blonde some more."

"Cassie."

He returned to the table, motioned toward the lone cookie on the plate with his chin and, when I took it, carried that to the sink, as well. "Gloria, from the Sexy Seniors group back home, was helping me set up a page. Maybe I can finish it and tap this fella or whatever it is you do on there to see someone's page."

"You don't *tap* them, you *friend* them."

"Then I'll friend him." He closed the curtain above the window the way I always did at bedtime and then turned back to me. "I'd like to know who did this before I head back on Friday afternoon."

"Head back? Head back where?"

"Home."

"*Home?*" I dropped my cookie onto my napkin, pushed back my chair, and crossed to the refrigerator and the ticket magnetized to the front. "But your ticket says Sunday night. We were going to squeeze in another weekend together before you left!"

He padded over to the doorway leading to the living room, his slippers making a soft tsk-tsk sound against my linoleum floor. "I've been sleeping on your couch long enough, Sugar Lump. And besides, weekends are for romance—time to hold hands, share secrets, and make love eyes at each other just the way Grandma and I did. Don't you remember the things we used to do on the weekends when your grandmother was alive? The parks we used to walk around? The museums we visited? The picnics we'd have?" "Of course I do. I remember everything." I followed him into the living room and over to the couch and the pile of bedding he kept tucked inside the first of two storage ottomans I'd purchased during his last visit. The other ottoman, I knew, kept some of his clothes so he didn't have to live out of his suitcase. "But I was always with you."

"Which is exactly how we wanted it."

I watched as he rolled the ottomans off to the side, transferred the couch cushions to a spot along the east wall, and then grabbed hold of the handle that would unleash his bed. "And having you around is exactly the way I want my weekend."

"You're not the only one in the romance, Sugar Lump."

"Hey…wait, right there." I stepped in beside him as the legs of the sofa bed snapped into place. "If you're insinuating that Andy doesn't want you around, you couldn't be more wrong. He thinks you're great."

"That doesn't mean he wants me around all the time." He stepped around me, opened the first ottoman, and pulled out the fitted sheet he made sure was always on top of the pile. With practiced hands, he snapped it open a fold at a time, until it was ready to be attached to the standard sofa bed mattress. "And who can blame him when he's got someone as cute as you by his side?"

I knew I should help him with the sheet, but I had a point to prove and only one way I could think to prove it, so I went in search of my phone. When I found it in the kitchen alongside the box of Cocoa Puffs I'd indulged in while waiting for the cookies to bake, I made a beeline back to Grandpa Stu.

"I'm going to call Andy right now so he can tell you himself."

I opened my contact list and was just about to press Andy's name, when my grandfather's hand stopped me. "Don't call him, Sugar Lump. It's late. He's probably sleeping."

"He's not. And besides, he *told* me to call him before I fall asleep."

"So the two of you can have time alone, Tobi…not so he can talk to me or about me." Grandpa Stu held my gaze until I lowered the phone to my side, and then returned to the business of making his bed. "Besides, I have my routine there. My friends. People to sit and laugh with over lunch. And before you say something about meeting me for lunch more, that's not what I'm saying. Sometimes it's nice to pass the time with other old farts just like me. There's a camaraderie there that makes me feel like I belong."

I dropped onto the ottoman that housed his clothes and splayed my hands across my lap. "Don't you feel like you belong here? With me and Carter and Mary Fran and Sam? Because you should. Heck, your bus back home is never more than a block down the road when one, if not all of them, are hounding me about when you're coming back."

A hint of a grin played at the edges of his mouth as he slipped his pillow into a case, fluffed it up with his hands, and then tossed it onto the bed. "And that's all well and good, but it's still nice to be around people my own age."

"Rapple is your age! And you have fun with her!" I tossed him the second of his two pillows and watched as he slipped a case onto that one, too. "Just about every member of our little crew here has commented on how much fun the two of you seem to have together."

He tossed the newly cased pillow alongside the first and then pointed at the ottoman on which I was sitting. I didn't budge. "You've cooled it with her because of me, haven't you?"

He said nothing.

"Oh, Grandpa." I looked up at him the way I had a million times in my life. Only instead of waiting to hear a life lesson or a silly joke, I knew that it was me who needed to do the talking. "I didn't mean for you to end your friendship with…" I stopped, swallowed, and looked away, the bitter taste kicking off a veritable furnace effect in my cheeks.

Crap.

"It's okay, Sugar Lump." Grandpa kissed me on the forehead and then reached around me to retrieve his SpongeBob pajama pants. "Your grandma was the love of my life, and we had almost sixty years together. That was a lot of happy, Sugar Lump—*a lot* of happy. I'd be a fool to forget that."

"Being happy now doesn't mean you've forgotten Grandma."

"But I have no business carryin' on like a damn fool. Your grandma deserves better."

"Whoa." I thwarted his trek to the bathroom with a firm hand. "You don't really think Grandma would begrudge you your happiness, do you?"

He waved the question away with a twinge of disgust. "Of course not. I'm sure she's laughing along with me when I'm sitting around with my friends back home, telling those jokes that always made her smile and roll her eyes all at the same time. And I know, when I'm spending time with you, she's glad."

"That's because Grandma loved you. She loved your smile, your laugh, your kindness, your gentleness, even your mischievousness. She wouldn't want you holding that back. Ever." Desperate to get through the doubt I saw clouding his eyes, I tried another road to get through. "In fact, I think denying yourself happiness in her name would actually *hurt* her, Grandpa. She loved you. And when a person loves someone—really loves them—they want that other person to be happy."

He tucked his pajama pants under his left arm and pulled me in for a hug with his right. "Then you understand why I needed to put a stop to it before it went any further."

I stepped back. "A stop to what?"

"My time with Martha."

My confusion must have been written all over my face because he led me over to the edge of the sofa bed and sat beside me. "It's like you said, Sugar Lump. When a person really loves someone, they want that other person to be happy. And that's how it is with me...for you. I should've considered you when I was thinking all those thoughts about Martha. I should've considered how seeing me with someone other than Grandma might hurt you. I only hope you can forgive me and we can get past this in a way that gets us back where we belong and doesn't ruin your friendship with Martha."

I took a moment to steady my breath in the event the cookies we'd recently finished eating decided to make an encore. When I was sure they'd remain in place, I ventured into uncharted waters. "Grandpa, there's nothing to forgive. I don't have any problem with you dating—I think it has the potential to be kind of neat, actually. And as for Rapple? Well, let's just say that referring to what we had as a friendship is, um, a bit of a stretch to say the least."

My grandfather's surprisingly bushy eyebrows rose toward his bald head. "I saw you earlier today, dropping her and Gertie off. You had your arm around her as you walked her to the door."

"She needed someone to pick her up and—"

"Martha needs that kind of affection. It's hard being alone all the time, especially someone who's had the life she's had. I'm only here every few months or so. Martha is here all the time. I don't want this thing that was building between us to affect your relationship. She needs all-the-time more than she needs some-of-the-time, Sugar Lump."

Especially someone who's had the life she's had?

I shook off the curiosity born on the back of that sentence and willed myself to focus on the matter at hand, even if I was finding it hard to meet his eyes. "Grandpa, what you heard me say the other night? To Andy? I-I didn't say those things because I was hoping you'd overhear me and break it off with Rapple. I said those things...*to Andy*...simply because that's the way we all"—I paused to clear my throat and, as I did, stole a peek at my grandfather and the genuine cluelessness he wore.

Somehow, someway, the hatred (okay, maybe intense dislike) my fellow neighbors and I had for Martha Rapple had escaped my grandfather. The thought was preposterous at first, but when I thought about my grandfather's visits—really thought about them—it suddenly all made sense.

Grandpa Stu's very presence made everyone happier. And while none of us ever willingly included Rapple in any of our movie nights or gatherings when my grandfather was around, we never really said much about her in his presence, either. So when he invariably recognized a lonely soul, he reached out and drew her in—

"That's the way you all, what?" my grandfather asked, forcing me back to a track I didn't want to be on at that moment.

Yes, I knew we had a problem. Or, rather, *I* had a problem. But honestly, I was at a loss on how to fix it.

Assuming, of course, I even wanted to fix it.

Drawing in a deep breath, I tapped the pair of pajama pants still waiting in the crook of Grandpa Stu's arm, and did my best to muster up a smile. "It's getting late, and in addition to my regular work, you and I need to do some investigating tomorrow. So let's table this for another time and get some sleep, okay?"

~Chapter Twenty-Two~

I walked Gina Poletti, co-owner of Pizza Adventure and one of my very favorite clients, over to the front door and then leaned my cheek in for the pinch I'd come to expect and accept.

"I know you'll help us unveil the new destination room in a way that'll have every table filled for the next month, at least." Gina followed up her pinch with a kiss on my forehead. "It's a given."

"*A given*? Gee, nothing like adding a little pressure."

Gina scoffed at my words. "I'm not trying to add pressure, Tobi. Quite the contrary, in fact. I just know how clever and creative you are. I've seen it countless times these past few months as you helped us introduce the St. Louis area to Dom's pizza. Not only did you get—*and keep*—people in our seats, you also achieved the unthinkable."

"Whoa. As much as I'd love to take all the credit for the line you've had every weekend since you opened, I can't. I mean, my ads may have helped get people to give you a try, but let's be honest, it's Dom's pizza that has them coming back." And it was true. Not even the most amazing advertising campaign on the face of the earth could make up for a bad product or a restaurant that failed to impress. Fortunately for Pizza Adventure, my campaign only told half the story. Dom Poletti's pizza told the rest. In fact, it could be said he'd singlehandedly versed St. Louisans in the true definition of good pizza.

"I'll concede that. But don't sell yourself short," Gina said as she hung a purse on her forearm and readied her keys for the walk out to the car. "As I said, you achieved the unthinkable, dear."

Amused, I crossed my arms and leaned back against the wall. "Okay… I'm waiting. What unthinkable feat did I achieve?"

"You got Dom to stop thrashing around in bed at night, you got him to stop muttering under his breath every time he looked at anything involving the restaurant, and you got him to tell me"—she inhaled a triumphant breath—"I was right!"

I heard JoAnna's soft gasp from just around the corner, the sound only serving to intensify the grin I knew was in danger of splitting my face open. "Dom mutters?"

"That's the part you heard? That he—" She held up her non-key-holding hand and then swept at me as if I was a bothersome, albeit endearing, gnat. "Do you know how many times I've replayed that moment in my head?"

"Just in your head?" I teased.

The telltale flush of embarrassment colored Gina's cheeks a beat before her grin knocked mine off the Richter scale. "Okay, so I might have reminded him that he said I was right a time or two since he did...."

I laughed. So, too, did JoAnna from the other room. "A time or two?"

"Well, maybe twenty—thirty, tops. Although Dom claims it's been thirty-six." Gina pushed open the front door of my agency and stepped out onto the sidewalk. "But don't worry. Even if he's exaggerating, I'm quite sure I'll reach that number soon."

My laugh and my eyes followed her across the street and down to her car before I turned and made my way back to the reception area and a still chuckling JoAnna. "She's a pistol that one."

"That's one word for it." I made my way over to the candy jar, inspected its contents, and then claimed the chair across from JoAnna without taking anything. "The first few months have been so wildly successful for them, they've decided to open another destination room."

JoAnna finished typing something and then rolled her chair out from behind the computer so we could have a better view of one another. "Why? They already have a tropical island room, a drive-in movie room, a Bat Cave room, and all those other wonderful spaces."

"They always planned on opening a few more if business was good. And I think Gina likes to decorate."

"So where are St. Louisans going to get pizza this time?"

"I'll tell you that in a second. But first, guess how they came up with the idea?"

"Shouldn't you tell me what the idea is before asking me to guess where it came from?" JoAnna asked.

I ran my finger along the lip of her desk and tried to stay focused. It had been a battle the whole time I was in my meeting with Gina, but somehow, even during those moments when my thoughts had successfully strayed to

Deidre...and Todd...and Cassie...and Grandpa Stu, Gina hadn't seemed to notice. I was glad for that, of course, but, in hindsight, I was also a little surprised. Gina missed nothing. Ever.

"Earth to Tobi, come in, Tobi..."

I shook my focus back into the present and leaned back in my chair. "They had a contest. Every time a person would come into the restaurant, the hostess would ask if it was their first time. If they said no, she gave them a slip of paper and asked them to suggest a destination room they'd like to see added to the lineup."

"That's clever."

"I know, right?" I fidgeted with a loose cushion thread next to my thigh and when I managed to free it, wrapped it around the tip of my finger. "Gina knew that if they'd already been there once, they liked it enough to come back. And she figured if they liked it enough to come back, they'd probably enjoy being a part of the decision process for the next few rooms."

JoAnna stink-eyed me until I unwrapped the thread and placed it in her outstretched palm. Then, and only then, did she re-engage in our conversation. "She's a smart cookie, that one."

"She is, indeed. So...the room. It's going to be a zoo."

"A zoo?" JoAnna cocked her head in thought. "How are they going to do that?"

"Would you have imagined a drive-in movie theater and a tropical island for restaurant rooms?" I countered.

"I see your point. But still, she can't bring in animals."

"They'll be stuffed...with the appropriate noises piped into each cage or enclosure. And the tables will be in with the animals. If you like lions, you'll eat in a lion's cage. If you like polar bears, you'll eat in their space—which, in case you're wondering, will require coats to eat in." I stood, made another visual inspection of the contents of JoAnna's candy jar and, once again, kept my hand to myself. "Gina did a much better job describing everything, and I took notes that I'll consult when I work on the ads, but really, I'm not doing it justice right now. Just know that it's going to be incredible."

"I have no doubt." JoAnna's chair creaked as she, too, stood. "So is this about that phone call you got just before your meeting with Gina or is it something else?"

"*This?*"

"You've looked at that candy jar twice and you've yet to dive in."

"I don't just dive in. I always ask permission."

"While your hand is removing the lid."

I started to raise an objection but stopped when I knew it would be overruled before I even finished my sentence. "Okay, so there's some truth in that, but if you actually said no, I'd stop. You know this, right?"

JoAnna came around the desk and perched on its lip directly in front of the chair I'd abandoned. Then, grabbing hold of my hand, she guided me back to a seating position. "Of course I know that, Tobi. You don't have to sell me on you. *You* know *this*, right?"

I nodded.

"Now that we're on the same page with all of that, let's get back to the main point in what I was saying—you never step away from candy. If you did, I'd only have to fill"—she hooked her thumb over her shoulder—"it once a month instead of once a week."

"Don't you mean, once *a day*?"

We both turned toward the doorway and the blond, green-eyed man that still made my heart flutter even after the nearly six months we'd been dating. "Andy!"

JoAnna didn't try to stop me as I stood and met Andy in the middle of the room, his arms encircling me with a strength and warmth I sorely needed at that moment. Why, I wasn't entirely sure, but I knew I'd felt unsettled for much of the morning and now, well, I didn't.

"Hi, JoAnna," he said over my shoulder.

"Hi, yourself. Tobi bypassed my candy jar. Twice."

Andy released his hold on me, stepped back, and made a show of checking me for any signs of illness. I played along for the fever, ear, and throat check, but teed my hands when he started pushing on my stomach. "Okay, you two, enough. I'm just not in the mood for candy right now. Is that really so out of the ordinary?" I let the rhetorical question go in favor of a shrug. "Yeah, okay, don't answer that. But really, I just have a lot on my mind right now. That's all."

JoAnna pushed off the desk, raised her right hand in a salute, and then nodded at Andy. "She's all yours, sir. As for me, I'm meeting an old friend for lunch at the Chinese place on the corner. I'll be back in thirty, and I have my cell if you need me."

I waited as she collected her purse from behind her desk and then caught her cheek with a kiss as she passed me en route to the door. "Take an hour and enjoy your friend. I'm pretty sure I can handle things until you get back."

When she was gone, I pointed toward my office and, at Andy's nod, led the way to my inner sanctum. "So to what do I owe this unexpected, yet very welcomed visit?"

"It's actually *to whom*, although, truth be told, I'd have made an excuse to stop by even without her." He caught me, mid-step, and turned me around for another hug, this one culminating in the kind of kiss that made me wish it wasn't twelve o'clock on a workday. Eventually, and with the kind of obvious reluctance that made a gal feel pretty special, he let me go and pulled a small envelope from his pocket. "Here. This is for you."

I looked down at the smattering of lilacs around the edges of the envelope and then back up at Andy. "Is this an invitation to a party or something?"

"I don't think so. You've never mentioned her having parties before."

"*Her*? Her *who*?" I asked, as I took the envelope and turned it over in my hands.

"Ms. Rapple."

I laughed and, yep, despite all the progress I'd made in breaking myself of the habit, I snorted, too. "In order to have a party, one would have to have friends to invite. So yeah, I'm pretty sure this isn't a party invitation."

"So then open it and see what it is."

"Translation: you're curious." I waved the envelope at him and then when he graced me with the sheepish nod I was after, I carried it around my desk, plucked out the letter opener JoAnna kept in my top drawer despite my propensity to rip things open, and sat down. "So how did you end up with this?"

"Sam asked if I'd take him out to St. Charles today."

"Doesn't he have school?"

Andy took the chair across from mine and hiked his ankle across his opposite knee. "He said something about teacher workshops."

A memory flashed in my head and I snapped my fingers. "Yes, okay, I remember now. He's got his photo job down for Callahan out in St. Charles today. I am just so proud of that kid, you know? He's going places and he's only sixteen."

"Anyway, I was only a block or two away when he called to tell me Callahan had sent a car for him." Andy chuckled at the memory. "You should have heard him when he told me that, Tobi. I swear, he's probably still pinching himself even now."

"Probably."

"Since I was almost here, anyway, I swung out to your house to say hey to Stu. But he wasn't there."

I sat up tall. "He wasn't?"

"Nope."

"Where'd he go?"

Andy made a face at me. "I don't know. He wasn't there, remember?" Then, before I could come up with the next thing to say, he pointed at my hand. "And that's when I saw Ms. Rapple and she asked me to give you that. Oh, and before you ask, she didn't know where Stu was, either. Side note here, I'm pretty sure I saw her eyes well up when I asked."

I didn't know what to say to that, so I said nothing.

"So, not wanting to leave her like that, I asked after Gertie. And that perked her up a little. Seems your favorite furry friend is showing signs of feeling better."

"You didn't have to do that, you know."

"Do what?" he asked.

"Stay with her."

Andy shrugged. "I know. But, honestly, I felt bad for her. I think she really cares about your grandfather. Like *really* cares."

A snarky thought regarding people with ice in their veins and their inability to care about anyone other than themselves rolled around on the tip of my tongue, but for whatever reason, I left it unspoken.

Weird.

"So? Are you going to open it?"

"I guess. I mean, I can't imagine why she'd want you to give this to me." I slid the tip of the slicer beneath the seal, liberated the note from inside, and began to read aloud.

Dear Tobi,

They say that true friends reveal themselves in times of crisis and I believe that is true. From the moment you moved in below Carter, you've struck me as kind. You stop and talk to me when I'm walking Gertie.

I laughed (and snorted). "Ha! So leading Gertie over to my lawn to pee is considered *walking* in her book? This woman is too much."

Andy rolled his fingers in a keep going gesture and I obliged.

You tolerate my penchant for nosiness, and even put up with me when I'm in a cranky mood, which probably seems like always to you, and sadly, you're right. I love Gertie. But I've always longed for people to gravitate toward me the way Carter, Mary Fran, Sam, and everyone else does to you. Carter drives me nuts, as you well know, but I get why he calls you Sunshine. You're like the sunshine every plant needs, even the temperamental ones like me.

I drew back, silently reread the last few sentences, and then looked up at Andy. "You sure this came from Rapple?"

Andy's laugh accompanied my eyes back down to the note in my hand.

When my mom died, I wanted to die, too. She was my mom, my confidante, my best friend, and my support system. But she wanted more for me and that's why she made sure I had Gertie before she passed away. Gertie has helped, don't get me wrong. She gives me someone to fuss over, to talk to, and to sleep beside, even when sleeping is made difficult by the late night comings and goings of you and your friends.

I rolled my eyes, but kept reading.

But as much as I love my precious Gertie, I miss that connection I had with my mom. I miss knowing that I wasn't alone during difficult times, and that I matter to another person.

You and Mary Fran have made me feel as if I matter these past few days. I know you covered the pet shop so Mary Fran could get Gertie and me to the vet. And when I called yesterday, you picked me up without a moment's hesitation, even though it took you longer to reach me than it should have.

"It took that long because I forgot you," I whispered.

I know I'm hard to like, and I'm sorry about that. I wish I could offer a reason for why I am the way I am, but even now, at my age, I still don't know. I want to be different, I always have, and for a brief time, thanks to your grandfather, I was. I just wish I could figure out why I'm different with him so I can be like that with everyone.

I'm sorry for the length of this note. I didn't intend for it to go on so long. I really just wanted to say, thank you. Thank you for being there for me and for Gertie this week.

Sincerely,
Martha (or Rapple, if you prefer)

I ran my tongue across the sudden dryness of my lips and slowly looked up at Andy. "Wow. I wasn't expecting that."

"What?"

"This." I shook the note. "This isn't the Rapple any of us know."

Andy's mouth opened as if he was going to respond, but then closed a beat or two later.

"What?" I took one last look at the note and then tossed it onto my desk. "What were you going to say?"

He dropped his foot back to the ground with a labored exhale. "I think that's the Rapple your grandfather knows."

"So she's good at turning on the charm when she wants to."

"I think it's more than that, Tobi. I really do."

I searched my immediate surroundings for any sign of a camera or other recording device designed to tape my reaction to this bizarre conversation, but there was nothing. So instead, I yanked open my emergency snack drawer. I hated that I looked to sugar to get myself through difficult moments, but it's how I rolled. A quick pass of the contents however, yielded nothing that jumped out at me as proper fortification for talk of Rapple. Instead, I closed the drawer, braced my elbows on my desk, and dropped my chin into my hands. "Okay, lay it on me."

"I think she's a different person around Stu because he *lets* her be a different person."

"Huh?"

"Prior to Sunday, obviously, I've never heard you or anyone else talk too badly about Ms. Rapple when he's around."

"Because his presence makes all bitter pills easier to swallow. It's just a fact."

"Agreed. But that's probably why he gave her a chance. And why she took it."

For some strange reason, my face was getting warm, so I grabbed Rapple's note and used it as a fan. "Can we talk about something else for a while?"

"Is this about whatever is bothering you?"

"Bothering me?"

He gestured toward my side of the desk and then hooked his thumb over his shoulder toward my door. "I heard what JoAnna said about you and not indulging in any candy out there... And you just did it again a minute ago with your emergency stash drawer."

"Okay, so I'm distracted."

"After everything you told me on the phone last night about Deidre's viewing and her husband's rope burns, and the apparent bad blood between Deidre and Cassie, I guess that's understandable."

I almost added in the part about my talk with Grandpa Stu, but I was still processing that. Instead, I merely nodded.

"So now what?" he asked.

"I called Cassie this morning right before my meeting with Gina."

"And?"

"I asked her why the envelope she carried onto the stage Saturday night was different than all the rest. Why it didn't have the same sparkles and trappings."

He waited as I indulged in a sudden need to fold Rapple's note, slip it back into the envelope, and stuff it into my backpack. When it was out of sight and thus, no longer distracting me, I continued. "Cassie said she didn't know. That when she walked over to the table to get the final envelope, she noticed it was different. She asked a few backstage people if the correct envelope had been moved somewhere else, but she was told that was the spot. So she chalked it up to some sort of last minute change that didn't allow for the normal glitz."

"Interesting..."

"Someone wanted Deidre dead so badly they deliberately replaced the correct envelope—with Lexa's name in it—with the plain one, containing Deidre's."

Andy stood, cupping his mouth briefly as he did. "So kill her in a restroom, or the parking lot, or wherever. Why go to such elaborate efforts in a place filled with witnesses?"

"Witnesses to her death," I clarified.

"What are you saying?"

"Think about what you just said—about the elaborate efforts and the public forum. Doesn't it seem as if a person who would go to that kind of effort in order to kill a person is after more than just the death itself?"

Intrigue propelled Andy around my desk until he was inches from my chair. "I'm listening...."

"Deidre's killer wanted to make sure her demise was"—I cast about for the right word to make my point—"*seen*—by colleagues and friends."

"But why?"

Holding up my finger to buy myself a second, I opened the drawer just above the one that held my secret stash and pulled out the piece of paper I'd shoved inside upon Gina's arrival. I unfolded it from the careless folding job I'd done, and smoothed it out across the top of my desk. "I called my grandfather after I got off the phone with Cassie to make sure I had them all. I'd forgotten mob contract, gang vengeance, and initiation, but I'm pretty sure we're not looking at any of those in this case."

Andy leaned around me to see my list, his breath, as he read each item aloud, both warm and comforting. "Hate crime, robbery, murder-for-hire, thrill killing, jealousy, crime of passion, obsession, revenge, greed, mob contract, gang vengeance, and initiation."

I nodded.

"Why did you underline and star crime of passion?"

"Because I think our killer was super pissed off. How else can you explain the planning that went into Deidre's death? Think about it Andy… The platform was rigged so it would drop when she stepped onto it with her award. Which would mean there would be a ballroom full of people there to watch her fall. A person who does that has to be angry, don't you think?"

"Okay, yeah, that makes sense. But if you take that thought process out a step further, a few other things on your list could use a little starring and underlining, too."

I knew where he was going and I was ready. Or as ready as I could be after a meeting that had required me to actually pay attention to my client… "So, operating on the assumption our killer was angry, the next step is figuring out why. Was it jealousy—like I suspect it was with *Cassie* as the killer?" I heard the pitch of my voice moving into excited now that I was getting to try out the theory that had started to form in my head as Gina was talking about lions, and tigers, and bears. "Killing her in front of everyone in our field would be the ultimate revenge, don't you think?"

"You've got a point, that's for sure. Although, the thought of it is pretty sick."

He moved his finger to the fourth motive from the bottom. "But you can't forget greed. Especially if there's anything to what you told me on the phone last night before bed."

"You mean with Deidre's husband?"

"You said he had rope burns."

"I did. Which is why, now that I think about it, my grandfather probably didn't answer when you knocked this morning. He was probably all over the laptop I left him, trying to find out what he can about Todd Ryan." I made a mental note to check in with him when Andy left and then moved on. "But even without knowing what, if anything, Grandpa Stu has unearthed, I just don't see this guy staging such a public killing of his wife to get his hands on life insurance money. Why not do something quieter—like poison her morning tea, or take her hiking and push her off a cliff? Something with less witnesses, less chance of things going wrong in front of a lot of people?"

Andy reached around me, opened my secret stash drawer, rooted around inside until he found a bag of pretzels held closed with a clip and, at my nod, helped himself to a small handful. "I guess I keep coming back to the rope burns if for no other reason than the timing, you know?" I mulled his words as I watched him make short work of the pretzels. When he finished the first handful, I told him to take another as a new scenario began to play out in my head. "I still stand by the fact that the very manner in which Deidre was killed implies anger—a lot of anger. So, if I stick with that, the life insurance aspect makes even less sense. I don't think greed spawns anger. Desperation, sure. But anger? Not so much."

He perched on the edge of my desk so we were facing one another as he munched and I continued to hypothesize. "Soooo, if *Todd* is our killer, it has to be because of something that made him really, really angry. Like an affair."

"Hmmm..."

"But I just don't see Deidre as the affair-having type, I really don't. Granted, I wouldn't have guessed she was behind *Bitch Pitch*, but still, every time I did see her, and our personal lives came up, she literally *gushed* about her husband and her kids."

"I'd say maybe she wasn't the one having the affair, but that wouldn't make any sense because—"

I ricocheted forward in my chair so fast I'm pretty sure the back legs left the floor. "Wait. Say that again!"

"Why? It doesn't work with the whole intense anger thing and Deidre is the one who was killed, not her husband...." Andy stopped eating. "Unless he was angry because she found out and she threatened to divorce him or something. But even if he were, he wasn't in the advertising industry, was he? So how he'd have access to backstage and why he'd want to do it in front of those people doesn't make—"

"Unless it wasn't him at all, but, rather, the person he was having the affair with." I grabbed a pretzel from his hand and worked at the salt with my teeth. "Maybe *she* is in the industry. Maybe *she* was the one who was angry because... I don't know... Maybe Todd called it off, said he loved his wife more. Many a thriller has been born on the notion of a scorned mistress, right?"

"True. But Todd had the rope burns."

And just like that, I placed the now salt-free pretzel back in Andy's hand and flung myself against the back of my chair. "Crap. I forgot that part."

He looked from the now salt-less pretzel to me and back again, and then, with a wink, stuck it in his mouth while I stewed. When he was done, he hooked his fingers underneath my chin and guided my gaze back to his. "Breathe, sweetheart. You'll figure this out. I know you will."

~Chapter Twenty-Three~

I was just starting to get into something resembling a productive flow when a soft tap at my office door brought it to a crashing halt.

Ugh.

Ugh.

Ugh.

Dropping my pencil onto my drafting table, I swiveled on the stool and waited for JoAnna to breeze in with a pink sticky note or a letter of some sort. But there was no breezing, and there was no JoAnna. Instead, my grandfather's bald head appeared around the edge of my door.

"Got a minute, Sugar Lump?"

"Grandpa! Sure. Of course." I slid off my stool and ventured over to the door. "Come in, come in."

He stepped all the way in, gave me a quick hug that was still lacking its normal oomph, and then, as I was stepping back, pulled a wrapped deli sandwich from the pocket of his windbreaker and handed it to me.

"You brought me a sandwich?"

"JoAnna said you skipped lunch."

"JoAnna talks too much."

"I asked. She answered. I was passing the deli."

I didn't have the heart to tell him my appetite was missing in action, so, instead, I leaned forward, planted a kiss on his weathered cheek, and then motioned him over to my desk. "Come, sit. We can share this."

"No need." He patted his opposite pocket and then pulled out another, slightly fatter wrapped package. "A ham and swiss for you, a Dagwood for me."

"Perfect." I looped around the side of my desk, plopped onto my chair, and made a show of unwrapping my sandwich even though I knew the likelihood I'd eat more than a bite or two was slim. "So, I came up with what I thought was a pretty solid motive for Deidre's death starring Todd as the murderer, until, well, it didn't exactly fit with the whole rope burn thing."

"He's a climber."

I stopped fiddling with my wrapper to look at my grandfather. "What do you mean he's a climber?"

"He's a rock climber."

"How do you know that?"

"I was doing research today, remember?"

"Right. Of course." I broke off a corner of the bread and nibbled on a smidge of crust. "So I take it you came across something that said he's a rock climber?"

"He's won a few competitions across the country over the past few years."

"So he's proficient with ropes then?"

My grandfather wrapped his hands around his sandwich and took a big bite, his eyes rolling back in his head in pleasure. "He was at a competition the morning of the award show—not far from where I live out in Kansas City. From what I can figure by a news clipping I found online, he had just about enough time to get home and showered before heading back out with his wife for her big night."

"Maybe he didn't go."

"He won both of his events, and he was in a few photographs."

"But you didn't go to the funeral so you can't be sure it was even him, right?" I knew I was grasping at straws, but that was preferable to being back at square one.

"The photos had captions, Sugar Lump. And I remember seeing him at the award show."

I felt my shoulders beginning to droop and didn't bother to fight them. "And to think I was starting to warm to him as a possible suspect—"

"Tobes?"

Together, my grandfather and I looked toward the door and the sixteen-year-old peeking back at us through tired eyes. "Hey, kiddo, come in... How'd it go down at Callahan? Did you completely wow them?"

Sam pushed the door open enough to accommodate both him and his camera bag, set the latter down in a place it couldn't possibly get stepped on, and then joined us at the desk, his gaze skirting our sandwiches a half second before his Adam's apple rose and fell with a swallow.

"Have you eaten?" I asked.

Tiny pinpricks of pink appeared on his cheeks as he temporarily refocused his attention on me, rather than my sandwich. "They brought lunch for me. Thai, I think. Either way, it was good."

"But you're still hungry."

He shrugged, but it lacked conviction.

"Course he's hungry." My grandfather reached across my desk, pilfered half of my sandwich, and handed it to the all too eager teenager. On a normal day, I would have protested, but since I'd done little more than eat a pea-sized piece of crust the whole time the sandwich had been within reach, it would've been silly. At least with Sam, I could rest easy knowing the pig hadn't died in vain. "He's a growing boy."

"My mom says I eat enough for five boys."

"I think she needs to up that assessment." I winked first at Sam and then, dodging my grandfather's eyes, surrendered the rest of my sandwich, as well. "So...tell us everything."

And he did.

He told us the gist of the ad he'd been asked to shoot, the models he'd worked with and how impressed they'd been by his direction, the ideas they'd had for shots, and the way his suggestions for tweaks had been well received.

And he told us about the people he'd met, his face noticeably clouding as he did.

A look at my grandfather showed that he, too, had noticed the shift in Sam's demeanor.

"Everything okay, young man?" my grandfather asked, setting what was left of his own sandwich back onto his wrapper and wiping his hands on the soft brown paper napkin he'd stowed inside his pocket along with his sandwich. "You look...troubled."

Sam swiped the back of his hand across his mouth and sank into the second of the two client chairs I kept in front of my desk. "I think I finally really got why my mom is the way she is with guys."

I traded glances with my grandfather over the unexpected change in topic and, at his nod, I took point. "Did something happen with Drew? Because I thought that was going okay."

"It is. But I know she's afraid of getting hurt. And until today, I never really got how hard it must've been."

Yep, it was official. I was completely and utterly lost.

I considered feigning understanding until I could actually catch up, but that took more energy than I had in my tank at that moment. Instead, I went straight for the most obvious question.

"How hard *what* must have been?"

"My dad cheating on her. Especially once I was in the picture, you know?"

I did know. About the cheating part, anyway. But it was the bigger picture relevant to the here and now that I didn't get, especially on a day when he'd just realized yet another professional dream at an age most of his peers were simply focused on grades and crushes.

"Did you get a call from your dad or something today?" I noted the way he clenched and unclenched his hands atop my desk and made a note to call Mary Fran the second he was gone. "Is that why you're bringing him up?"

Sam exhaled into his clenched fist, puffing out his cheeks in the process. "No. Christmas doesn't come around for another seven and a half months, so it'll be that long before he calls again."

I could feel my grandfather stiffen with disgust and rushed to head him off before he gave it words. "Okay, so do you want to tell us where this came from then? This stuff about understanding your mom better now?"

Since Sam's hands were now below the sightline afforded by my desk, I had to rely on other visual clues to know he was fidgeting—movement in his elbows, a few restless glances at his lap, and, finally, a rise back onto his feet that kicked off what quickly revealed itself as aimless pacing. "He has two of them. One is maybe four, and the other is really little... like not even walking yet. I played with them both for a little while when their mom brought them out to watch. And"—he turned when he reached the window overlooking the alley and then headed back in our general direction—"they're really cute, Tobes. *Really* cute. And she was super nice. Pretty, too...for a mom."

I gave some thought to chastising him for that caveat, but something told me to let it go. And (surprise!), I listened.

Sam, in turn, reached my desk, turned back to the window, stopped mid-way, and then sighed as he swung out and around my grandfather to reclaim his chair. "I guess I wasn't supposed to see them behind that one building, but Mom had asked me to check in with her when I had a chance and so I stepped away from the models and stuff to find a place and... There they were."

"*Who?*" Grandpa Stu and I asked in unison (a very impressive one, I might add).

"That lady's husband and the one you were so sure was going to win your category on Saturday night."

I stared at Sam as my brain worked to not only catch up with my ears, but to also make some sense out of—

"Wait! Are you talking about Lexa Smyth?" I asked. "The bleached blonde in the royal blue gown?"

My grandfather stopped me with his best impression of a crossing guard (minus the whistle) and leaned across the divide between their chairs. "The bleached blonde in the *low cut* royal blue gown?"

I tamped down the impulse to roll my eyes and shifted my attention back to an emphatically nodding Sam. "Mrs. Callahan was so nice to her, too. I mean like, super nice the whole time I was taking my shots. Mrs. Callahan even invited her to come out to her place to see her horses after work tomorrow. Told her to come alone so they could bond."

"You lost me again, Sam."

He leaned forward against my desk and then threw himself back against the chair, clearly agitated. "Sorry. I guess I just keep thinking about those kids. And..." He stopped, swallowed, and took a deep, audible breath. "He had her pressed up against the building when I walked around the corner, and her blouse was almost completely unbuttoned. And if that wasn't gross enough, they looked to be playing a pretty intense game of tonsil hockey."

I was no longer lost.

Only now, I wished I were.

"You're talking about Kevin Callahan, aren't you?" I asked, although I knew the answer without Sam having to say a word.

Mary Fran had been right.

The interaction between Kevin and Lexa in the bathroom hallway of the funeral home hadn't been two colleagues chatting. No, it had been a snippet of something much bigger.

Suddenly, Sam's agitation made all the sense in the world.

So, too, did the fact that I now felt the same way.

"Do you think she knows?"

I pulled myself out of my own funk to meet Sam's troubled eyes. In them, I saw a young man who wanted to believe the world was good—that people didn't knowingly hurt one another, and children didn't have to suffer the ill effects of a parent's deplorable behavior.

"I don't know, Sam." But even as I said the words, I found myself wondering if maybe Susan did know. If she did, it would explain the exchange between her and Mavis at the funeral home when Susan expressed a need for a break. It could also explain Mavis's promise that she would never let Cassie—another well-known flirtatious type—work for Callahan.

I snuck a peek at my grandfather to see where he was in all of this, but if he'd been paying attention when Sam dropped the bomb about Lexa Smyth and Kevin Callahan, he'd since moved on to something different based on the way he was looking off. There would be time to ask for his feelings on the subject when we headed back home in just a little over an hour. For now though, I needed to find a way to help Sam.

"Sam, I—"

He stood, crossed to his camera bag, and hiked it onto his shoulder. "I'm okay, Tobes. I just want them to be okay, too."

~Chapter Twenty-Four~

The car ride home from work was quiet, with me thinking about Sam, Mavis's daughter-in-law, and Deidre, and Grandpa Stu likely thinking about the same things based on the way he was thumbing through his notebook and running his finger down an occasional page.

"I feel like we're getting close, Sugar Lump," he said as I pulled to a stop in front of my house and turned off the car. "Like we just might wrap this up before I leave on Friday afternoon."

I pulled the key out of the ignition and sank back against the driver's seat. "I thought we talked about this. About you staying through the weekend as originally planned. Or, even better, staying another week."

"I think you're right. About what you told me you told Andy... About the killer being angry."

"Grandpa, I—"

"The fact that he set it up so it happened in such a public way really smells like revenge. Which makes me think we've been going about this the wrong way."

I reached around the back of his seat, retrieved my backpack from the floor, and hoisted it onto my lap, the note from Ms. Rapple deliberately placed in an outside pocket for easy removal. But just as I was pulling it out, my phone rang inside the cup holder between our seats.

A check of the screen revealed JoAnna's name and face.

"I'm sorry, Grandpa, I've got to take this. It's rare for JoAnna to call me after hours." I pressed the green button and held the phone to my cheek. "Hey, JoAnna, is everything okay?"

"I'm not sure, but I figured I'd let you decide."

"Okay..."

"I was just heading out when I heard the phone ring. I almost let it go to voicemail since it was after closing, but, well, you know me."

I did, and it's why I smiled despite the little voice in my head that was telling me to brace for cover at the semi-ominous tone to my secretary's voice. "So who was it?"

"Cassie Turner."

"Cassie Turner?" In my peripheral vision I could sense a straightening of my grandfather's posture and held him off with a flash of my index finger. "Why?"

"She didn't say. She just asked to speak with you, and when I told her you'd just left, her voice got fidgety."

I pulled the phone closer to my face. "Did you just say her *voice* got fidgety?"

"Yes."

For some reason, Carter appeared in my mind's eye, his hands propped on his hips, his mouth doing that twist-thing it did just before he gave the kind of retort that left me in stitches. But I wasn't Carter, and I certainly wasn't as funny. So, instead, I drummed the fingers of my free hand on the steering wheel and waited for more.

"I told her you'd get back to her in the morning, but figured I'd let you know now in case you want to follow up sooner."

I looked at the note peeking out of my backpack and thought about the conversation I knew I needed to revisit with my grandfather, but when I turned my head to look at him and ended up grazing his chin with mine, I knew he'd kill me if I waited.

"Get her number so we can call her back," he whispered.

"Tell Stu to get his pencil ready and he can write it down as you repeat what I say."

My grandfather whipped his pencil out of the front pocket of his flannel shirt, thumbed forward in his notebook until he found a clean page, and gave me his best *I'm waiting* face.

Alrighty then...

"Okay, he's ready."

"It's her mobile number: 555-2463."

I repeated the number back, checked my grandfather's chicken scratch for accuracy, thanked JoAnna, and told her I'd see her first thing in the morning. Then, I slipped my phone into the pocket with Rapple's note and motioned toward the house with my chin.

"Aren't you going to call her?"

"I don't know...maybe. Later. After we talk. There's something I need to—"

"Call her now, Sugar Lump. She might be ready to confess."

I didn't mean to laugh, but the second I did, and the excitement drained from his face in response, I regretted it. My grandfather lived for this kind of stuff. I knew this. Besides, hadn't I already caused him enough pain? "Actually, you're right. JoAnna did say she sounded…fidgety." I grabbed my phone back out of the pocket, swiped my way into the keypad, and pressed in the digits my grandfather rattled off.

Cassie picked up on the first ring.

"Hello?"

"Hey, Cassie, it's Tobi, Tobi Tobias. My secretary called and said—"

"I remembered something!"

I didn't need to look in my rearview mirror to know my eyes had widened to the size of dinner plates. A glance to my right showed the same expression on Grandpa Stu just before he picked up his pencil again and prepared to write.

Closing my eyes quickly, I sent up a prayer of forgiveness to my grandmother for the lie I was about to tell, and then hit the speaker button so my grandfather could hear all. "I'm driving right now so I need to put you on speaker, okay?"

My grandfather's mouth opened only to close again (thank God) when I shook my head and held my fingers to my lips.

"Whatever." Cassie's inhale filled the space between us and I matched it with what I hoped was a quieter version. "Remember earlier? When you mentioned the envelope for your category being different?"

"I do."

"The writing wasn't in gold, remember?"

"I do."

"It was black."

"I know. I saw that in Sam's picture. It was why I asked you about it—"

"A few categories before ours, I saw Callahan's wife in the restroom."

"Mavis?"

"No. Kevin's wife."

A peek at my grandfather showed his hand was no longer poised to write. Instead, he was leaning so close to the phone I was afraid he'd topple onto it. I tapped his shoulder, swept him back into his seat, and then continued the conversation. "*Susan*, right?"

"I don't know. I guess that's it. I just know she has two kids, does nothing but the whole wife/mom thing, and is either the most clueless woman on the face of the earth or loves money more than one might guess looking at her clothes."

Grandpa Stu rolled his finger forward and I verbalized the sentiment. "So you saw her in the restroom…"

"She had the kid on the changing table but she must have finished before I walked in," Cassie said. "Because he was just lying there making gurgling noises and she was capping up a black marker."

I hoped my answering gasp helped mask my grandfather's, but in the event it didn't, I skipped the whole processing step and went straight to blabbering (okay, lying). "I'm sorry, I…uh…just got cut off by an idiot. Did you say a black marker?"

"Uh huh. Weird, right?"

That was one word for it.

My grandfather's hand practically flew across the page on his lap. When he was done, he turned it so I could read it from my seat.

As if envy.

I looked at my grandfather and waited. He, in turn, tapped his pencil next to his chicken scratch.

I muted the call.

"Grandpa, I have no idea what that says."

"Ask if she saw an envelope."

I nodded and shut off the mute feature. "Any idea what she'd been writing on? I mean was there any sort of paper or—"

"I didn't really look because, honestly, I really didn't pay her much mind other than the usual pity job. But today, at work, when I walked past Lexa's old office, something about it triggered the memory about the marker and it made me wonder. You know, in light of the whole envelope thing."

"Did you see an envelope?"

"No. But that doesn't mean she hadn't already stuck it in the bag or her pocket before I walked in."

My grandfather shrugged.

"Okay, so then what?" I prodded. "After you saw her?"

"I went into a stall, and she was gone when I came out."

"Did you see her anywhere backstage after that?"

"Nope. Best Overall was almost up and I had to get ready."

In a flash, I was back in the banquet hall, sitting next to Andy, waiting for my category to be up, and, sure enough, I'd seen Susan and the baby returning to the Callahan table just as Carl Brinkman stepped back onto the stage to announce Cassie. And just like it had that night, my stomach roiled. Only this time it had nothing to do with nerves and everything to do with a growing sense of dread.

"Anything else?" I managed to ask as I leaned into my headrest and held a groan in check.

"Maybe Susan figured out Deidre was the bitch behind *Bitch Pitch*." I felt the weight of my grandfather's glance and tried hard not to let it derail me. "Excuse me?"

"Think about it. That little bitch could try to smear me in one of her clever little posts, but prattling on about getting even after losing a campaign eight years earlier could refer to anyone in this business. It's just *the way things are done* in our field, am I right?"

Before I could dispute her statement though, she continued. "But a post about a floozy who slept her way into a primo office at one agency only to leave and start fooling around with a top level exec at the most prestigious firm in the city? Trust me, people would know the identity of the floozy before the end of the first paragraph. And as for the top level exec she was sleeping with? That, too, would be a no brainer if our blog writing bitch made the whole *like father, like son* correlation."

I felt my mouth go dry as I stole a look at my grandfather. He, in turn, mouthed two single words.

Motive.

Means.

"But I didn't see a post like that," I countered.

"Not yet. But maybe Susan had reason to think one was coming. And if she did? She certainly wouldn't be the first woman to show loyalty to a person who has none for her in return."

I tried Cassie's words on for size and realized they could fit.

"Okay, well thanks for telling me this."

"Yeah, no problem."

I waited until I was sure she was gone from the line before I ended the call and turned my head to look at my grandfather. "I wanted to figure this out, but I didn't want it to go this way."

"Maybe it's not what it seems," he said in a tone that held little belief in the words making their way out of his mouth.

"Crap."

~Chapter Twenty-Five~

There were times when no matter how hard I tried to justify my actions to myself, I still felt like a heel.

Like when I ate Rudder's kiwi (in all fairness, I had missed lunch and he was being a brat) and he looked as if he'd been struck.

Like when Carter worked hard to prepare a feast "guaranteed to make me like greens" and I filled up on Cocoa Puffs (I. Hate. Greens.), instead.

Like when I opened my big fat mouth about Rapple (something I'd done a million times before) without looking to see if my grandfather was near.

And like now, as I zipped down Highway 40 alone (aka, sans Grandpa Stu) toward St. Charles County and a coffeehouse named Perk-It! I could (and did) try to justify my decision to slip out of the house after dinner without sharing details of my destination in several ways.

But no matter how I spun my decision to confront Susan Callahan without my trusty mystery-solving sidekick in tow, I still felt like a heel. Hadn't I done enough to hurt him already? Didn't I want him to rethink his earlier-than-planned departure?

I shook off the guilt provoking questions, pushed on the radio, and began flipping stations in the hope a Bruce Springsteen song was playing and I could lose myself in a little singing (or, as my grandfather calls it, *screeching*). Unfortunately, instead of Bruce, I got Culture Club (hell, no), The Hooters (a wee bit better), and Justin Bieber (there are no words), the latter bringing an immediate end to my station surfing (and radio listening) with one decisive push.

Dejected, I focused on the GPS app guiding my every mile from atop my cup holder and, before long, I was parked and headed toward the coffee bean-brown door (nice touch) and torn between wanting to find justice for

Deidre's children and worrying about two very different children—children that had left such an impression on Sam earlier in the day that he'd shown up at my office needing to vent. A few feet away from the door, I stopped and looked between the P and the E on the large plate glass window. Although not a coffeehouse I'd know living in the Central West End, it was obvious that the people in the immediate area of Perk-It! knew it well. A dozen or so tables, in a variety of heights and widths, were scattered around the well-lit room with all but one boasting at least two patrons if not more. If one party at a two-person table was sipping from their coffee mug, the other was animatedly talking or leaning close as if telling a secret. At the tables where there were more than two seated, there was laughter—the kind of laughter I'm sure would be present at a table taken up by me, Carter, Mary Fran, and Sam.

I smiled at the image and made a mental note to bring them back here with me another time, assuming, of course, the coffee was good (not that this die-hard hot chocolate drinker would know). And that's when I spotted Susan Callahan, the room's lone single drinker, at a small table in the back left corner.

I stood there for a while, watching her and making the kind of assessments I usually did when people watching. The difference, of course, was for every basic assessment I made (she was preoccupied, she didn't touch her mug, she swiped at her eyes a few times), there was that follow-up voice in my head spinning it in a direction I really didn't want to go (she was going through a play-by-play in her head of the moment Deidre fell to her death, the guilt was making it so she couldn't hold her hand steady enough to take a sip, and now that the deed was done, she felt bad).

"None of which you'll know if you don't go inside, dummy."

A laugh from somewhere over my left shoulder caught me off guard and I turned to find a guy, about my age, staring at me. I couldn't quite make out his face thanks to the shadow cast by the interior light streaming onto the sidewalk, but I was pretty sure he was grinning.

"I said that out loud, didn't I?"

"Yep."

I looked up, found the trio of stars I'd had to follow every night for a month when I was in third grade, and deflated my cheeks with what could only qualify as a pretty impressive exhale. "I do that sometimes."

"I know. I do it sometimes, too."

I lowered my gaze so I could try to make out more of his features, but since the light was still in play and neither of us had moved, it was futile. "Thanks."

"Can I buy you a cup of coffee?" he asked. "Assuming, of course, you listen to yourself and go inside."

"Thanks, but I'm meeting someone."

"Another blind date?" he asked.

Even now, with Andy in my life, I still shudder whenever I hear those two words, thanks, no doubt, to Mary Fran. In fact, all those stories people think when they hear the words, *blind date* were tame compared to the ones Mary Fran arranged for me.

I shuddered again.

"And you're still playing along?"

I shuddered a third time. "Uh, no. Been there, done that, never going back."

"Does Mary Fran know this?"

I startled so hard and so fast I had to steady myself against the window with my hand. "Y-you know...Mary Fran?"

He stepped forward, out of the direct path of light streaming through the window, and smiled. "Don't you remember me? Mary Fran set us up last summer. I'm—"

"Oh my God, you're..." I swallowed back *foot-fetish guy* and, instead, made myself insert what I hoped was his real name. "B-Brian, right?"

"Brent," he corrected as the smile slipped from his face. "Brent Dalton."

"Of course. Brent. I'm sorry. I-I knew that, I just..." Again, I let my words trail off for a moment, only this time I remained silent rather than add yet another lie to my day's total.

He waited me out for a few seconds and then, when I didn't finish, he turned and made his way back across the street, sans coffee.

I considered calling out to him, but when I really thought about it (and the fact that it was because of him, I'd sworn off blind dates forever), I simply turned, headed inside, ordered a cup of hot chocolate, and carried it over to Susan Callahan's table.

"Oh, hey, *Susan*...right?" I mentally patted myself on the back for remembering some of the acting tips Carter had shared over the past few years and followed it up with a smile for the woman now looking at me with a mixture of confusion and...*apprehension?*

I set my hot chocolate mug on her table and extended my right hand. "I'm Tobi. Tobi Tobias. I met you last night at Deidre Ryan's viewing. I was in the back, talking to your mother-in-law."

It had taken a moment or two, but based on the hint of familiarity making its way past the confusion, I was pretty sure I was ringing some bells.

"Oh. Sure. Yeah."

I pointed at the empty chair across from hers and, at her eventual nod, sat down. "I love this place."

"I thought we'd have come sooner but..." Susan's voice, along with her eye contact, faded off for a few seconds before returning with a shake of her head. "I decided to come myself." She gestured around the room. "I take it you're here alone, too?"

"I am."

She ran her finger along the top of her mug for a few moments and then looked up at me. "You're okay with that?"

"Okay with what?"

"Doing stuff like this"—she pulled her finger back long enough to gesture around the room a second time—"like being at a place like this by yourself?"

"Sure." I took a sip of my hot chocolate, moaned a little over how good it tasted, and set it back down between us. "I love to do things with my friends. They make me laugh, you know? But sometimes, it's just nice to be alone—to think, to plan, to dream..."

Susan laughed, although there was no humor in the sound. "I'm not sure I even know what it is to dream anymore. I thought I was living mine so I...stopped, and..." Something that sounded like a strangled sob made its way past her lips before she dropped her head into her hands. "I wanted to be a good mom. I wanted to be a role model. But, now, because of him, I'm not any of those things."

Now, I realize I'm not always the epitome of decorum, but I'm usually pretty smart in the basic rules of life. I know when to use my magic words (my mom was big on instilling those), I get the whole *different strokes for different folks* thing (my sister is a hippie), and I've gotten where I am in the business world by knowing when to listen and when to talk (thank you, Grandpa).

So, long story short, even *I* was surprised when I decided to confront her with what she'd done...in the middle of a coffeehouse...without my grandfather or Carter or Andy for backup. "You switched the names, didn't you?"

For a minute, I wasn't sure she heard me on account of the fact her head remained down and I heard nothing even resembling a sound from her general vicinity. But just as I was revving up to say it a little louder, she lifted her head, her eyes seeking mine as tears escaped down her cheeks.

"I didn't know that was going to happen," she whispered as the tears came faster. "I-I swear I didn't."

"But you changed the name in the envelope."

Her gaze lifted above my head, but I didn't bother to turn around. I knew she was no longer in Perk-It! Instead, if I were a gambler, I'd bet my agency *and* my car on the fact she was back at the banquet hall, watching as the platform gave way beneath Deidre. "I couldn't let Lexa's name be called. I couldn't watch my daughter clap her little hands for the woman her daddy has been sleeping with for months. I-I just couldn't let that happen."

"So you're saying Lexa was supposed to win?"

Susan's focus returned to the room and to me. "Mavis said you were in the field, yes?"

I nodded.

"So surely you know."

"Know?" I echoed.

"That Lexa Smyth is sleeping with my husband. Everyone knows that."

I grabbed my hot chocolate and took a big gulp. "I don't pay attention to that stuff... Benefit of working for myself instead of one of the big agencies, you know?"

She stared at me for a minute. But just as I was trying to decide whether the expression she wore was one of pity (for my being out of the loop) or shock (I was leaning toward pity), the tears started again. "I see the looks every time I walk into the office or the foundation. All these people who used to smile when I came in with Kevin, now avert their eyes like they're afraid to look at me. And the ones who actually speak to me? They're no doubt whispering about me and my kids when we leave. They all assume I'm the clueless wife, and they pity me and my children. But I've known about Kevin and that little tramp for a while."

"How?"

"He butt-dialed me about a month ago. I heard...everything. Every word, every groan, every...*noise.*"

I willed away the image of walking in on Nick and the waitress from our favorite restaurant and, instead, reached across the table and patted Susan's hand. "I'm so sorry. He doesn't deserve you."

"On some level, I know that. But then, when I look at my kids and think of uprooting them from their home and trying to raise them alone back in the northeast, I find myself wondering if Mavis is right...if it'll stop like she says it will."

"Once a cheat, always a cheat."

"You really believe that?" Susan asked, pulling her hand out from under mine.

"There's a reason we've all heard that expression."

Silence sat alongside us for a few moments as I tried to figure out what to do. Did I call the cops? Did I encourage Susan to turn herself in? I really wasn't sure. And that's when it hit me. Susan assumed I knew about her husband. Which meant her motive for killing Deidre didn't work.

Before I could get my bearings though, Susan spoke again, her voice hushed and raspy. "I keep thinking about Deidre's kids. They looked so *lost* last night...because their momma was their world just like she should've been... But then, I think of mine, and how lost they'll be if I go to jail for what I did. But Tobi? If I'd known that platform was going to give the way it did, I'd have let my daughter clap for her daddy's mistress."

~Chapter Twenty-Six~

My grandfather was sitting on the couch, watching television, when I raced into my house some thirty minutes later, my head reeling from the about-face brought on by Susan's parting words.

I'd been right. Lexa had been the intended winner in my category on Saturday night. Her name had been in one of the same sparkly gold-edged envelopes used for all the winners since the award show's debut some forty-one years earlier.

But just before the show started, Susan swapped the envelope with one containing Deidre's name under the guise of changing her baby. Then, she returned to her seat beside her husband, waiting for the moment Deidre—rather than Lexa—was called onto the stage as the night's big winner. Only instead of getting to enjoy the chance to lash out at her husband, she'd watched a woman who was not her husband's mistress fall to her death… from a platform that had, ironically, already been sabotaged.

I tossed my keys onto the little table next to my door, watched them go flying off the other side, and kept right on walking until I was standing in front of Grandpa Stu. "Lexa was the target, not Deidre."

He shut off the TV. "Are you sure?"

"I'm positive." I ran into the kitchen for my Cocoa Puffs and popped the lid open as I returned to the living room and the vacant spot on the sofa cushion next to Grandpa Stu. "I talked to Susan tonight."

His mouth gaped, closed, and then gaped again. But not a sound came out.

"I know, I know. I should have told you where I was going. But I thought maybe she'd be more open if I approached her alone—as someone who'd just met her the previous night."

"Go on."

So I did. I told him everything, my eyes widening right along with his as I rehashed the evening in a way that made him feel as if he, too, had been there. When I got to the last thing she said to me (or, perhaps, the last thing I *remember* her saying to me), I stopped, mid-crunch, and splayed my hands out from the sides of the box. "Changing the envelope to make Deidre the winner was Susan's way of striking out at Lexa. But the real strike was already in place."

"For Lexa."

I nodded so hard I almost fell off the couch. "Exactly. So while I think the whole anger thing is still very much in play, we've been sniffing around the wrong places because we had the wrong victim."

"So Todd and his rope burns are out, like I suspected."

"Yup."

"And Cassie is back in play."

I paused my hand inside the box and mulled my grandfather's words. Still, as much sense as they were starting to make, I needed to play it out. "Are you asking that because of what she said on the phone earlier?"

He nodded. "There's no love lost between her and Lexa, correct?"

"Correct."

"She had access to backstage, correct?"

"Correct, but—" I stopped, unsure of what, exactly, was bothering me.

"But what?"

"What you described...about how the stagehand said the platform was sabotaged... That had to take a little time, right?"

"Some, I guess. Ropes like that would take time to cut, and even the loosening of the bolts wouldn't be fast."

"And let's not forget, Cassie was in a gown with a slit. I'm thinking that wouldn't be easy to maneuver around in for something like you just described."

"The last safety check was at five o'clock, Sugar Lump. The show started at eight."

Crap.

I'd forgotten that part.

I shoveled up a handful of puffs, popped them into my mouth, and waited for the sound of my own crunching to clear my head. It was one of my odder quirks, but one I'd come to embrace as one of my truths over the past half year or so.

"You look tired."

I glanced up from my box and swallowed my chewed puffs. "I am. It's been a long day."

"Then get some sleep. This will all still be here in the morning."

I opened my mouth to protest but none of what I said made any sense thanks to the yawn that took over mid-way through the first word. A second, even bigger yawn let me know my grandfather was right. If I continued pushing, I'd end up making no sense *and* I'd be useless at work the next day.

"Okay, okay, you're right." I closed the lid on my puff box, and leaned over to my grandfather for my good night hug. "Thanks for listening, Grandpa."

"My pleasure, Sugar Lump."

I pressed my head into his chest and savored the feel of his arms around my shoulders and the warmth of his kiss on the top of my head. I wished, as I did every night he was here, that I could be little again if for no other reason than to relive every moment we'd spent together. But we couldn't, and I knew this. All we had was now. "We need to talk, Grandpa Stu. Before you leave. There are some things I need to say."

"You love me, right?"

"More than all the stars in the sky."

"Then that's all I need to know."

"Grandpa, I—"

"Not tonight, Sugar Lump. You need your sleep."

* * * *

I slept the sleep of the dead. Which, translated, meant I slept through my alarm, was forced to skip my morning round of Cocoa Puffs, and drove a wee bit faster than I should have in order to find myself standing in front of a clearly amused JoAnna roughly two hours late.

"They say there's a first for everything and you seem hell bent on proving that true this week, don't you?"

"Meaning?"

"You rebuked candy yesterday, and you-who-is-never-ever-late-for-work is, well, late for work."

I considered rolling my eyes, but JoAnna was right. So, I pulled the lid off her candy jar, asked permission to dive in, and, when I had it, pilfered a butterscotch candy and a fun size bag of M&Ms. "I slept hard that's all. Did I miss anything important?"

"No."

"No calls?"

"No."

"No appointments?"

"You had one, but I rescheduled the moment Stu called and told me you were still asleep."

"My grandfather called?"

"Yes."

"What did he say?"

"Just that you were asleep and he didn't have the heart to wake you."

I unwrapped the butterscotch candy and slipped it in my mouth. "He wasn't anywhere to be found when I woke up."

"He said he had an errand to run and to tell you he'd be in touch soon."

"That's all he said? No specifics?"

"You know Stu."

"If he calls, patch him through. If he shows up, send him back." I replaced the lid, tossed my wrapper into the trash next to JoAnna's desk, and headed down to my office and the concept ads I needed to work on for the upcoming zoo room at Pizza Adventure.

It was hard to concentrate thanks to the way my mind kept playing over Susan's words, but I stuck with it until I had a few workable ideas in draft form that I could show Dom and Gina at our next scheduled meeting. It had been slow going, no doubt, but I was pleased with the result, if not myself, for the whole sleeping-in debacle.

"Tobi?"

Stretching my arms high above my head, I spun around on my swivel stool and stood. "Yes, JoAnna?"

"Mary Fran is on line two."

"Line two. Got it." I started toward my desk but stopped shy of my destination to call out to JoAnna as she headed back down the hall. "Any word from my grandfather yet?"

"No."

Hmmm...

I walked around my desk, flopped onto my chair, and grabbed my desk phone, pressing line two as I did. "Hey, Mary Fran."

"Did Sam tell you about that Callahan creep?"

"If by Callahan creep you mean Kevin...yes."

"He was so upset last night he almost didn't want to go back today."

"Sam has another day off?"

"Technically, no, but since yesterday was a teacher in-service day and he wasn't missing anything because of that, I agreed to let him take today off when he got the call. Though now, after yesterday, I'm pretty sure he's wishing he hadn't taken the job at all." Mary Fran's voice dipped with what was likely an adjustment of the phone between her cheek and her shoulder as she moved about the pet shop doing any one of the dozens of tasks she did at about this same time every day. "Which doesn't help this irresistible urge I have to go down to that agency and rip this guy's eyes out."

I yanked open my secret stash drawer, fished out a box of Milk Duds, and popped a few into my mouth. "Prob...ably...not...a...goo-d...idea."

"Are you chewing?"

"Yup."

Mary Fran said something to someone in the background and then continued with me as if I hadn't just gotten busted eating and talking at the same time. "Sam said he wasn't sure what was worse...wondering if the wife knew or knowing that the grandmother did."

I stopped chewing and pushed the remaining duds into the corner of my mouth so I could speak as intelligibly as possible. "Excuse me?"

"The grandmother. She's the one who suggested Sam go behind the building to make his call. Even pointed the spot out to him, herself."

"Mavis Callahan knows about Kevin and Lexa?"

"Sam said she was angry but not surprised. That implies knowledge, Tobi."

"Snort! Snort! S-nort!"

This time, I rolled my eyes.

"That's right, Rudder, I'm talking to Tobi!"

"Snort! Snort! S-nort!"

It was on the tip of my tongue to ask her why she encouraged my nemesis' nastiness, but my thoughts zipped right back to Mavis. "Wow. That has to be so hard. I mean, she loves those grandkids like crazy... You could see it all over her face at that table Saturday night. And think about it...this creep's father did the exact same thing to her. Right down to the award and—"

Oh. My. God.

"Tobi, you still—"

"Snort! Snort! S-nort!"

"Mary Fran, I've gotta go! I know who did it!"

"Did what?"

"I know who killed Deidre Ryan!"

~Chapter Twenty-Seven~

I'm not sure where I thought I was going, or what my plan was once I got there, but I was running. I ran out of my office, I ran past JoAnna and her desk, I ran out the front door of my agency, and I ran to my car (a slightly longer process than expected thanks to the momentary brain fog regarding the location of my parking spot). I'd like to say all that running helped birth a plan, but I can't. Because it didn't.

I pressed the unlock button on my key fob, heard the answering echo of the driver side door, and slid into place behind the steering wheel with my phone at the ready. I was virtually positive I knew who had killed Deidre (albeit by accident), but what to do with that information was a little less clear. Sure, I could take it straight to the police, but I was pretty sure they'd look at me like I was nuts if I came in off the street claiming to have solved a crime. Besides, my grandfather would have my head if I denied him the thrill of apprehending a killer.

I dialed my home number, counted six rings, and then hung up as I asked myself to leave a message after the beep. Next, I dialed Carter's number in the event my grandfather was hanging out upstairs, but six rings (great minds!) morphed into his canned greeting and I hung up without leaving a message there, either. I almost tossed the phone into the cup holder but opted to try my grandfather's cell in the rare event he actually had it turned on.

He picked up on the second ring.

"Stu here."

"Hey, Grandpa, it's me. I need you to tell me where you are at this exact minute, and then I need you to stay put in that spot until I can pick you up."

"Where's the fire?"

"I know who did it, Grandpa."

A pause gave way to something that sounded almost squeal-like. "I just left Fletcher's and I'm on the way to see you."

I stuck my key in the ignition, turned on the car, and shifted into drive. "Don't move a muscle. I'll be there in three minutes—tops."

Two and a half minutes later, I pulled to a stop less than a block from the newsstand and welcomed my grandfather into my car with a kiss on his cheek and a reminder to buckle up. He accepted the first, groused about the second, and then rubbed his hands together as if he were preparing to warm them over an open fire. "It was Cassie, wasn't it? Why, I—"

"It's not Cassie." When I was sure he was buckled, I checked my side view mirror and pulled back onto the road, my destination suddenly crystal clear. "It's Mavis."

"I said her name that very night, remember? I thought..." My grandfather stopped the hand-rubbing thing as my words finally registered in his ears. "Mavis? Who's Mavis?"

"Kevin Callahan's mother, or, rather, stepmother."

"The old one?"

I turned right at the stop sign and headed toward the highway, my answering laugh seeming both inappropriate and needed all at the same time. "The *old one*? Seriously? Isn't that a little like the pot calling the kettle black?"

"Maybe. But she wasn't even on our radar."

"Because she wasn't... But we also thought *Deidre* was the target then, remember?" I pulled onto the highway, heading east, and did my best to fill in the gaps the way JoAnna had explained it to me earlier in the week. I told him about Shamus Callahan and his prominence in the advertising community back in the day. I told him about the first award show and how Shamus had started it as a way to fawn over his pregnant mistress. I told him how the awards, themselves, had been designed by Shamus's wife, Mavis—a woman who'd had a real talent in art yet given it up to support *his* career and *his* goals. And I told him how Shamus had knowingly asked her to design the evening's biggest award for his mistress.

"Did she know?"

I stole a quick glance at my grandfather before looking back at the road in front of us. "You mean, did Mavis know about her husband's affair when she was doing all this for him? JoAnna seemed to think everyone in town knew except Mavis in the days leading up to the event, and then when he had to tell her he was finally going to be a father, Mavis was absolutely humiliated."

"Going to be a father by way of the mistress?" my grandfather asked.

"Uh huh." I got off the exit for Market Street and continued east. "Care to venture a guess as to who that child is?"

Grandpa scratched his head for a few seconds before the reality train stopped at his station. "That young man? The one you pointed out as running the whole award show?"

"The award show, his father's agency, the family foundation, all of it."

"He's the one that had Sam so upset the other day, isn't he? The one that was fooling around with that one you were up against for that same award?"

"Lexa Smyth. The one we now know was the intended target on Saturday night." When another peek at my grandfather revealed a healthy dose of skepticism, I filled in a few of the gaps I'd managed to piece together myself. "My guess is that Kevin's affair with Lexa stirred up repressed feelings or something for Mavis and she lashed out. Or tried to before Susan went and switched the envelopes.

"And if you think about it, Grandpa—really think about it—it makes a ton of sense. I mean, you saw how inconsolable Mavis was in the immediate aftermath of the accident, yes? You heard her screams, you saw her face... And it wasn't much different when she was interviewed by that reporter afterward. She became so inconsolable, in fact, that Kevin stepped up and fielded the rest of the reporter's questions without so much as a flinch."

"But if she set it up... If she loosened the bolts and somehow managed to cut the safety rope... Then she would have to have known it was going to happen."

"*To Lexa*, not Deidre," I reminded.

My grandfather grew silent as he tried my theory on for size. I, in turn, pulled into the parking lot behind the Callahan building in time to see Sam coming out the back door with his camera bag in one hand and a white envelope in his left.

I slowed to a stop and lowered the passenger side window. "Hey, Sam, is Mrs. Callahan inside by any chance?"

He leaned into the window, greeted my grandfather, and then shook his head. "No. Today's the day she's meeting what's-her-name for some bonding time at her stables, remember? Which, for the record, is pretty screwy if you ask me."

"*What's-her-name?*"

"You know, the one her son is cheating with."

I felt the weight of my grandfather's stare as he turned his attention from Sam to me. "Are you thinking what I'm thinking, Sugar Lump?"

I hit the unlock button for the back door and motioned Sam inside. "Do you know where these stables are?"

"No, why?"

I hung a U-turn in the middle of the parking lot and sped toward the exit, tossing my phone to my grandfather as I did. "Call JoAnna. Ask her to figure out where the Callahan stables are—STAT."

* * * *

By the time we got out to Wentzville (thank you, JoAnna), Sam was not only up to speed on Mavis Callahan as the killer, but also on our shared suspicion that her purported bonding time with Lexa was really about righting a wrong.

Translation: Lexa was in danger.

I drove through the gates of the Callahan ranch and watched as plumes of smoke, kicked up from the dirt beneath my tires, followed us up the driveway to the stables. When we reached what appeared to be the main door, I threw the car into park, tossed my phone into the back seat with Sam, and ordered Sam and my grandfather to stay in the car and call the police.

Neither listened.

Fortunately for them, time was of the essence and I took off inside with Sam and my grandfather close on my heels.

"Tobes, you take the stables on the left, I'll take the stables on the right," Sam said as he caught up to me.

"And what am I supposed to do?" my grandfather groused.

I looked left as Sam looked right. "Keep your focus straight ahead."

Stall by stall we made our way through the building. We passed a light brown horse, a black horse, a white horse, a gray horse, another gray horse, and then we heard it....

It was fast.

It was faint.

But it was definitely a woman's cry.

I held my finger to my lips and slowly, step by step, led the way in the direction the sound had come—toward the last stall on the right. Unlike the other stalls we'd passed thus far, the stall appeared to be lit. As we drew closer we saw two shadows on the wall—one low—as if sitting, and the other looming above the first.

"I know your type, Lexa. You set your sights on things and people that don't belong to you because *you can*. You don't care if you destroy lives. Hell, I think that's half the fun for women like you, isn't it?"

I signaled to Sam and my grandfather to stop and, when I was sure they had, I bent forward at the waist and made a beeline for the half wall separating me from Mavis and Lexa. With the only sound beyond Mavis's voice that of my pounding heart, I worked to steady my breath and remain calm.

"Someone just like you ruined my life more than half a lifetime ago. And like you, she didn't care who knew it. Looking back, I was a fool to stay...to write off my own happiness in favor of playing a role my husband never respected to begin with. But that was the old Mavis...the *weak* Mavis.

"But I'm not that Mavis, anymore. And I'll be damned if I'm going to sit by and let another heartless run-of-the-mill hussy rob me of the two greatest things in my life."

I heard muted footsteps and guessed, thanks to a peek at the shadows, that Mavis was on the move. But she didn't go far. "Do you know what happens to a horse if they get into just a wee bit of rat poison?"

I saw the top half of the lower shadow move. By process of elimination, I figured the shadow belonged to Lexa and that she was likely sitting on the ground, shaking her head in response to Mavis's question.

"They go crazy."

A soft whinny on the other side of the wall let me know that Mavis and Lexa weren't alone. A check of the sign just above my head told me Muffin Man was the likely third party.

"Did you know a horse can trample a man—or, in your case, a woman—to death when exposed to something like rat poison?" The muffled cry I heard next let me know Lexa was likely gagged.

"Fortunately for me, Muffin Man doesn't need to ingest rat poison to get a little wild. All I have to do is put his bit shank in wrong and then pull on it really hard. When that happens, he rears up like a crazed beast. So that's what I'm going to do now...with you in stomping range. Because I'll be damned if you're going to be the reason I lose my grandchildren."

I started to stand but stopped as my grandfather motioned for me to wait. Before I could respond via a shake of my head or a pointed widening of my eyes, he grabbed hold of a shovel that was propped against a nearby wall and headed in my direction. I tried to hold him off, to tell him I'd come to him, but my grandfather was on a mission.

He also wasn't the most dainty of souls.

Translation: he bumped the handle of the shovel on a wall as he approached, silencing Mavis in the process.

The silence, however, didn't last long thanks to the sound of approaching sirens and a responding flurry of movement that told me it was now or never.

I grabbed the shovel from my grandfather, ran the length of the half wall, and dashed into the stall just as Mavis guided Muffin Man closer to Lexa.

"Please, Mavis!" I shouted as I inched my way toward Lexa while using the shovel my grandfather gave me as a makeshift shield. "This isn't the way."

"It's the only way, Tobi." Shoving the horse forward, Mavis pulled on the male horse's shank and then stepped back as Muffin Man reared up on his hind legs in anger.

"No!" With a speed I had no idea I possessed, I tossed the shovel to the side and lunged forward, wrapping my hands around Lexa's feet and pulling with all my might. Seconds later, Muffin Man's front legs came crashing back down, narrowly missing Lexa's hair as it dragged behind the rest of her body.

I wanted to stop, wanted to plead with Mavis to think about what she was doing, but there was no time. Before I'd even made it halfway across the stall, Mavis was at it again, steering the incensed animal toward Lexa (and now me). I tried to pull harder, faster, but I tripped over the shovel and went down just as Muffin Man's front legs flew into the air above us. "No!"

With the last bit of strength I could muster, I pushed Lexa to my right and rolled to my left as Muffin Man's front hooves crashed down between us, drowning out everything but the steady beat of rapidly approaching feet.

"Police! Mavis Callahan, put your hands above your head, now!"

~Chapter Twenty-Eight~

I saw his rolling bag the second I stepped out of my bedroom. It was there, next to my couch, with a single bus ticket sitting atop the handle.

Even without getting any closer, I could see the details imprinted across the top half:

One Way.
Depart: St. Louis, 4:30 p.m.
Arrive: Kansas City, 7:45 p.m.

"Good morning, Sugar Lump, how did you sleep?"

I turned toward the voice I'd loved my whole life and mustered the smile he deserved. "As much as I hated to do it, I think calling JoAnna and taking today off was a good idea."

"Still sore like you were last night?"

"A little, I guess. But it'll go away."

"Susan Callahan called last night. She heard what happened and she wanted to apologize."

"What happened in that stable wasn't Susan's fault. Mavis... She let her pain, her anger, and old wounds guide her actions. And that's never a good idea." I pointed toward the kitchen. "I know I slept in, but I'd love to make you breakfast. Maybe some eggs? Or...French toast?"

"Do you even know *how* to make French toast, Sugar Lump?"

I shifted my weight from one foot to the other while I tried to remember if I'd ever attempted to make French toast. "Honestly, I'm not sure. But even if I haven't, how hard can it really be?"

"I'm good. I actually scrambled some eggs for myself a few hours ago."

I glanced around him and into the kitchen, my eyes narrowing in on the clock above my back door: Twelve thirty.

Oops.

"I could make you some lunch, instead. Maybe a grilled cheese sandwich...or some peanut butter and jelly?"

"I'm not really hungry, Sugar Lump. But I'll sit with you while you eat, if you'd like."

"I would." I stepped around him and led the way into the kitchen, my desire to make things right winning out over any and all hunger pangs. Still, I knew I'd get a lecture if I didn't eat something, so I popped a piece of bread into the toaster and joined my grandfather at my kitchen table. "Thanks for being by my side yesterday, Grandpa. I don't know what I'd have done without you."

"You'd have done exactly what you did—which you did without me, I might add."

"*I* didn't call the police."

"Neither did I. *Sam* did."

"Because you told him to."

"Trust me, he'd have done it whether I told him to or not."

"Maybe. Maybe not. Either way, the fact is *you* told him to call. And because of *that*, Lexa is still alive."

"Because of *you*, Lexa is still alive."

My grandfather leaned back in his chair and studied me with an expression I couldn't quite read. I considered asking him about it, but figured he'd get to it in due time. Besides, there were things I needed to say. Mistakes I needed to correct. Forgiveness I needed to seek.

"Grandpa, I need you to know how sorry I am about what I said about Ms. Rapple. It's just that we have a bit of a history and, well, I was acting like an immature brat."

"Not wanting to see me with someone other than Grandma doesn't make you an immature brat, Sugar Lump."

"But that's the thing, Grandpa. I don't have anything against you dating. I really don't." I stood, transferred my toast to a plate, and carried it— along with a small glass of milk—to the table. "You sure you don't want anything? A glass of milk? A piece of cheese? Anything?"

"I'm sure."

I set everything at my place but left it behind as I pulled my chair closer to my grandfather's. "While I wanted to believe my issue with you and Ms. Rapple being together was one hundred percent about her propensity for nastiness, I realize my refusal to see the same changes in her that Mary

Fran, Andy, Sam, and even Carter noticed when she was around you was because I was jealous."

"Jealous?"

I looked down at my hands, tried to find the best words to hit home my point, and then met my grandfather's gaze, head on. "Before Rapple—I mean, *Ms.* Rapple—you came to see *me.* Yes, you and Carter go off and do whatever it is you two do together when I'm staring down a deadline... and you toss a ball around with Sam in the backyard on occasion...and you help Mary Fran carry her groceries inside when Sam is manning the pet shop... But I always knew you came to see me. But since this thing between you and Ms. Rapple started up, that's not the case anymore. Sure, you're happy to see me when you arrive, but you're just as excited to see her now, too."

"Tobi..."

"No. Please. Let me finish." I reached behind me for a sip of my milk but refrained from taking a bite of the toast lest I lose my courage to say everything I needed to say. "And that's where the immature brat part comes in. I know I matter to you. I know nothing and no one in the world will ever change that. I also know I'm a better Tobi Tobias because of your input in my life. So if I can be a better me because of you, why can't I accept the fact that you make Ms. Rapple a better person, too?"

He captured my hands in his and brought them to his chin. "The *fact?*"

"Grandpa, she's been every bit as lost without you these past few days, as you've been without her. And you know what? I *want* you to be happy. I *need* you to be happy."

"I am happy, Sugar Lump. I have you."

"You're right. You do. Forever and always. But that doesn't mean you can't have Ms. Rapple, too."

A smile the likes of which threatened to melt my heart right there, in the middle of my kitchen, spread its way across my grandfather's face. "You're really okay with this?"

I started to nod but stopped myself before I lost my golden opportunity. "I am...under three conditions."

"And those are?"

"One, you rip up that ticket and stay through the weekend as originally planned."

"Deal." He stood, retrieved his ticket from the living room, and carried it back to me. "You can do the honors, if you'd like."

I ripped that sucker to smithereens and tossed it into the trash beneath my sink. "One down, two more to go."

My grandfather laughed. "Okay, let 'em rip."

"Two, I need you to get Gertie and her high octane pee out of my shrubs."

"I'll see what I can do."

"Thank you." I stopped, took a deep breath, and tried to hold my instinctual shudder at bay as I shared my final demand. "And third, you know that whole matching clothes thing with Rapple and Gertie?"

His eyebrows shot up. "Yes…"

"No. Just…no."

~THE END~

About the Author

As a child, **Laura Bradford** fell in love with writing over a stack of blank paper, a box of crayons, and a freshly sharpened number two pencil. From that moment forward, she never wanted to do or be anything else. Today, Laura is the national bestselling author of several mystery series, including the Tobi Tobias Mystery Series, the Emergency Dessert Squad Mysteries, and the Amish Mysteries. She is a former Agatha Award nominee, and the recipient of an RT Reviewer's Choice Award in romance. A graduate of Xavier University in Cincinnati, Ohio, Laura enjoys making memories with her family, baking, and being an advocate for those living with Multiple Sclerosis.

DEATH IN ADVERTISING

When Tobi Tobias decided to open her own ad agency, having to moonlight in a pet shop wasn't part of her vision . . . of course, neither was murder.

Sometimes when opportunity knocks, the door you open leads to a closet. That's certainly the case for Tobi, whose weekends spent cleaning cages in her best friend's pet shop may soon be over. She's just landed her first big break—Zander Closet Company needs a catchy campaign slogan ASAP, and Tobi thinks she's got the right hook to knock 'em dead: "When we're done, even your skeletons will have a place."

But when a real dead body topples out of a showcase closet, she's about to discover there is such a thing as bad publicity. To save her fledgling business and not get killed by the competition, Tobi takes on a new pet project: solving the murder. But with a stressed-out parrot as the only witness to the crime, Tobi will really have to wing it to put the cagey killer behind bars.

30 SECOND DEATH

To help an old friend, Tobi Tobias gets a third-rate thespian a part in a commercial, and learns that in the advertising business, bad acting can lead to murder . . .

When Tobi Tobias opened her own advertising agency, Carter McDade was there for her every step of the way. A brilliant hairdresser, Carter has just landed his dream project: doing hair and makeup for a theatrical production of Rapunzel. But the dream turns into a nightmare when he runs into Fiona Renoir, a cruel, talentless starlet who won't let Carter touch a hair on her head.

To get Fiona out of Carter's hair, Tobi hires the difficult actress for a bit part in her latest commercial. But true to character, Fiona is a terror on set, and Tobi is starting to think she's made the biggest mistake of her life. But things get even worse when Fiona drops dead in the hairdresser's chair, and the only suspect is the man left holding the tainted hair dye, Carter McDade. And unless Tobi can prove his innocence, he'll never do hair in this town again.

Printed in the United States
by Baker & Taylor Publisher Services